PRAISE FOR THE BUCKET LIST MYSTERIES

Murder Under the Covered Bridge

"The second in this series spices up Perona's usual recipe with a little fantasy." —*Kirkus Reviews*

"If you miss getting new episodes of *Murder, She Wrote* every week, you should definitely check out the Bucket List mystery series. Thank goodness Perona has given these senior sleuths long bucket lists, so we can hope for many more adventures with them."

—Donna Andrews, author of
The Meg Langslow series

Murder on the Bucket List

"Bubbly characters keep this cozy debut lively as you search through the red herrings for the big fish." —*Kirkus Reviews*

"A well-crafted mystery." —New York Journal of Books

"Do yourself a favor and treat yourself to Elizabeth Perona's charming debut, *Murder on the Bucket List*. This warm and witty caper features delightful characters, hilarious antics, and a celebration of friendship. *Murder on the Bucket List* is this year's must-read for fans of amateur sleuth mysteries. Don't miss it!"

—Julie Hyzy, *New York Times* bestselling author of the White
House Chef Mysteries and the Manor House Mystery series

"Elizabeth Perona mixes murder, mystery, and a charming cast of characters to concoct an engaging and fun read. High on ingenuity and imagination, low on gore, *Murder on the Bucket List* keeps the reader guessing. Looking forward to many more stories from this promising new author."

—Mary Jane Clark, *New York Times* bestselling author
of the Wedding Cake Mysteries and the KEY News Thrillers

"*Murder on the Bucket List* is the best kind of cozy mystery—inviting, engaging, intelligent, warm, and witty. Elizabeth Perona's ensemble cast of senior sleuths puts out a welcome mat I couldn't refuse, and you shouldn't either. What's on my bucket list? Moving to Brownsburg, Indiana, and joining the members of the Summer Ridge Bridge Club for their next adventure. I can't wait!"

—Molly MacRae, national bestselling author
of the Haunted Yarn Shop Mysteries

"*Murder on the Bucket List* is the best combination of female friendships, quirky characters, and an intriguing mystery. Elizabeth Perona has created a wonderfully light read, with a fun combo of race cars, suburban life, adventurous seniors, and a killer I did not see coming. Can't wait for the next adventure of the Summer Ridge Bridge Club!"

—Clare O'Donohue, author of the
Someday Quilts Mysteries

Murder
under the
Covered
Bridge

Murder
under the
Covered
Bridge

Elizabeth Perona

MIDNIGHT INK
WOODBURY, MINNESOTA

FIRST EDITION
First Printing, 2016

Book format by Teresa Pojar
Cover design by Lisa Novak
Cover illustration by Greg Newbold/Bold Strokes Illustration, Inc
Editing by Nicole Nugent

Midnight Ink, an imprint of Llewellyn Worldwide Ltd.

This is a work of fiction. Names, characters, places, and incidents are either the product of the author's imagination or are used fictitiously, and any resemblance to actual persons living or dead, business establishments, events, or locales is entirely coincidental.

Library of Congress Cataloging-in-Publication Data

Names: Perona, Elizabeth, author.
Title: Murder under the covered bridge / Elizabeth Perona.
Description: First edition. | Woodbury, Minnesota : Midnight Ink, [2016] |
    Series: A bucket list mystery ; 2
Identifiers: LCCN 2016003100 (print) | LCCN 2016007210 (ebook) | ISBN
    9780738748054 | ISBN 9780738748627 ()
Subjects: LCSH: Murder—Investigation—Fiction. | GSAFD: Mystery fiction.
Classification: LCC PS3616.E74975 M88 2016 (print) | LCC PS3616.E74975
    (ebook) | DDC 813/.6—dc23
LC record available at http://lccn.loc.gov/2016003100

Midnight Ink
Llewellyn Worldwide Ltd.
2143 Wooddale Drive
Woodbury, MN 55125-2989
www.midnightinkbooks.com
Printed in the United States of America

DEDICATION

To all the dreamers out there, keep dreaming and working toward your dreams! Perseverance matters.
—Tony

To Isaac, I'm so glad that God chose me to be your mommy and have you join our family. I'm so looking forward to watching you grow.
Love you, Goober!
—Liz

ACKNOWLEDGMENTS

First, as always, I thank God. For everything. Were it not for his peace, this book would never have found its way to completion. There were many early mornings he shaped, prodded, and manipulated me as well as my writing in ways I still don't understand. But I am grateful.

And I am grateful to my co-author and "Elizabeth Perona" partner, my daughter Liz Dombrosky. Thank you for making this series and this book possible.

A number of people contributed to this book, and for that I want to acknowledge their help. First, the genesis for this book was a long time coming. It was first suggested to me more than five years ago by Doug Weisheit, a cousin who was involved with the Covered Bridge Festival. Thank you, Doug! I also want to acknowledge the staff of the Rockville Public Library, who helped with the research for this book. The manager of the Rock Run Café and Bakery, which is located just outside the Roseville Bridge as described in the book, provided much lore about Doc Wheat—who really did exist, though I have enhanced his legend quite a bit. The Rock Run owners also have allowed me to use their wonderful café as a location in this book. Their food and hospitality are well worth the drive. Please check them out.

I also wish to thank Parke County Sheriff Justin Cole and Deputy Sheriff Jason Frazier for helping me with their expertise about the county and law enforcement details. The Parke County Highway Department also provided some historic details about bridge fires and how they have tried to stem them in modern times, although for dramatic purposes I have not chosen to include some of them. Plainfield Police staff, especially Capt. Jill Lees, Lt. Gary Tanner, and Det. Scott Ardnt, also provided their expertise, as did Fire Chief Brian Russell. Any mistakes in this manuscript are mine as the author, and not theirs.

My aunt, Nancee Margison, has helped in a great number of ways with this series, all of which shall remain a mystery to the general public for now.

The character of Joy McQueen is named for reader Joy McQueen, who won the right to have a character named after her in a contest. I hope she continues to enjoy this series.

I am privileged to be a member of an incredible writers group, the Indiana Writers Workshop, and I wish to acknowledge their help with this manuscript. It is so much better because of their critiques: David Ballard, Teri Barnett, Pete Cava, John and June Clair, Steve Heininger, Sylvia Hyde, Cheryl Shore, and Steve Wynalda. I also want to acknowledge IWW member Lucy Schilling, who passed away during the writing of this manuscript. She was a marvelous writer, and I miss her friendship and her critiques. I also appreciate the support of the local Speed City Chapter of Sisters in Crime, of which I am a member (a Mister Sister).

Midnight Ink has a great staff to work with! Special thanks to our editors, Terri Bischoff and Nicole Nugent, and to our publicist, Katie Mickschl. They make it a pleasure to be part of the Midnight Ink family.

None of this, of course, would have taken place without the love and support of my wife, Debbie. Thank you, Deb! And I appreciate the support of my daughter and son-in-law Katy and Taylor Jenkins as well as Liz's husband, Tim, who have all been troopers about this book business. I am blessed to have such a marvelous family.   —Tony

First, I'd like to thank God for granting me this opportunity. I never in my wildest dreams saw myself on this crazy journey with my dad, and I'm just so thankful that He saw fit to make it happen.

Thanks Dad, for inviting me along to do this with you. It's been a blast, and I'm looking forward to more books!

I'd also like to thank my husband, Tim, for continuing to cheer me on and spend a little extra time entertaining our kids, so I can write, edit, and do appearances. I love you!

And finally, I'm thankful for nap time, a little bit of quiet time to get stuff done. Kidding, kind of. ;)   —Liz

ONE

"Is Joy NERVOUS OR is she just cold?" Francine whispered to Charlotte. "Her microphone is shaking."

Francine McNamara and Charlotte Reinhardt shivered in the cold morning air as they stood and watched their friend Joy McQueen fumble the intro for her television spot again. Joy was the correspondent on senior living for the local ABC affiliate as well as an occasional reporter for *Good Morning America.* She'd landed the job after she and the other members of their Summer Ridge Bridge Club gained widespread notoriety for a skinny-dipping party with an uninvited guest. A dead body. Francine would later quip during a Dr. Oz show on seniors staying in shape, "I don't usually have that effect on people."

"She's cold. That Channel Six jacket they make her wear is form-fitting enough to look stylish, but it has no insulation whatsoever. And God knows Joy needs the insulation. How many seniors our age can wear those skinny jeans the kids have without looking ridiculous?"

Francine had to admit Joy's wardrobe alone made her look a good ten years younger than the other seventy-somethings in their Bridge Club. Joy was thin as a rail. She could shop at J.Crew and leave with a bagful of clothes that actually fit. Francine, though more physically fit than the rest of them, was usually assumed by clerks to be shopping for her grandchildren. Which, truthfully, was usually the only reason she would set foot in J.Crew.

"Joy, what's wrong with you today?" Marcy Rosenblatt, Joy's forty-something agent, pulled off her headset and let it dangle around her neck. Marcy served as the cameraman for the segment because the Bridge Club did not want people from the news station around. Coverage of the opening day of the Parke County Covered Bridge Festival was designed to divert attention from their real reason for being there: another bucket list item they didn't want anyone to know about. Though Marcy wasn't a part of the Bridge Club, she knew what was going on. "You usually whip this stuff out in two takes, ten minutes maximum."

Joy threw her an icy stare. "I'm cold."

"Told ya," Charlotte whispered. "And I don't blame her. The skies were clear last night and the temperature got down to freezing. It may be early October, but the frost, as they say, is on the punkin.'"

Francine raised an eyebrow at Charlotte's paraphrase of the James Whitcomb Riley poem. Charlotte, a white-haired, short, plump woman wearing an orange down jacket, looked like a pumpkin with frost on her top. Francine, on the other hand, was tall and wearing a tan Burberry raincoat that was not warm but long enough to cover the rented costume underneath it.

"By the way," Charlotte added, "have I told you yet that you look like a flasher in that raincoat and those high-heel laced-up leather boots? Aren't you cold?"

"Yes, I'm cold. And if Joy doesn't get the intro done soon, I'm going to yank that microphone away from her and do it myself."

Francine had high hopes for Joy's next try, which was going well until Marcy cut her short. "You're a professional," Marcy said. "I need more enthusiasm. Tell me how these bridges are living history. Use that line from five takes ago about practically being able to hear the clip-clop of horses' hooves coming through the bridge a century ago when the structure was rebuilt after the fire. Then introduce Francine to tell the story of her great-grandmother. Then get out. The segment isn't supposed to be that long, anyway."

Joy paused for Marcy to get the camera going.

"All this week we'll be out here in Parke County at the Covered Bridge Festival," Joy said in reporter mode. "Today's opening isn't for a couple of hours, but I wanted you to get a look at one of these historic bridges this morning." She stood off to the side so Marcy could do a close-up. "This is the Roseville Bridge. Two hundred sixty-three feet long with beautiful barn-red siding and a shingled roof that protects anyone inside. Can't you just hear the clip-clop of the horses' hooves echoing through the expanse as it pulls a carriage across? I've got a story for you today from Francine McNamara, whose great-grandmother was one of those carriage riders at the turn of the twentieth century."

Joy indicated for Francine to join her on camera. Francine hurried to do so before Marcy demanded another take.

"Francine, tell us a little about this bridge and how it fits into your family's history." She tilted her microphone toward Francine.

"My great-grandmother became the black sheep of the family as result of riding through this very bridge. She was secretly in love with her carriage driver, and when she was being driven from Rockville back to the family homestead, a storm blew up. While they waited out the storm, the physical attraction was too much. With no one to chaperone, they surrendered to temptation."

Francine was getting ready to add another sentence, but Joy whipped the microphone away. "Oh, my! What happened to them then?"

"When my great-grandmother showed signs of being with child, the obvious questions led to the carriage driver being dismissed. She was married off quickly to a widower who needed someone to help him take care of his family."

"Did they ever get back together?"

"We never knew. She outlived her husband but she didn't marry after his death. My grandmother, her daughter, wanted to believe they found each other again before they died, but we have no record that it happened."

Joy brought the microphone back in front of her and looked straight into the camera. "The story of star-crossed lovers and the Roseville Bridge. We'll be bringing you more from the Covered Bridge Festival tomorrow. I'm Joy McQueen."

Joy and Francine held their poses for a few seconds.

"And we're out," Marcy said. She held up a hand. "High five!" Joy clapped it in the air.

Francine was relieved to have it over with, and now that they had established their alibi, she wanted to move on. "I'm freezing in this outfit. I'll see you inside."

She hustled into the covered bridge and made her way toward the center, where they had set up a photo shoot. A carriage much like the one her family had owned a long time ago was in the middle of the set, surrounded by lights. Jonathan, her husband, was inside the carriage waiting. Francine stopped when she reached the circle of lights, taking in the warmth. "That feels glorious."

Jonathan stuck his head out. "What took you so long?"

"Joy had issues. It's fine."

Francine heard Charlotte's cane clicking on the floor of the bridge as she caught up. "How come you didn't mention the fire?" Charlotte asked as she made it to Francine's side. "The one that burned down Roseville Bridge the first time."

"It had already been rebuilt. It really isn't pertinent to the love story. Besides, I was in a hurry to get my part done once Joy got through hers okay. She's not usually like that."

Charlotte stood in front of one of the lights, hogging its warmth. "I'll say. She's usually quite the talker."

Francine unbuttoned her raincoat. "I guess I'm warm enough for the photo shoot."

"Good," Charlotte said. "Yours is the last photo we need for the pinup calendar."

As Francine pulled off the jacket, she wondered why she'd even suggested the complicated photo shoot for her part in the calendar. The idea of doing racy photographs had been Charlotte's. Each of the women had made a Sixty List of the top sixty things they'd like to do before they died. Francine didn't understand why this one was so important that it couldn't have waited until after the Covered Bridge Festival was over. As far as she knew, Charlotte wasn't going to keel over anytime soon. But once Charlotte got a notion in her head, it was hard to change. Francine had learned over the years it was often easier just to humor her.

She was surprised, however, that Jonathan had been so accommodating. He'd agreed to re-create the historic scene between long-ago lovers, arranged for the carriage and the horse, made the trip from the horse barn to the Roseville Bridge this morning in time for them to do the photo shoot, and even went with Francine to the costume shop to try on his clothes. "Might as well make sure they fit," he'd said. Francine wondered if maybe this hadn't been something of a fantasy turn-on for him.

She handed her raincoat to Charlotte and stripped off the white blouse that she'd worn over the costume. At first she'd been appalled at what the costume store had in stock as a "naughty Victorian," but Jonathan's reaction had been so eye-popping she'd decided to go with it. Her undergarment was a lacy see-through chemise with its hemline shortened so that it dropped only a few inches below her buttocks. Over that was a red and black lace corset that emphasized her bust. The boots were a little too dominatrix for her, but it was a package rental.

"What am I supposed to do with this?" Charlotte held up the raincoat.

"I don't know. It's not warm but it's my good raincoat, so I don't want it on the dusty floor. We can't have it in the carriage. It would be historically inaccurate."

"Like your entire outfit isn't historically inaccurate." Charlotte looked around for something to hang it on.

"Let's call it a variant on historically accurate. At least we know they wore chemises and corsets."

Francine opened the door to the carriage and placed the blouse in a corner where it wouldn't be seen by the camera. She was thankful Jonathan had tied the horse to a tree outside the bridge. She felt a general unease around large animals. And as Joy said, animals can be unpredictable and you don't want to be upstaged by one. Joy's other camera, the one she used for photography, was sitting on a tripod aimed inside the carriage's open window. Francine pointed to it.

"Maybe you could hang it here, at least until Joy gets back to take the photos," she told Charlotte. "Where has Joy gotten to, anyway?"

"I'll go find her." Charlotte threw the coat over the camera and started back toward the entrance to the bridge. Francine noticed Charlotte seemed to be more interested in checking out the features of the bridge than hurrying to retrieve Joy. Or maybe she was tired.

"What happened to Joy and Marcy?" Jonathan asked as she climbed in the carriage.

"I have no idea. I want to get this photo shoot done as much as the next person."

"I *am* that next person, and I definitely want it done."

Francine eased into the space next to him. He lifted the wool blanket he was using to stay warm and she nestled under it, trying to get comfortable. Jonathan's costume was a white, long-sleeve shirt unbuttoned to the navel and the pants a working coach driver would have worn, well-constructed but stiff. His boots were shiny, black, and heavy. "I really appreciate your humoring me."

"When you said we were going to re-create a historical event, I thought maybe you were getting into reenactment, not something out of your family's scandalous past. Until then, I didn't realize your family had a scandalous past."

"Didn't want to scare you off at first, but now that we've been married forty-eight years, I supposed it was okay to let it out."

"I still find it hard to believe it was Charlotte's idea to do a nude calendar."

"It's not a *nude* calendar. A sexy pinup calendar. Like men used to hang in their garages back in the 1940s, when times were innocent."

"You know what I mean. I can't believe Charlotte had that on her Sixty List."

The items were still something of a secret to anyone except the ladies, but the fact that the Summer Ridge Bridge Club members had lists wasn't—not since the Friederich Guttmann Incident. Guttmann was a race car mechanic whose body had been discovered at the skinny-dipping party, high on Joy's list (#10 Go Skinny-Dipping). The whole nightmare ended with Charlotte checking off her top item (#1 Solve Murder Mystery), though it hadn't been as easy as all that. Francine shuddered at the thought of Friederich's dead body, even though she felt secure with Jonathan right beside her.

"It's not even all that far up on the list. Something like thirty-nine, Be a Sexy Calendar Girl."

"I'm sorry, but the last one of your friends I want to imagine nude is Charlotte."

"Jonathan!" Francine said disapprovingly. She may have agreed with him in a physical sense, but Charlotte *was* her best friend. And besides, it was not fair to assume that just because a woman might be older, or overweight, or had a face that looked a bit grumpy when she wasn't smiling, that meant she didn't have a sexy side or wouldn't look desirable under the right conditions. "First of all, I've seen Charlotte's photograph. She is not nude, and it reveals a side of her that people never see. I'm sure Philip found her desirable." Philip was Charlotte's husband who had died in his mid-fifties of a heart attack.

"You're right. I'm sorry." He leaned over and kissed her, then brushed his lips against her ear. "But you are still a 'ten' on my sexy list."

His warm, gentle breath in her ear made shivers go down her spine. "Let's not do that in here, okay? We're just pretending for the camera."

Jonathan's finger's loosened the strings of her corset. "I think we need to see a little more cleavage."

"Jonathan!"

"Come on. She doesn't intend to distribute this calendar you're making, does she?"

"Goodness, no. None of us would have agreed to participate if she had. This is just for us." She affected a Southern accent. "It's supposed to be a surprise for our gentlemen friends."

Jonathan kissed her bare shoulder. "Not to worry. I'll still be surprised when I see Charlotte's sexy side."

She gave him a quick kiss on the lips to stop him from taking this any further. "This outfit is so scratchy I'll be applying hydrocortisone cream like it's body lotion for weeks."

They heard the echo of footsteps in the bridge. "Francine and Jonathan, you're still in there, aren't you?" Joy called out in her chirpy voice, the one Francine tolerated better in the afternoon. At half past nine in the morning in the middle of the Roseville Bridge where they could theoretically be discovered at any moment, the voice was grating.

"We're here," Francine answered. "Where did you go?"

Joy stuck her head in the carriage so she could look at them as she updated them. "False alarm. We thought we heard a car coming, which would have completely shut this photo shoot down. I stationed Charlotte out there in case." The bridge had only one lane, a quaint remembrance of long-gone, gentler days. Since there was no other way across Big Raccoon Creek, an oncoming car would have forced them to hook up the horse and pull the carriage out. The Roseville Bridge was one of the less-visited bridges, quite a distance from the center of the Festival in Rockville, but they still needed to rush to get the photo shoot done.

"I'm not trying to be difficult," Jonathan said, "but I already talked the owner of the horse and carriage into opening early so I could get this here for the photo shoot. I don't want to return it late."

"This is the perfect time for an old cliché," Charlotte cracked. "Jonathan, hold your horses."

"What are you doing here?" Joy asked her. "I thought I stationed you at the front."

"The lights make it toasty warm in here."

Joy removed Francine's coat from the camera and dropped it on the dirty bridge floor.

Francine winced.

"Since you're here," Joy said to Charlotte, "move that light a little to the left." She looked through the lens of the camera and flicked into "director" mode. "Jonathan, I need to be able to see your boots in the picture. Spread your legs a little more. Are your pants unbuttoned? I can't tell from this angle. Francine, prop yourself a little higher above him and open that corset more. We want to see more... eager flesh. And smile, for heaven's sake. This is forbidden love. You're supposed to be delirious with anticipation."

"She's delirious, all right," Charlotte muttered.

"I heard that, Charlotte," Francine said. "Shouldn't you be guarding the bridge?"

"Marcy's doing that. I talked her into it."

That must've been some talk, Francine thought. "But what about the other end?" While the intersection of Coxville Road and County Road 350W was the busier end, it was always possible cars could come from the Coxville Road side.

"That? It's a gravel road, for heaven's sake. We'd hear someone coming a mile away."

"We'd still have to move for them," Francine argued. "There's no quick way around the bridge. They'd need to go through it."

"Quiet!" Joy said. "All the more reason to get this finished."

Joy began snapping photos. She took the camera off the tripod and moved around, photographing Francine and Jonathan from a variety of angles and making them shift positions. She gestured to

Francine. "I need passion. Remember, you're Victoria. You're the one who instigated seducing your coach driver. Jonathan, could you look like you're enjoying it more?"

"Of course," he said dryly. He tossed the blanket aside. "Though I think he and Victoria were fifty years younger than we are when they were doing it in a carriage."

Francine bent down and gave Jonathan a long, sexy kiss. "You mean you're not aroused?"

Jonathan pulled Francine down on top of him. "Joy, step back from the carriage. I'm confident we can give you what you're looking for."

Joy's camera clicked away. "I like your attitude. Francine, could you come up for air? We need to be able to see your heaving bosom."

"My heaving bosom? Do you need for my thigh to quiver too?"

"Let's see Jonathan's manhood," Charlotte joked.

"Let's not," Jonathan said. "And Charlotte, get back to guarding the front of the bridge."

"Easy for you to say in the heat of passion and with all those warm lights pointed at you. It's cold out there. If the Rock Run Café on the hill opened earlier than eleven o'clock, I'd be up there getting a cup of coffee." Charlotte didn't budge.

Joy continued to look through the lens of her camera. "That's good, Francine. Push yourself up over Jonathan a little more. Good shot of your boobs. And let's see a little more hunger in your eyes."

"For heaven's sake, I'm not going to eat him." The words no sooner left Francine's mouth when she realized what she'd said. She laughed, a little embarrassed at first, but then it rolled into a satisfied chuckle.

"That's perfect!" Joy's camera continued to snap photos. "Loved that look of surprise when you realized what you said, and then the wide eyes. Now give me determination. Show me you want this as much as he does."

"Glad you're almost done," Charlotte cracked. "Because otherwise I'm going to have to leave my post and hope there's a vibrator in those woods down by the creek."

"Charlotte!" they exclaimed in unison. It echoed in the bridge.

In the instant that followed, they heard shots.

And not the kind Joy was taking.

TWO

Marcy's feet echoed in the expanse of the long bridge. She was inside and running toward them. "Someone's shooting. What do we do?"

Francine could hear the horse snorting and whinnying, clearly distressed. They had it tied to a tree near the creek bank. She hoped it was okay.

Jonathan tried to maneuver between Francine and the carriage door. "Get on the floor!" he ordered. "What's happening out there?"

"Some guy is running for his life through the cornfield. He's being shot at. He's headed toward us. At least, he was."

More shots rang out. Francine tried to count them. Six, maybe seven total. It was difficult to tell because some of them came so quickly on the back of another. Rifle fire, she guessed.

"Two shooters," Charlotte said.

Francine nodded.

Jonathan bounded out of the carriage, fastening the buttons on his shirt. Francine put her hand on the carriage door and tried to get out. Jonathan reached in behind her and grabbed something from his stash of regular clothes just as they heard another shot. He squatted down. Then he moved to edge of the carriage and peered out from around it.

Despite problems with her leg, Charlotte had grabbed hold of the rear of the carriage and eased herself onto the dirty floor of the bridge. Francine stepped out and sat beside Charlotte. She could feel Charlotte trembling and hugged her. Marcy, who had thrown herself down when Jonathan ordered it, now crept toward them.

Two more shots fired. They came directly through the window in the bridge. One of them went through the back side of the bridge, splintering the board it hit. The second took out a light stand, shattering the box. The light fell to the floor.

The women screamed.

What seemed like an hour went by, but Francine guessed it was only a few minutes. There were no more shots.

Jonathan, keeping low, worked his way to the window in the bridge.

Francine whispered, "Be careful."

He lined up on the left side of the window and took a quick peek, then ducked below. He did it again. No reaction. He crept under the window and repeated it on the right side. Again, no reaction. Slowly he stood up, keeping out of the line of sight from anyone who might be able to see through the window.

"I can see the cornfield and the creek bank. There's a pretty steep drop-off from the bank to the creek."

Marcy blinked back tears. She tried to wipe the tears away with her hands, but her hands were dirty, leaving dark streaks on her face. She wiped the dirt off on her clothes. "Can you see if the guy is being chased? I saw cornstalks behind him rustling like there was a second person. Those shots had to come from somewhere."

"I don't see any other movement in the cornfield. The man being shot at must have fallen down the bank. He's lying by the creek almost directly under us. He's not moving."

Charlotte grabbed her cane and leveraged herself to a standing position. She beckoned the other women. "C'mon. I have to see what's going on. This could be another murder."

Murder was the last thing Francine wanted to hear, but she, too, was curious. She and Marcy took Charlotte's circuitous route around the carriage while staying out of direct view of the window. When they were all next to Jonathan, they could see what he was talking about. The man's lower body had landed up to his knees in the waters of Big Raccoon Creek. His upper body was on the bank, his face turned away from them.

"If we don't get to him soon, he's going to be dragged into the creek," Jonathan said.

"He's unconscious," Francine noted. "He won't survive if he slips into the water." She surveyed the photo shoot. The video camera was missing. Joy was missing. Her heart skipped a beat. "Joy?"

"I'm down here at the far end," she answered. The camera sat on her thin shoulders. "Do you think it's safe to go outside? I want to find out who came running out of the cornfield."

Francine noticed that Jonathan now held his handgun. He moved in Joy's direction. "Let me go out first," he said.

Francine had had mixed feelings about the fact her husband owned a gun, something she had discovered at the end of the Friederich Guttmann Incident. That he'd kept it secret all these years was disturbing, but on the other hand, he was so adept with it that it made her feel more secure. Still, she didn't like guns.

Despite Jonathan's orders, Joy went out ahead of him. "Whoever was firing on him seems to be gone." She looked into the LCD screen of the camera. "The man in the water might be dead. The close-up shows blood."

Francine put the white blouse back on over the corset and tried to button it up. She found her hands were shaking. She fumbled with the buttons as she moved to follow Jonathan.

Big Raccoon Creek ran high thanks to a rainstorm the day before. "The waters are pulling him in," Jonathan said. "I'm going down there."

"There's no cell service here!" Marcy's voice was shaky. Francine looked back to see that she was fiddling with her phone. *Marcy the publicist would think of that,* she thought. Marcy gave Francine a helpless look.

She waved her out. "Go up to the Rock Run and see if there's anyone up there yet who can call for help. If not, check at a nearby house."

Marcy sped out the opposite end of the tunnel and headed toward the restaurant.

Francine joined Joy at the top of the creek bank. Joy was filming the scene. Charlotte trailed Jonathan as he headed for a clearing where he could climb down to reach the unconscious man.

"Charlotte, stay where you are!" Jonathan ordered. "It's too steep. I'm not even sure I can make it myself."

Francine thought he sounded pretty sure of his own abilities, though. He made eye contact with her and motioned her back inside the bridge. "I think it would help if you watched from the window. You'll have a more direct view from there if I need advice."

Francine was a retired nurse. She knew he meant advice in treating the victim. She hustled toward the bridge only to see that Charlotte was still hobbling after Jonathan along the upper bank.

Francine used her "urgent voice," the one that usually worked on her best friend. "Do what he says, Charlotte! Your knees can't possibly negotiate that decline." Charlotte gave her a pouty look but fortunately did what she asked.

Francine found herself being slowed by the high-heel boots. *How did women ever walk in these things?* She made it back to the carriage without falling over. She unlaced the rented shoes and threw them in the carriage, trading them out for tennis shoes. She rushed to the window. She stuck her head out in time to see that Jonathan had successfully navigated his way to the creek. He slipped along the muddy bank, his feet sinking partway into the water.

She found herself gripping the sill.

Jonathan reached the fallen man. He bent over and examined him. "It looks like he hit a lot of brush on the way down," he shouted up to Francine. "He has cuts and bruises on his face. I've got to stop him from going farther into the water, but I'm worried he might have hurt his neck."

"Can you tell if he has a pulse?"

Jonathan put a finger to the man's throat. "He's alive but not responsive. I don't see any gunshot wounds, so I think he escaped that. I know I shouldn't move him but I can't hold him in place until the medics get here. I don't have enough stamina. I've got to move him to drier ground."

"Do what you have to. Try to keep his head stable if you can."

Jonathan put one hand under the man's neck and gripped him tight around the belt. He slowly moved backward until the man was on drier ground. He sat in the muck and gently set the man's head on the ground so it was stable.

"Nice work!" Francine let out the breath she didn't know she'd been holding.

She heard footsteps rumbling through the covered bridge and turned to see Marcy jogging toward her. She slowed as she got to Francine. "The manager was at the café," she said, gasping for breath. "He called 911. Rosedale's Fire Department is responding, but it might be ten minutes before they get here. It's a volunteer force. They're also sending the Parke County Sheriff's Department because of the shots, but the nearest sheriff is in Rockville." Rosedale was the closest town, just a few minutes away; Rockville was the county seat and a good ten minutes away.

Marcy continued out of the bridge to where Joy had set up the camera to film. Francine followed and picked a spot next to Charlotte.

Jonathan kept looking into the face of the man. He used his free hand to explore the pockets of the man's coat. "Well, this is interesting," he called. He pulled something out of one of the pockets and held it up so they could see it. "It's a vial of something."

"What's in it?" Francine asked Joy, who was seeing it in close-up view.

"Something clear and liquidy. Looks like water to me," Joy said.

"Can you find his wallet?" Francine shouted to Jonathan.

Jonathan laid the vial to the side and carefully eased the wallet out of the man's pants. He opened the wallet one-handed and flipped to the driver's license. "I have some bad news, Francine. I thought he looked familiar but I didn't want to say it until I was sure. It's your cousin William."

"William?" Francine's voice cracked. She was concerned, but she could hardly believe what she'd heard.

"Is this the cousin you were telling me about?" Charlotte asked. "The one who owns the funeral homes around here? Weren't you going to visit him this week?"

"William is a cousin of sorts. He and his wife, Dolly, own a string a *nursing* homes, not funeral homes. He lives in Montezuma, which is about fifteen minutes up the road. I hadn't talked to him yet, but I did plan to visit."

"What do you mean by a sort-of cousin?"

"He's not a first cousin. His grandfather Earnest and my grandmother Ellie were brother and sister, which means my mother and William's father were first cousins. Don't ask me what version of cousins that makes us."

"What's he doing out here in the outerlands of Parke County this early in the morning?"

Francine glared at her. "I don't know. What are *we* doing out here in the outerlands of Parke County this early in the morning?"

Francine no sooner asked the question when her hand flew to her mouth in realization. What would *they* tell the Parke County deputies about this? Her immediate reaction was panic. She looked at the horse pulling at the rope holding it to the tree. Their bucket list item was sure to be discovered.

But the more she thought about it, the more perfect Joy's story for the Indianapolis news station seemed as a cover. They were out here celebrating a moment of Francine's family's past. The rented stagecoach and the 1920s clothes all fit into a neat little spin they could make. Even with their reputation as the "Skinny-Dipping Grandmas," no one would suspect what the photo shoot was really all about. She was glad the segment was only for local news too. As long as the story about William didn't generate too much curiosity,

Joy wouldn't be asked to do a *Good Morning America* segment on the Covered Bridge Festival. It was way too tame.

But then there was Marcy. Marcy the publicist was the loose cannon in the whole scenario.

"You know what this is like?" Marcy said. "This is just like when you found Friederich Guttmann's body in Alice's shed."

Charlotte craned her neck toward Marcy. "Indeed, it is. Maybe we're just magnets for dead bodies."

There was no mistaking the twinkle in Charlotte's eyes, but Francine wanted to put a stop to this idea before Marcy got too excited. "It is *nothing* like that. He's just unconscious. And we've already recorded a segment that has us covered." She explained herself.

Joy spoke without looking up from the camera. "That is *not* what you argued for last time, Francine. Last time you argued that we should tell the authorities the whole truth. And what are you worried about? Look how well it turned out."

"It didn't turn out so well for Alice," Francine said.

In the aftermath of their skinny-dipping episode that ended with the discovery of a dead body, Joy landed the job reporting on the adventurous activities of senior citizens, Francine was a guest on Dr. Oz's show about senior fitness, and Mary Ruth went on to become a contestant on the Food Network's hit show *Chopped*. But the husband of their friend Alice was discovered to have had a long-ago affair that produced a child, and they were now separated.

"I know it's been a rough time for Alice and Larry," Joy said, "but they're on the road to getting back together. And Alice *loves* the idea of having a stepson. There's nothing wrong with saying we were doing a photo shoot here. We can tell them we were doing it for a *Good Morning America* segment. I'll clear it with the producers as soon as we're out of here."

Francine eyes opened wide in alarm. "We don't have to tell them about the *calendar*, that's all I'm saying. Let's just stick with the notion that it was a photo shoot. *Good Morning America* doesn't have to be involved."

Charlotte surprised her by agreeing with Joy. "Even if it got reported, it would all be fine. It's not like we got buck naked. The photos were tastefully done."

Francine looked down to see how Jonathan was doing. She found he was examining something else besides William's wallet. "What's Jonathan got?" she asked Joy.

"I don't know. Looks like it might be a book. He found it in the other back pocket in a plastic bag."

"What's that you've got, Jonathan?" Francine shouted down at him.

"I'll tell you later. When do you think the ambulance will get here?"

Francine turned to Marcy. "What did they say? Ten minutes?"

Marcy's hands were dug deep into her plaid wool coat and her shoulders were hunched against the cold. She might have been nodding her head yes, but Francine couldn't tell. "About ten. The same for the sheriff's department, but I don't know how long ago that was. Maybe another five minutes?"

Before Francine could tell Jonathan anything, he called back up. "I'm only asking because Joy needs to take down the lights and pack everything away before the ambulance gets here. It won't be able to get through to this side. See if someone from the restaurant can hook up the horse and move the carriage out of the bridge. There's a spot just off the road on this end where it can be parked."

Francine realized how much there was to do. "Oh my gosh! He's right! We've got to get packed up."

"I grew up with horses," Joy yelled to Jonathan. "I'll take care of that." Joy turned off the camera and handed it to Marcy. "Marcy, you're in charge. Francine and Charlotte, do exactly what she says. You helped unpack; you know how to pack it up. We'll be out of here in no time."

No time was exactly what Francine was worried about. How long would it really be before the ambulance got here? And how much time had passed since the shots were fired? Was someone in the cornfield still watching them? The shooting had stopped and they didn't seem to be in danger. But Marcy had reported seeing the cornstalks rustled by William's pursuer. Was their presence preventing the shooter from finishing off William, or was he waiting for them to bring the body up top so he could shoot him again? If so, would that make the rest of them dispensable? If he was waiting, she thought, he'd be disappointed, because they weren't doing anything until after the emergency medical technicians got there and the sheriff's department arrived.

Marcy took the camera and rushed into the bridge. Francine and Charlotte did their best to keep up with her.

But Francine couldn't help glancing back at the cornfield. There was no wind to speak of this morning, and the rows of withered cornstalks stood upright and stationary. The trees and undergrowth lining the creek wound to the north as far as she could see, about a quarter of a mile away. She saw no one in that direction. The dampness of the still morning air hung on and Francine shivered. She needed her jacket. She needed to change clothes.

Francine glanced Charlotte's way. Her expression was somewhere between delight and excitement. *Either she's energized by the attempt on William's life or she's up to something. Or maybe it's just that she's always fascinated by mysteries.*

Francine linked arms with Charlotte to help her go faster. They had a lot to do to make things look as normal as possible before the ambulance arrived.

THREE

Joy untied the horse from the tree, brought it inside, and hooked it up to the carriage while Marcy instructed Francine and Charlotte in packing up the equipment.

"What are we going to do about this light that got trashed by the rifle shot?" Charlotte asked. "I can get it back in the case, but it's in pieces."

Joy mounted the coach driver's seat. "The station's not going to be happy about that light stand."

"I guess that's the price of getting this story," Charlotte said.

"Not much of a story if I don't record it. Remember to keep out the video camera for me." She coaxed the horse and pulled the carriage out of the bridge.

The women finished dragging the equipment to one side of the bridge just before the fire truck arrived from Rockville. They'd hoped to give the vehicle room to edge past them, but the truck was either too heavy or too big to use the narrow bridge. The driver parked it on CR 350W, which would have blocked traffic had there had been any that time of the day.

A nimble fireman ran across the bridge with a radio. The women pointed out William and Jonathan. He radioed back once he assessed the situation, and soon two men from the fire truck joined him. They carried rope bags and wore life jackets with a metal loop on the back. Francine watched as they threaded a rope through the loop and tethered themselves to a sturdy sycamore on top of the bank. They made their way down carrying a backboard.

A brown sheriff's car came screaming up from the south. He dodged the fire truck and pulled in front of the bridge, blocking access to it. He got out of the car and rushed across. Once the fresh-faced deputy saw the firemen rescuing the victim, he turned to the women, who were with Joy and the horse near the creek bank. He looked at Francine. She was now back in her raincoat covering the costume. "What's with the horse and carriage?"

"I'll give you the shortened version," she said. "It's a photo shoot." She hoped it was the only time she'd have to give an account for this, but she wasn't optimistic.

He seemed satisfied with her explanation. He pointed to Charlotte, who was waving her hand like she knew the answer to the difficult problem in a classroom. "You. Let's step away from the others and you can tell me what happened."

Despite his instructions, they all began to talk at once again. He held up a hand. "Only her," and he motioned Charlotte to come to him.

Together they stepped several yards away from the group. The deputy nodded. "Go ahead."

Francine could hear Charlotte anyway. "We heard shots and we—that is, Marcy—saw the unconscious man down there run from the cornfield. He was in a rush from being shot at and he must have fallen or slid down the embankment and hit his head. Jonathan—that's Francine's husband, he's the other man down there—went to keep him from slipping any farther into the water and drowning."

"Who's Francine?"

"That's me," she said, waving a couple of fingers at him. She realized she shouldn't have let him know she could hear, but he seemed to forget because he directed his next question at her.

"Your husband ran out while the shots were being fired?"

"No, he waited until the gunmen had gone."

"Okay," he said. "Step over here." He waited until Francine had joined them. "There was more than one gunman?"

Charlotte interrupted. "They were shooting rifles, and the shots came on top of one another, so there had to have been more than one."

"Did you see any of them?"

Francine shook her head. "No. They must have stayed hidden in the cornfield or left once William fell down the creek bank."

"You know the victim?"

"It's weird, but I do. He's my cousin. I have no idea why he was here or why he was being shot at."

The deputy took notes. "Did you know the gunmen were gone, or did you just assume it?"

Charlotte answered, "We didn't know for sure, but they stopped shooting. And they didn't fire at us when we left the bridge."

Everyone turned their attention to the scene below as the fireman helped Jonathan back up to the top of the bank. A second fireman checked him over. Jonathan handed over the wallet and the vial he'd retrieved. Francine didn't see the book but presumed he had turned it over as well.

Meanwhile, the firemen below hoisted William up on the back-board. Another two steadied them with the tethered rope.

The ambulance arrived. It couldn't get across the bridge because the sheriff's car blocked the entrance. The deputy ran back across the bridge to move his car out of the way.

In spite of the circumstances, Francine had to chuckle over the Barney Fife moment.

The ambulance made it across the bridge and backed into the turnaround space while Marcy steadied the horse and Joy continued filming the rescue. The paramedics loaded William into the ambulance and the firemen prepared to leave, but not before the deputy obtained the vial and the wallet. Then the ambulance sped out onto CR 350W, sirens wailing.

More deputies arrived. Once the group assessed the situation, they moved into the cornfield, cautiously spreading themselves out.

"They're going to establish a perimeter," Charlotte said, "and search for evidence."

Another sheriff's car arrived. The man who got out had a long, leathery face accentuated by thinning white hair parted to one side and a full, bristly white mustache. He carried a white Stetson, which he put on when he got out of the car. He reminded Francine of an Old West character who stayed on the job because he needed to keep busy. After he'd been briefed by the first deputy on the scene, he crossed the bridge to where the women and Jonathan had been placed for safety's sake.

"I'm Detective Stockton," he said. He glanced at Jonathan, now wrapped in the wool blanket that had been in the carriage. "Since it's cold, let's go up to the Rock Run. I'm confident the owner will let us in, and we'll talk further up there. In the meantime, please don't talk among yourselves about what happened."

Francine carried Jonathan's change of clothes as well as her own as they made their way to the restaurant. The detective allowed them to use the men's and women's restrooms to change, but made everyone else sit at separate tables far apart from each other. Once Francine and Jonathan were out, he slid "Volunteer Witness Statement" forms in front of each of them.

"I need you to fill these out," he said, "without talking to each other."

"How long is this going to take?" Joy asked. "Our friend Mary Ruth Burrows is running a food stand back in Rockville. You might have heard of her? She was on *Chopped*. You know, on Food Network? Anyway, we have jobs helping her out. We need to get back."

"It should take as long as it needs. Give me as much detail as you can remember. Now is the best time for you to do that, while it's still fresh in your memory."

"I may need extra paper," Charlotte said, checking over the single-page form. "I have excellent powers of observation."

"If you need more," he said dryly, "let me know. I have plenty."

Francine didn't like being separated at a time like this, especially from Jonathan. But she understood the need for an unbiased assessment from each of them. The story would only get muddled if they had a chance to talk to each other. And they'd already talked a lot. She hurried through the document while giving as much detail as she could remember.

Joy finished first and brought the form to Stockton. He asked her a couple of questions and then the two of them signed the form. Marcy was next. Francine began to feel pressure to finish up, like she was back in school taking a test and everyone but her was having an easy time of it.

Charlotte, indeed, asked for extra paper, making Joy grumble. "I wish we had more than one car so we could leave."

Marcy plopped down at a table. Joy sat next to her. "I'm hungry."

Marcy grabbed a menu. "Me too. We should make the best of this."

A man with salt-and-pepper eyebrows and a receding hairline approached them. He was carrying a pot of coffee and two cups. He introduced himself as the manager. "We're not open for business yet, but the sheriff asked me if I could get something to warm your group up. Can I pour you some coffee? I've got cinnamon rolls heating in the oven. They'll be ready in a minute."

"That's kind of you," Joy said. Then she took notice of what he'd said. "Sheriff? He said he was a detective."

He put the cups in front of them. "Detective now, but he was the sheriff until he hit his term limit. He's a good guy to have on the force still, so the new sheriff let him stay on in a special capacity. Some folks even still call him sheriff."

"That would never have happened in Hendricks County where we're from."

"Helps that his son is the new sheriff."

Marcy laughed. "It's like a mini-Indianapolis. Or Chicago."

He poured them both coffee. "I'll be back in a minute with those cinnamon rolls. On the house."

Joy whipped out her cell phone. "We need to let Mary Ruth know what's going on." She punched a few buttons on the phone before Marcy reminded her, "There's no cell service in the area."

"We have a phone in the back you can use," the owner said as he was leaving. "Follow me."

Francine finished up her form and handed it to Detective Stockton. Jonathan was right behind her. Charlotte was still writing. Francine and Jonathan pulled chairs up to the table and Marcy told them where Joy was. Even though she knew the restaurant wasn't open for business, Francine still looked through the menu. She was stressed, and stress made her hungry.

Joy returned. "She didn't answer her phone, so I left a message. Since she can't reach me here, I told her to send me an email. The sign says they have WiFi in here. I let her know we would be there just as soon as the detective lets us leave."

The owner carried a plate of cinnamon rolls into the room. He slid it on the table and looked at Francine and Jonathan. "Can I get you coffee too?"

Jonathan nodded eagerly. "Strong and black, please."

The man brought more cups and poured coffee in them. He saw Joy fiddling with her cell phone. "If you need the Internet password, it's on the menu."

She thanked him and he left. She bit into a cinnamon roll. "These may be good," she whispered, "but they are nowhere near as flaky and gooey as Mary Ruth's."

Francine cut a piece for herself and handed the rest of it to Jonathan. "No matter how good they look, I can't afford too many of these calories, not with the temptation we'll face at the food booth. If we ever get there."

Joy's phone made a dinging sound. She checked it. "It's an email from Mary Ruth." Everyone quieted down and watched her read the message. "Oh my gosh! She says there's a huge line already and she keeps delaying opening. She wants to know when we're going to get there." Joy put the phone down. "She sounds frantic."

"But she's got Alice and Toby helping her," Marcy said. Alice had become an investor in Mary Ruth's catering business and was learning the trade. Toby was Mary Ruth's grandson who lived in her basement while he tried to figure out what to do with his life. "It must be desperate if the three of them can't handle it."

Joy put the last bite of cinnamon roll in her mouth and wiped the icing off her lips. She handed the cell phone to Marcy. "Email her back and tell her to keep frying up as many of those corn fritter donuts as she can ahead of time. We may have to drag Charlotte out of here." She went over and stood next to Detective Stockton. "We need to leave," she said. "We've got to get to Rockville."

He smiled but seemed not to be in a hurry. He picked up the Volunteer Witness Form she had turned in. "You're Joy McQueen, aren't you? The reporter on Channel Six?"

She gave him a high wattage smile. "Yes, that's me."

He used a wave of his hand to indicate the rest of the group. "And you all are the Skinny-Dipping Grandmas, correct?"

Jonathan put his cup down. "Not me."

"Sorry. I meant the ladies."

The women all nodded. Francine didn't know where this was headed but she hoped it would get them out of the café and back to Rockville as quickly as possible.

Joy continued, "Our friend Mary Ruth is being featured at the festival. So you can understand how important it is that we get back to help her out."

"Then why would you be out here in the Rosedale area in the early morning instead of back in Rockville helping your friend?"

Joy shifted her eyes toward the group. "I'm doing segments all week long about the Covered Bridge Festival. We were here filming one this morning."

"With a horse and carriage?"

"Well, we …"

"It's my fault," Francine spoke up. "My ancestors were from the area, and the Roseville Bridge played a part in a scandal from the early 1900s. I thought it would be fun to hire a horse and buggy and re-create a scene from the scandal, but we didn't want to do it when there were a lot of tourists around. Who would have thought something like this would happen?"

After she finished, she bit her lip. *Too much detail*, she thought. *It sounded rehearsed. I wonder if he thinks we're hiding something.*

Stockton tilted back in the seat, balancing it on two legs. "Given your recent troubles, I would have thought you might anticipate it." His crooked smile indicated was probably jesting, but Francine wasn't sure.

"So can we go?" she asked.

"What's your maiden name? I assume it's not McNamara."

"Miles."

He nodded knowingly. "Your family didn't live too far away, between Rosedale and Bridgeton, didn't they?"

Francine didn't know whether to be flattered that he recognized the name or alarmed because this could lead to more questions and further delays.

"It's been a long time since my father sold the farm and moved us to Evansville. I'm surprised you remember."

Stockton eased the front two legs of his chair back on the floor. "Our memories are long in Parke County. Being from here, you should know that."

Joy drummed her fingers on her forearm. She gave Francine a glance that Francine interpreted as *Hurry this along.*

Stockton noticed the gesture. "Mrs. McQueen, I enjoy your reports on senior citizens, but that gives me reason to be concerned. I saw you filming a bit when I got here. Do you plan to report on what happened?"

"I expect the station will ask me, but I haven't heard that. There's no cell reception around here."

"So you haven't called it in? How much footage did you get of the incident?"

Joy's back straightened. "I got most of Jonathan's rescue. I don't know how good it is. Why?"

She knows why, Francine thought.

He leaned forward. "We're going to want it."

"I'm confident I don't have to give that up right away. But I'd be happy to make a copy of it for you."

"I could confiscate the camera right now."

"Please don't." She took a conciliatory stance. "Look, we really need to get back to Rockville. You have our statements. Can't we leave?"

"Not until your friend finishes."

They all looked at Charlotte, who was now on her third page. She shrugged. "I'm good at remembering details. Plus, I'm giving them suggestions on how they should investigate it."

Joy exhaled noisily. "I'm confident Detective Stockton has had a lot of experience and knows how to run an investigation."

"Thank you," he said.

Francine knew Alice didn't do well under pressure, and Toby was not always the help he should be. They really did need to get to Rockville. "I'm sure Charlotte's finishing up right now." She said the last two words through gritted teeth.

"No more than five more minutes," Charlotte replied.

Francine had an idea. "Perhaps Charlotte can ride in the carriage with Jonathan back to the horse barn and then come to Rockville with him in his car. That would enable the rest of us to leave right away." She knew Jonathan and Charlotte chafed at each other when they spent too much time together. Both would hate it if she weren't there to keep the peace.

Stockton checked Joy's form. "Is this your cell phone number so I can get hold of you?"

"Yes. If you can find a place with cell coverage."

"You may come to appreciate our area," he said. "But in the meantime, you can go."

"Well, look at that," Charlotte said. "I just finished."

Jonathan smiled. "Good. Then I'll just head back to the barn by myself." He gathered up his costume clothes, gave Francine a quick kiss, and left.

The rest of the group rushed to gather up their belongings. Charlotte snatched a cinnamon roll to take with her. "Those things are pretty sticky," Joy said. "I don't want sticky fingerprints all over my seats. Put it back."

Charlotte frowned. "But I haven't had one yet."

"That's what you get for giving the detective so much advice." Joy winked at Stockton.

Charlotte defiantly took a bite and chewed slowly. "Then we'll just have to stand here until I finish it, won't we," she said with her mouth full, "now that Jonathan's gone."

"I'm sure I can still catch him." Joy's comment made the detective laugh.

Francine handed Charlotte a napkin. "Wrap it up in this. I've got wet wipes in my purse."

Charlotte set her mouth. "I don't know. I'm kind of messy."

"You'll likely have it finished before you reach the car," Marcy said.

That's for sure, Francine thought.

Charlotte reached for her cane as Marcy and Joy headed out the door. Francine juggled her costume but still managed to hurry Charlotte out of the restaurant, the bell above the exit ringing as the door slammed shut behind them.

FOUR

"The sheriff thinks Joy is cute," Charlotte said, almost in a sing-song voice.

Francine hung back with Charlotte, who was making slow going. They'd just entered the covered bridge while Joy, Marcy, and Jonathan were almost out the other end.

"You mentioned that already." Francine tried not to sound annoyed, but she was fairly confident Charlotte would read through all that. She was annoyed not only because Charlotte was trumpeting the flirtation between Joy and the detective, but also because she knew—they all knew—Charlotte could walk faster than she let on. For the most part, they all played along. But Charlotte was seriously slow right now.

"Don't you think it's about time she started dating again?" Charlotte asked.

"I do, but don't think I'm going to stand by and let you ruin that relationship, if any develops, just because you want in on what happened to my cousin William."

"Me? I wouldn't get involved in Joy's relationships. Why would you even think that?" Charlotte winced as she put her weight on one of her knees.

Francine considered that perhaps all the walking they'd done, especially on the uneven ground at the top of the creek bank, actually was taking its toll. She resolved to be more charitable. But she still found herself annoyed. "Because you already offered to 'help' the sheriff several times, that's why." Francine crossed her arms. "And we both know you can't resist a mystery."

Charlotte let a beat go by. "It's on her Sixty List."

There was some interpretation to be made as to what exactly Joy's bucket list item meant. *#5 Romance!* was all it said. Between themselves, without Joy around, they'd debated it. The general consensus was that Joy eventually wanted to date again, but it had been a long, long time since her husband, Bruno, had left her for another man. The scars lingered. Shortly after the divorce, she'd dated a few men—losers, according to the Summer Ridge Bridge Club—and she retreated into the shell she'd now been in for more than a decade. It was only with the Friederich Guttmann Incident and her new role as a reporter that she'd started reclaiming the vivacious person she once was.

"That doesn't mean you wouldn't be above using her to get what you wanted."

Charlotte didn't respond but stopped near the window through which they'd been fired upon. She looked out. "One of the bullets came in through this window perpendicularly and hit the light stand." She showed the direction the bullet must have traveled.

Francine's eyes followed to where Charlotte's hand pointed. "So?"

"So, that means one of the shooters was located down the creek bank, not in the cornfield. Otherwise, it would have come through at a slant and gone the long way down the bridge before it hit anything."

Francine thought about that. "That would make sense, because the second bullet that came in through the window went straight out the other side." She walked the width of the bridge to where the bullet had exited, leaving behind splintered wood.

"That means they were shooting at us, not William."

A chill went down Francine's spine. "You're right."

"Why did they fire on us?"

"Because we could see what was happening to William?"

"Maybe." Charlotte stuck her head out the window. She looked toward the cornfield to the left and then the Rock Run on the right. "At one point the two rifles were firing almost simultaneously. But someone at that distance along the creek bank wouldn't be able to see William in the cornfield, would they?" She pointed to a spot hundreds of yards upstream.

Francine looked out the window, trying to judge the trajectory of the bullet that had hit the light stand. "I agree. They probably would have been out there where the creek makes a bend."

"Why was the other person stationed there?"

That didn't seem like a difficult question. "Because they couldn't be sure which way William would run out of the cornfield."

Charlotte gave a protracted sigh.

"You don't like that answer?"

"No, it's an okay answer. But the second shooter had a much cleaner bead on William. Yet he wasn't hit."

"If the second shooter wasn't after William, what was he after?"

"Good question. Was William sneaking out or sneaking in when he was discovered? If he was sneaking in, he might have surprised one shooter, but not two. Unless they knew he was there. Otherwise, they wouldn't have had time to set up in two different locations. They would have both shot at William from the same direction."

Francine looked down at her short friend. "You're getting at something, Charlotte. Just say it."

"I'm just theorizing here." She limped to the spot in the bridge where they had done the photo shoot. "William ran toward this bridge. He must have done that for a reason, wherever he was coming from. Suppose it was our presence that surprised the second shooter? What was it we were seeing that he or she didn't want us to see?"

Francine took a moment to scan the immediate area looking for clues. The light around the window was better now that the sun was higher in the sky. She was so caught up in looking for clues she forgot they were on their way to the car to join Joy and Marcy. She was jolted back into the present with the noise of the horse and carriage entering the bridge.

Jonathan hailed her from the carriage driver's seat. "What's keeping you two? Joy and Marcy are getting impatient."

Francine and Charlotte moved out of his way. Jonathan pulled up beside them and handed a book the size of a small paperback to Francine. She recognized it as the book he'd pulled out of William's pocket. "I forgot to give this to the fireman," he said. "I meant to give it to the detective, but by the time I'd finished his witness form I'd forgotten again. It fell out of my clothes when I tossed them in the back of the carriage. You might want to look at it before you do anything with it, though. If I read the first page right, it's your grandmother's journal."

Francine stared at the cover. She knew her grandmother had been quite the journalist. She remembered watching her write an entry once, using a loose-leaf sheet of paper as a guide to keep her penmanship level across the page. Francine had been seven at the time her grandmother passed away. She hadn't seen any of the journals when the family went through her house.

But what struck her about the book was the cover.

"I know I've seen this graphic before," she said.

"Of course you have," Charlotte said. "It's a heart pierced by an arrow. There are probably thousands of them carved into trees all over Parke County. There's probably fifty in the graffiti on this bridge."

"As observant as you are, you haven't noticed that there's very little graffiti on the bridge?"

Jonathan snapped the reins on the horse and the carriage started moving again. "I'll leave you ladies to battle that out, but I wouldn't do it for very long. You need to get back to Rockville."

As Jonathan left, Charlotte moved toward the window. "I know we need to leave, but you're right. For as remotely located as this bridge is, there's almost no graffiti."

"Maybe someone comes along and cleans it up."

Charlotte indicated the sides of the bridge nearest them. "You could cover up spray paint with other paints, but you couldn't cover up carvings, and I don't see a lot of paint or carvings. Where did you see this heart and arrow?"

Francine pointed at a spot directly below them. "There." The beams that ran parallel to the river holding up the bridge were beyond their ability to reach, but they could see what was on the one below the window. "The graphic is a heart pierced by an arrow. I spotted it when we were crouched below the window with Jonathan."

Charlotte was skeptical. "I don't know. It seems pretty crude."

Francine juggled the costume she was carrying and pulled out her cell phone. She used the flashlight app to shine a light on the beam. "Look at the arrow. There are three vertical slashes on the back end of the arrow, just like on the journal."

"You're right. Better take a photo."

Francine turned off the light beam and switched on the photo app. She snapped a picture.

Joy's SUV entered the bridge noisily, startling Charlotte and Francine. She beeped the horn and rolled down her window as they approached them. "Get in or we'll leave you behind," Joy said.

The two women threw their stuff in the back seat.

"I'll give you this," Charlotte told Francine. "Those wooden beams are pretty old. The graffiti engraved in that wood could go way back."

Marcy turned around from the front seat. "What are you talking about?"

"Nothing," they said at the same time.

"Now you've got me curious. Francine, what was it you were taking a photo of?"

"Graffiti. Could be something, probably not. We'll worry about it later."

Charlotte buckled in. "Could you get some heat going in this car?"

"It's trying," Joy said. "Soon as the engine warms up, I'll put the heater on full blast."

Joy took the bridge at a slow pace, but once they were on CR 350W, she got her speed up as fast as she could.

Francine turned around to look back at the Rock Run Café & Bakery. There were still a few sheriffs' cars in the parking lot. "I hope William's all right. I wonder where they took him."

"You won't find out till we get back to Rockville and can make a call." Marcy sounded disgusted. "You remember there's no cell service out here."

"How could I forget? I hope the detective is able to find the person who was shooting at him quickly before this gets pushed to the back burner."

"I'm confident he will," Joy said. "I'll be following up on this as a reporter, so I'll keep the pressure on him."

The car got quiet. "What?" Joy asked.

"Nothing," Charlotte said. Francine could see her smirking. She wondered if Marcy was doing the same.

Joy continued, "Plus, he used to be the sheriff, so he knows what he's doing. Don't you think he looks like a sheriff?"

They could all agree on that.

"I think what Francine is saying," Charlotte said, "is that if William turns out to be okay, and we hope so, there will be other things to keep the sheriff busy. With none of the rest of us hurt and tourists flocking to Parke County like lawyers to a twenty-car pileup, this could drop off his radar in no time."

Joy and Marcy started discussing television, which always bored Francine. She slipped the journal Jonathan had given her out of her stash of costume clothing and examined it. When she'd looked at it back at the bridge, there hadn't been a lot of light. Now she saw more detail than she had before. The front cover had been blank, but her grandmother had *stenciled* the drawing on it. *That means this is a pattern of some kind,* Francine thought. She briefly wondered if it were simply a popular symbol of the times. Maybe she'd put too much stake in the similarity to the graffiti she'd seen carved into the beam of the bridge.

"What's in the diary?" Charlotte asked.

Francine suddenly realized she couldn't possibly do this with Charlotte around. She'd have to share it, and since it was her grandmother's, she didn't want to. Not yet.

"Nothing, really." She put it in the pocket of the raincoat. She'd look at it later.

FIVE

Once they got closer to Rockville and had cell reception again, Francine made a phone call to William's wife, Dolly, and learned that he was at Union Hospital in Clinton. Dolly was distraught and couldn't seem to say anything about William's condition, other than he was in a coma. Francine promised that she would be over soon to visit them.

On the outskirts of Rockville, the women drove past a large, gaudy billboard that read, Visit Mary Ruth's in Rockville! As seen on Food Network! The accompanying photo was of the front of Mary Ruth's Fabulous Sweet Shoppe at the festival.

"That's odd," Francine remarked. "I don't remember seeing that yesterday when we came in."

"You were driving."

Two hundred yards later they drove by another sign, this one a temporary wooden placard painted in Mary Ruth Catering pink, set by the side of the road on private property. Try the corn fritter donuts, as seen on Food Network! Mary Ruth's Fabulous Sweet Shoppe!

That just doesn't sound like Mary Ruth, Francine thought. She turned her head, continuing to stare in disbelief at the sign as the SUV sped by. On the other hand, she knew the festival was anxious to capitalize on Mary Ruth's notoriety. This would be just the kind of homespun advertising that would appeal to fair-goers. Perhaps Mary Ruth had nothing to do with it.

When the Covered Bridge Festival Committee approached Mary Ruth about operating a food booth at the Festival, what sealed the deal was the large home in downtown Rockville that a rich patron offered her as a place to stay and prep food. The patron hated the crowds and went on vacation during the event. Once Mary Ruth saw the mansion and its complete commercial kitchen, she'd agreed to do it. The rest of the Bridge Club had been willing to stay for ten days and pitch in to help get the food ready each day. Jonathan had stayed the night last night just to do the photo shoot in the morning.

The traffic backup got bad the instant they made it into Rockville. "It was a big mistake to come this way," Joy said. "Francine, can you guide us around the back roads?"

Though she hadn't grow up in the area because they'd moved to Evansville when she was a little girl, Francine had been there often over the years and knew her way around. Joy followed her directions until they hit another backlog. This one wasn't moving.

Joy drummed her fingers on the steering wheel. "At least we're closer than we were."

"If we're going to help Mary Ruth anytime soon," Francine observed, "we'll need to hoof it from here. Are you ready, ladies? Charlotte, do you feel up to it?"

"I guess I'll have to be." Charlotte grabbed her cane and, without hesitation, opened the back seat door.

Francine was glad Jonathan wasn't with them. Charlotte was grumbly but Jonathan would have been worse. He hated lines of any sort, especially traffic. Plus, he'd said to her more than once that the whole concept of the Covered Bridge Festival had been corrupted in favor of the American public's worst indulgences—purchasing junk and eating junk food.

It was hard for her to argue against that as Joy quickly parked and they got out in front of a pork rinds shack, which was next to a three-booth display of handmade clothing made exclusively for dressing wooden goose statues parked on geese fanciers' front porches. The three booths were divided into themes like Halloween, Christmas, and sportswear. A sign hanging at the entrance to the shop read, IF YOUR GOOSE IS NUDE, I'M YOUR DUDE.

The women had to walk two blocks to the Rockville courthouse grounds. Marcy made her apologies but said she needed to go work with another client. This surprised Francine, but when she thought about it, Marcy had never promised to help Mary Ruth. She was only there that morning because of Joy.

Francine had to keep Charlotte on task and prevent her from wandering into shops like the Beef Jerky Emporium, but they made it to the corner of Ohio and Jefferson. Mary Ruth's Fabulous Sweet Shoppe was at the far corner from them. There was a huge line that went all the way up Jefferson Street past a tent full of vendors, but the crowd didn't appear to be purchasing from the vendors. They were in line for something else. Francine and Charlotte went up Ohio and turned on Market Street.

The courthouse square was packed with people. A female duo near the stairs of the courthouse played guitar and sang country-western songs with a Carrie Underwood feel. Groups with political ties sought to influence voters for the upcoming November election.

Tour bus promoters hawked trolley tours of varying lengths covering the most popular of the bridges of Parke County, several "leaving from the square in just ten minutes!"

Despite Jonathan's raw assessment of the festival, Francine loved the sights and smells of the Covered Bridge Festival vendor areas. It was eleven o'clock and she could smell the sweet smoke of the pulled pork vendor tending to his meats, see the steam rising from the huge pots of ham and beans cooked over outdoor wood fires by the local Presbyterian church, and hear the chugging of the popcorn vendor's vat as it turned freshly popped popcorn into kettle corn. But the *pièce de résistance* was the heavenly scent of Mary Ruth's latest creation: fried corn fritter donuts with honey-cinnamon glaze. Francine discovered her booth was the source of the line that wrapped itself down High Street and along Jefferson.

The pink food truck gleamed in the sunshine. Mary Ruth had "tricked out" her catering truck and made it more functional by replacing the warming equipment with a stove, fryer, and refrigerator. She'd had to lose some of the shelf space, but it needed to become a small, fully functional kitchen. The "booth" part was something the Festival had built for her in front of the door of the truck. It was a small shack that had a large window for handling money and selling the baked goods. The window also had room for a bakery-style display case of Mary Ruth's offerings: the corn fritter donuts, gooey iced cinnamon rolls, five kinds of cookies, three types of scones, and her signature flourless chocolate cake.

Alice was heating up cinnamon rolls and icing them, Mary Ruth was frying the corn fritters to order and glazing them before handing them up to Toby, who was their front man, collecting the cash and distributing the product.

"It's funny to see people's reactions when Toby hands them their food," Charlotte said. "There's this hesitation, like, 'Do I want to eat something from this big, rough-looking tattooed guy?' but then they can't resist and gobble it right up."

"It helped that Mary Ruth made him clean up that neck beard. He's starting to look handsome, especially when he's not wearing all the piercings."

Toby spotted the women and hailed them with a desperate look in his eyes. "I think you'd better help Grandma. We're so backed up, the crowd is starting to get unruly and it's not even lunchtime yet."

"I thought we'd decided we weren't going to offer lunchtime food," Francine said.

"We're not, but that doesn't seem to have had an effect. We may want to start sedating them with samples."

Charlotte looked doubtful. "That might only create more customers."

Francine yanked her away. "I don't think he needs to hear that right now," she said *sotto voce*.

Joy snatched a corn fritter donut out of the display case. "We'll get right on it," she assured him. "I love these things," she told Francine and Charlotte as she took a bite into it.

They had to go around the long line to enter the truck, but before they got there they heard Marcy. She was standing in front of a tent parked behind Mary Ruth's place. She had changed into the red and navy-blue uniform of an old-fashioned carnival barker and was calling out in a shrill, high pitched voice, "Get your fortune told by the Great Merlina! Want to know your future? The Great Merlina sees all!"

Joy acted like she was not surprised by this and went in to help Mary Ruth, but Charlotte tugged on Francine's arm and pulled her over. "This is your other client?" Charlotte asked Marcy.

Marcy rolled her eyes. "I agreed to help my niece publicize her fortune-telling business." Then, as if she realized how rolling her eyes had come off, she added, "Not that she's not good. She's really good! She has THE GIFT."

That sounded ominous, Francine thought. "How nice," she said. "It looks like she's got a line so she certainly doesn't need us."

"Speak for yourself," Charlotte said. "I want to get my fortune told." She winked at Marcy. "Can you get me a discounted price?"

"Uh, sure."

Francine cleared her throat. "Charlotte, I think Mary Ruth might need you more. We need to get going."

Charlotte jerked her hand back. "Not until after I get my fortune told. What price was that again, Marcy?"

"For you, ten dollars. The Great Merlina usually charges thirty for a fifteen-minute reading. Better get in line now or it'll be noon before she can see you." She gave Charlotte a nudge toward the line, now about five persons deep. "I'll be there in a minute to see you get the discount rate. I need to talk to Francine."

Charlotte made her way to the end of the line. The shadow of the Great Merlina's tent absorbed her.

"Now that I've got you alone," Marcy said, "are you looking for any more television appearances? You did a great job back there at the Roseville Bridge, and I think I could get you on a couple of—"

Francine was mad. Last night they'd worked together in the big mansion's kitchen getting food ready for today and she thought she'd been pretty clear about this. "No. I don't want to be on television."

"Okay, radio, then. I could get you some radio spots."

"No!"

Marcy exaggerated a sigh, though Francine could tell she had anticipated her response. "Look what happened when I finally succeeded in getting Mary Ruth on *Chopped*. If she hadn't gotten to the dessert round, she would never have created the corn fritter donut."

"She still didn't win."

"Winning is relative. Would you look at her line? Mark my words, when the folks at Food Network hear about this, they'll come around to putting her back on the air."

"I wasn't aware you were still her publicist. I thought you only stayed the night last night because Joy needed you this morning."

"Okay, I'm not her publicist, at least not in the way you're thinking. But she'll come around too."

Francine wasn't sure how to answer that. Was Marcy working for Mary Ruth on her own? That was a scary thought.

"You sure you don't want a reading? I promise you she's pretty good. And I'm not just saying that as a publicist or a relative."

"I don't believe in that stuff."

"Let me take a look at your palm," Marcy said, snatching up Francine's hand and flipping it over. "She's taught me a couple of things."

Francine gave her a skeptical look but let her continue. "Let me guess, I have a short life line."

Marcy's eyebrows went up, far enough above the dark sunglasses that Francine could see them. "Quite the contrary. It's a very *long* life line. Look at this." Marcy traced it across Francine's palm.

"Is that long?"

"Compared to most people's, yes. In fact, it's the longest I've seen. Not that I've seen that many. Only since I've been helping out

Merlina. I think you should let her read your palm. Or your fortune with Tarot cards."

"Or maybe we should invite her over for a slumber party and have a séance," Francine said, and then regretted it immediately.

Marcy brightened. "Great idea! Does someone have that on their bucket list? Because the Great Merlina does séances too."

"Nope. Bad idea. I was just kidding." Francine averted her eyes. Alice, in fact, had this on her Sixty List. It was on the low end, somewhere in the forties, but it was there.

"Hmmm. Maybe I'll just have to check that out with Charlotte."

Francine spotted Toby hustling toward her. "Gotta go, Marcy. Good luck with the Great Merlina." She scurried off. As she left, Marcy had a big smile on her face. *Nothing good will come of this,* Francine thought. She'd thought that before, too, and had been right. "What is it, Toby?"

"Grandma needs you right away."

"What's going on?"

"She's nearly out of corn meal, she has zero time to go get some, and everyone's starting to notice we're running out of food."

"Does she need me to run to the store?"

"Yes, but it may already be too late."

A great murmuring swept the crowd at that moment, a wave of growing dissatisfaction like the stir of the ocean before it gathered strength and overwhelmed the shore. People began to push and crowd the booth. Fists struck the display case trying to seize whatever Fabulous Sweets were left. Joy gasped and took a step back from the register. Mary Ruth's hands went up in the air in alarm. Alice gripped the cross medallion at her breast.

Francine swallowed hard.

And then a reedy voice from two booths over cried, "Free pork rind samples! Get your free pork rind samples here." Another nearby vendor yelled, "I've got beef jerky, elk jerky, any kind of jerky you need!"

The crowd's ear perked up.

And then they dispersed to other booths.

Francine exhaled.

And knew she would never look down on pork rind or beef jerky vendors again.

SIX

Mary Ruth squirreled away the remaining few cookies, scones, and slices of flourless chocolate cake and closed the booth.

"Whew!" She wiped her forehead, sweeping the damp auburn hair to the side where it tucked naturally behind her ear. "I've never felt so threatened in my life."

"Second time today for me," Joy said.

"Oh my gosh, that's right! You said you'd been shot at while you were at the bridge. What happened?"

Joy and Francine filled in Mary Ruth and Alice in while they cleaned up the booth and got it ready for the next day.

"Do you know how your cousin is doing?" Alice asked. She stooped over and picked up loose change that had been dislodged from the cash register tray, holding back a lock of her graying hair so she could see where it had landed.

"I made a call to his wife once we got in cell phone range. I didn't learn much other than he was in a coma."

"Oh. You'll be wanting to go visit him this afternoon, won't you?" There was a hint of disappointment in Mary Ruth's voice. She double-checked that the stove and the fryer were turned off and didn't make eye contact with Francine.

"I'm sorry, but yes, I do need to go as soon as we finish up here. Jonathan should have turned in the horse and buggy and driven here by then." It was clear Mary Ruth needed her, but William was family and besides, it was the right thing to do.

"I understand, of course," Mary Ruth said.

Francine knew it was the truth. She wiped down the stainless countertop. "I'll come back as soon as I feel I can leave the hospital. I'll see if I can persuade Jonathan to stay an extra night. That way you'll have both of us to help once we get back. If today is anything like tomorrow, you'll need an extra hand."

"That would be nice."

"So what do we do now?" Joy asked. She leaned against the countertop.

"First, we head back to the house, make out a deposit slip, and get that cash in the bank," Mary Ruth said. "Rule number one of catering: deposit the money. Then we plan for tomorrow and head off for the store. We're going to need to do a lot more cooking and prep work. But I guess we have all afternoon now as well as the evening."

"We can't leave until Charlotte gets back," Francine said.

Mary Ruth put a hand to her hip. "And where is she?"

Francine pointed to the tent behind her. "Getting her fortune told by the Great Merlina."

"Great."

"How did Merlina end up getting booth space right next to you?"

"I have no idea. They didn't tell me who'd be around me when they offered me the space. All I knew was it was free, so I didn't ask many questions. I think they're trying to build up a food tradition here in Rockville since they don't actually have a covered bridge. They don't like the idea that Bridgeton and Mansfield get most of the action."

———

Since Mary Ruth didn't want to wait for Charlotte, Toby agreed to stay behind with the truck. The house was in walking distance of the booth for most of them, but not Charlotte, not with her bad knee. "I'll find something to keep me happy," he assured them. When they left, he was plugged into his phone and seemed content to wait however long it might take.

Francine made a call to Jonathan and found he was stuck in traffic not too far from them. "I'll come to you," Francine said, "and then we'll head for Clinton." She told him that's where William had been taken.

"That's fine. I don't expect to move from this spot. Not anytime soon." Francine walked up two blocks, found him, and got in his truck. She directed him around on side streets.

"I found out a few things," he said. "The person who owns the cornfield by the Roseville Bridge is named Zedediah Matthew. It's a large property, over three hundred acres. Apparently Mr. Matthew is very protective of his land and has a history of running people off his property. He probably pursued William, but we have no proof of that."

"Why would William chance an encounter with someone like him?"

"Probably for the fortune that's supposedly buried somewhere on the property. Zedediah bought the land from Doc Wheat, who acquired it in the 1920s. During the Depression he developed an interest in herbalism. At one time his home remedies were popular and shipped all over the world."

"You know how I feel about herbalism. It's unscientific."

"I'm not arguing with you. The advent of the modern pharmacy killed his business. But supposedly he acquired a lot of money before that. He had a deep suspicion of banks, bred from the Depression. Rumors were he buried all the money on his property. For decades since, people have been trying to find it."

"How did you find all this out?"

"I asked the owner of the horse barn."

She finally got them to US 41 south, and the traffic eased up. They drove toward Clinton.

She wondered why William would have been after a fortune. As far as she knew, his nursing home businesses were doing well. "William must have had a powerful reason to believe in the hidden fortune. Otherwise he wouldn't risk his life for it."

"I hope it doesn't cost him that."

"Me too."

Francine connected her phone to the truck's radio and scanned the playlists for something soothing. "Do you think it's just anger that's got Mr. Matthew shooing people off his property with guns?" Francine thought of *The Beverly Hillbillies* when Jed ran "revenuers" off his land. "If there's no treasure, what's he got to hide?"

"That sounds like a Charlotte question, so I'll give you a Charlotte answer. Maybe he's one of those survivalists. Maybe he's got a whole arsenal stored on his land and he's doesn't want anyone to find it."

Francine laughed. "I can't imagine why William would be looking for a bunch of guns, *Charlotte*."

"Maybe William is a federal agent. Maybe being a nursing home owner is just his cover."

"William does not look like he's even remotely capable of being a federal agent."

Jonathan leaned over and raised an eyebrow a couple of times. "Then he's perfectly unassuming. No one would suspect."

Francine smirked. "That is exactly what Charlotte would say."

"I've been around her a lot lately."

"I have to say, though, Zedediah does sound like the name of someone who would be a survivalist."

"I'm not sure I know enough survivalists to make that call," Jonathan replied.

They finished joking and settled into their own thoughts. Francine fretted over the situation with William.

Neither she nor William had had siblings, and neither had their parents. However one defined cousins, she and William were about it when it came to blood relatives. She found the lack of family lonesome, and it played into the decision she and Jonathan made to have three children, all of whom turned out to be boys. In contrast, William and Dolly had no children. Of course, they'd gotten a late start in life, and Francine presumed that was the reason.

Dolly was an odd duck. She and William were clearly devoted to each other, but Dolly wasn't the woman Francine would have guessed he'd marry. They found each other when Dolly was in her mid-forties, divorced from a man she'd let on had an unsavory past, though nothing more specific than that. If it hadn't been for Dolly's looks and her pursuit of William, who was then in his fifties, the two would not have gotten together. At least that was Francine's opinion.

Dolly came from a blue-collar background. She had been working as a bartender before they married. While Francine respected

Dolly as a hard worker and knew that without her help William would never have built up the successful chain of retirement homes, she was more shrewd than smart. In fact, Dolly could be ruthless when called for, which had served the business well in taking over existing retirement homes. There was no question who was in charge. William was probably good with it, though. Dolly was as social as William was introverted.

The last time Francine had seen William and Dolly had been at the wedding of her middle son, Adam. In some sense, the encounter had been a microcosm of their relationship. As family, Francine made certain her cousin was seated at her table. Yet, William had seemed uncomfortable and hardly talked, even when he was asked a question directly. He mostly drank. Dolly, on the other hand, talked nonstop, none of it worth hearing. The only time she stopped was to seethe at William's drinking, which led Jonathan to compare her to a volcano with an active lava flow: "You know any minute it could just explode."

Had it been some kind of remorse on William's part, that Francine had a son to be married and two other sons seated at the table of bridesmaids and groomsmen? Had Dolly's verbosity simply shut off William's need to speak? Or had William never conquered whatever demons had made him a socially backward teenager? Francine could easily see William running an efficient set of nursing homes, filled with elderly or infirm people whose basic needs were supplied by people he hired to do that. As the owner, with whom did he really need to communicate besides the few managers who worked under him?

Francine remembered when they were very young, when they shared secrets and played together in the attic of her grandmother's house. How differently they had grown up. But because of the good times, she still felt an attachment to William.

When they came to State Road 163, they turned onto it and crossed the Wabash River into Clinton. They followed the blue *H* signs until they found Union Hospital. Even given the traffic, it hadn't taken more than a half hour to get there.

Dolly was in the ICU when Francine and Jonathan finally succeeded in getting admitted as visitors. Dolly looked like she'd just spent an hour in front of the mirror despite having a husband in the ICU. Her makeup was perfectly applied, down to the faint blue eye shadow and red lipstick. She wore a casual white blouse and black jeans.

"I'm so glad you came." Dolly gave Francine a quick awkward hug. She shook hands with Jonathan. "It's been so difficult to just sit here, watching him sleep."

Dolly walked to the hospital bed and they followed. William looked like himself, his bald head sporting scraggly stands of gray hair that popped up indiscriminately over the shiny dome. It was scratched and marred with angry red wounds, though. A thick fringe of salt-and-pepper hair curled around the back and sides of his scalp. His color was good, but he was hooked up to a ventilator to help him breathe and his neck was in a brace. As a former nurse, Francine knew the odds William faced. "What did the doctors say about the coma?"

"They say he has a head injury, probably from the fall, that's caused swelling in his brain. The swelling is minor, and they're hopeful he'll regain full consciousness. But they don't know how long. A few days, a few weeks. Weeks, Francine! Weeks!"

Since their initial hug had been fast and uncomfortable, Francine didn't go there again. Instead, she put her arm around Dolly's shoulder.

"They say the prognosis is good," Dolly continued, "but it's too difficult to predict how he might respond when he wakes up. I'm thankful you were there, Jonathan, to pull him out of the creek. Even though it might have injured him further."

Francine released her hold on Dolly's shoulder momentarily as the thought ran through her mind that Dolly might try to file some kind of lawsuit against them because of Jonathan's action. She hoped she was being paranoid.

Jonathan seemed to be of similar mind. "It was a difficult decision to make. But I couldn't let him slip into the creek."

Francine gently finished his thought. "If he'd been pulled any farther into the water, he would have drowned since he was unconscious."

"Oh, I know. I understand. Jonathan saved his life."

Francine wished that last sentence was on tape, just in case. "None of the shots that were fired at him touched him, did they?"

Dolly tenderly traced the red scratches on the top of his head. "No. He had some bleeding, but that was likely caused by hitting tree branches when he fell down the bank."

Francine wasn't sure how to ask the next question because she didn't want to look like she was prying, when in fact she was. "What was William doing out at the Roseville Bridge anyway? Who was shooting at him?"

Dolly turned away. "I don't know why he was out there."

"I found out the property he was running across belonged to a man named Zedediah Matthew," Jonathan asked. "Did William know him?"

"Everyone around here knows who Zedediah Matthew is. He's a mean man, cranky and threatening."

Francine rubbed Dolly's upper arm supportively, though she worried the gesture came across as a means to coax more information. "Did you know he was carrying two items? One of them was a diary that belonged to my grandmother. The second was a vial of some kind of liquid. Do either of those make sense to you?"

Dolly stiffened at the question. Francine wasn't sure if that was because she didn't know, or if she knew and was alarmed to discover that Francine also knew.

"I didn't know," she said. "Do you know who has them now?"

"The sheriff's department." It was only a half lie. The police did have the vial. She didn't qualify her answer further. She made eye contact with Jonathan to make sure he didn't give her away, but he sat there with a smug look on his face.

"He fancied himself a historian," Dolly said. "I knew he'd found a copy of your grandmother's diary at some flea market. Why he had it there, I don't know. As for the vial, I have no idea what might have been in it."

"So William just left your house this morning and went out there carrying those two items? He didn't say why or what he was looking for?"

Dolly answered testily. "He said he was going into Rockville. You know one of our nursing homes is there. It operates twenty-four hours a day, so the fact that he was heading there very early wasn't out of line."

Francine pictured William leaving their home, a Victorian manor out near the tiny town of Montezuma. He should have taken Coxville Road toward US 41 and then turned north toward Rockville. For whatever reason, he went straight across US 41, continued down Coxville past the Roseville Bridge, and went traipsing across a dangerous man's property, a man who hadn't been happy to see him. She wondered where he had parked. "Have you looked into where his car is, Dolly? Has anyone seen it?"

Francine saw something cross Dolly's face. For a moment she thought it was a look of panic, but on second thought it settled into one of surprise. "No. It hadn't crossed my mind. Sheriff Roy was in and he asked what kind of car William drove, but I didn't put two and two together, not until now."

Sheriff Roy? Then Francine remembered that Roy Stockton had been the sheriff before he'd settled into retirement as a detective. "Finding the car could be the key to discovering who was responsible for shooting at William."

"Well, I assume it was Zed Matthew."

How odd that she called him Zed. It felt almost familiar. But if he's that notorious, everyone probably had nicknames for him, and Zed would be kinder than most.

Jonathan had crossed the room to a visitor's chair and let the women talk. But now he spoke up. "While that's likely, everyone is innocent until proven guilty."

Francine agreed, but she didn't need him prickling Dolly's mood while she was fishing for clues. "The sheriff has to operate under that premise. I'm sure that's what Jonathan was saying." She flashed her eyes at him. "Just out of curiosity, do you still own the Buick? What was that, a light blue Lucerne?"

Dolly focused back on William. She took hold of his hand and held it in hers. "Yes. We had OnStar too. It should be easy to track."

"Do you want us to help you with that?"

"You're being a dear, Francine. I can't concentrate on anything but William. Yes, it would help. What do you need?"

"The license plate number and the keys. If we can find the car, we should be able to retrieve it for you."

Dolly indicated a small table on the other side of William's bed where a knock-off Vera Bradley purse tote lay open. "The keys are in my purse. Let me get it for you."

Francine was thinking that the bright orange and pink paisley pattern was one she would never be seen carrying when her eyes spotted something else inside the purse: a small vial, similar to the one Jonathan had pulled out of William's pocket. This one, too, had a cork stopper on it. Francine couldn't tell whether it was full or empty, not without picking it up.

Dolly reached the purse and found the key to William's car. "Here it is. I put a light blue dot on the key. It was easy to remember that way." She looped the handles of the purse over each other so it was no longer easy to see inside.

"Thanks," Francine said, taking the key from her. "Didn't the Buick have a vanity license plate number?"

"It still does. 'WRM MMIES.' He thinks it advertises the retirement community, but I think it could also be 'Worm Mummies.'" She smiled at Francine, but Francine could see the pain in it. "Everything closer to 'Warm Memories' was already taken."

Francine eased into a second visitor chair, identical to the one Jonathan was in. It was simple in design—a cube on legs—but upholstered in a rust pattern and comfortable to sit in. She noted how hospitals had changed over the years that she'd been a nurse. Rooms used to feel cold and sterile. Now hospitals tried for a hotel feel. She patted the other chair in the room, which was next to her. "Let's sit for a while." The gesture was genuine even if she felt a little strange doing it.

Dolly left William's side. She plopped into the chair by Francine, but she leaned forward with her elbows on her knees as though she would lurch out of the seat any moment. "Thanks. My sister is coming up from Memphis to stay with me, but she won't be here for another couple of hours."

Francine couldn't remember ever meeting Dolly's sister, though it probably would have been at William's wedding and that was decades ago. "I'm glad to know she's coming. So, how are things going at the retirement homes? You and William are certainly the king and queen of the elderly set, at least in western Indiana."

She half shrugged. "Business is okay, although the rules change constantly. The government is giving a lot of financial support to encourage folks to stay in their homes and get end-of-life care. William says we have to adapt by offering different services. He's so business savvy. I could never do this by myself. He's got to recover."

"I'm sure he will." Francine caught Jonathan's eye and tried to implore him to help the conversation.

Jonathan steepled his fingers. "What are you doing now, Dolly? Are you managing any of the properties?"

"One of the Terre Haute properties, and also the one in Clinton. They're good, both profitable. I'm also responsible for all the memory care units. The one in Rockville is full and we have a waiting list." Dolly concentrated on the perfectly manicured nails she was picking to imperfection.

Jonathan seemed to feel he'd done his part of the socializing and sat back in his chair.

Though Francine had difficulties relating to Dolly, at least at the hospital she was in her element. The antiseptic smell of the room, the whispers of concerned visitors in the hall, and the scrolling LED lights of the EKG equipment monitoring William's heartbeat were all features of a scene she'd watched play out over and over again. "Memory care is a growing business. It's good but it's sad. Once a person can't function and becomes difficult to deal with, it's good to have a place where they can get proper care. But some relatives dump them into a care unit and hardly visit them."

"I see it all the time," Dolly answered. "We have this one older woman. She tells the most interesting stories." Dolly hesitated like she realized she shouldn't be talking about it.

Francine wanted to keep Dolly talking. It was easier that way. "What about the stories?"

"They ... she ... they're just unusual. It's like she's living in the late 1800s. I feel like I'm listening to an audio book of *Little House on the Prairie*, only set in Indiana."

"Does she get visitors?"

"Her husband. I don't know if he works odd hours, but he only comes in very late at night, and only once a month. I've never met him in person. He stays a half hour, then leaves."

The nurse came in and checked the monitoring devices. "Mrs. Falkes!" she said. Dolly stood and went over, completely absorbed by the nurse's concerned look.

Francine took that as the right moment to end the visit. Jonathan apparently had, too, because he stood up at the same time she did.

"Maybe this would be a good time for us to get going," Francine said. "We'll see if we can find William's car for you." She approached Dolly and handed her a note. "Here's my cell phone number and the address of the place we're staying in Rockville. Make sure your sister has it too. Call if you need anything."

As Jonathan opened the door for her, she glanced back at William. Would she ever see him alive again? She hoped so, but the figure under the hospital blanket twitched like something was very, very wrong.

SEVEN

"I can't believe you volunteered us to go look for his car," Jonathan said after he'd climbed into the truck and shut his door. Francine was already buckling up.

"Was that so wrong?"

"Not necessarily, but with all you've got to do today? Mary Ruth needs your help, and you know I can't stay."

"You can't?" In truth, she'd forgotten to ask him. She only remembered now she'd told Mary Ruth he would. "Why not?"

He started the truck and drove out of the hospital parking lot. "I have to go back this afternoon. I have an evening meeting tonight and several client meetings scheduled for tomorrow. I thought I'd mentioned that."

Though he was semi-retired from his accounting firm, Jonathan still maintained a few long-time clients and hadn't yet given up his partnership. She knew he'd arranged his schedule so he would be free yesterday to come with them to Rockville and today for the early morning photo shoot. *I guess it is an imposition to expect him to stay longer*, she thought.

"Let's hurry back to Rockville then. If Mary Ruth has everything under control, I'll recruit Charlotte to help me."

"Even if she doesn't have everything under control, she still may be better off if you take Charlotte off her hands to go look for the car."

Francine chuckled at that. Charlotte and Mary Ruth got along far better playing cards than when they were in a kitchen together. Charlotte wasn't much interested in food preparation except for sampling.

Since it was nearing two o'clock, they made a quick stop at the Dairy Queen on the way out of Clinton and ate in the truck while listening to songs from the 1950s.

The stately home Mary Ruth was using for the week was in an old, historic section of Rockville. Being the county seat for Parke County, Rockville had a number of homes that dated back to the turn of the twentieth century, but few of them were as grand as the Mansfield Estate, an Italianate home on Market Street that also had a carriage house and a gardener's cottage on the grounds. Inside, the house had been renovated several times, most recently to add a state-of-the-art kitchen and modern bathrooms to six of the ten bedrooms.

There were four unrecognized cars in the driveway, so Jonathan had to park on the street. "Do you know what's going on?" he asked Francine.

"No," she said. But she suspected Charlotte was up to something.

They rang the front door bell even though they could have just walked in. It wasn't like the owner was there. But with the extra cars, Francine thought it be better to announce their entrance. Plus, she couldn't get used to entering a house this nice without asking for permission.

"Oh, it's you." Charlotte seemed disappointed when she opened the door. She wiped her hands on a kitchen towel she'd carried with her.

"You were expecting someone else?"

"Ummm. No. Just surprised to see you back so soon."

Jonathan wiped his feet on the mat before entering. "We've been gone a couple of hours."

Francine admired the wide staircase in front of them and the balcony that surrounded the second floor above them. "I don't think I could ever get used to making a grand entrance into this place."

"This *is* some house." Charlotte leaned back to admire the high ceiling.

Francine did likewise. The ceiling was plaster and had a significant amount of crown molding around the walls. A large chandelier with what looked to be a hundred flame-shaped light bulbs hung from the center.

Mary Ruth came in from the kitchen, clad in her pink catering apron. Francine still did a double-take when she saw how Mary Ruth's clothes now flattered her body. She'd lost almost fifty pounds thanks to her Bucket List item and the hiring of a personal trainer. It was probably the reason she showed none of the exhaustion she had earlier from the tense morning in the food booth.

"I have to say, you do have friends with impeccable taste," Francine told her.

"And money," Charlotte added.

Mary Ruth laughed. "Friends of friends, not friends. But it's good to have people who are fans of my food." She motioned toward the kitchen. "C'mon back. The last of what we're making for tomorrow is in the oven."

Francine wrinkled her forehead. "How did you accomplish so much in such a short period of time?"

"Two things. One, Marcy persuaded me that I really didn't need to make that much more food, that shortage only made my food more desirable. We did the scones, cookies, and cakes today, leaving us only the cinnamon rolls to bake in the morning. The donuts, of course, we fry as needed." They followed her around to the back side of the staircase where they entered the kitchen through a swinging door.

"I imagine this is where the butler and servants used to come to get the food from the cook when the house was first built," Francine said. She held on to one of the swinging door and fingered the wood grain. She wasn't sure if the doors were original, but they looked like could have been used in the early 1900s, when food have been plated in the kitchen and then whisked away to the formal dining room for serving. "What's number two?"

Mary Ruth ushered them in. "I added staff." Besides Alice, who was working on scones, there were six other women in Mary Ruth Catering pink aprons at work. Two of them were tackling a mountain of dishes to be washed, and the other four were either manning the wall ovens or mixing up what looked to be batches of corn fritter donut dough.

Francine guessed the new recruits to be in their fifties. *Young*, Francine thought. "You hired them?"

"Technically, no. They're volunteers. The Covered Bridge Festival Committee sent them over after lunch. The Committee was apparently really impressed by the crowds we drew."

Francine walked over to the wall ovens. She didn't know what was in them, but she smelled cinnamon. She found a switch that turned on a light inside the top oven. "Those scones look divine," she said.

"Thanks," said Alice, who was using a spatula to transfer from a baking sheet to a cooling rack the biggest apple-cinnamon scones Francine had ever seen. "I've been begging Mary Ruth to let me make them. I feel like I've been a good apprentice and ready to try my hand at some of her recipes." She was dressed in the standard Mary Ruth Catering outfit of black pants, white shirt, black shoes, and a pink apron. Of course, the pants were Michael Kors and her shoes were Kate Spade, but that was Alice.

Charlotte nudged Francine aside so she could look. "Those things are cresting perfectly, and that fall-ish smell of cinnamon has been calling to me all afternoon. I can hardly wait to slather one in icing and take a bite."

"It's a *glaze*," Alice said. "And we don't slather them. We drizzle them."

"If I get hold of the icing, they'll be bathed in the stuff."

"That's why you will not get near them," Mary Ruth said. "They are Alice's to drizzle. She did exceptionally well making them. And all the help enabled me to get several batches of cookies ready for to-morrow." She uncovered a space on a countertop to reveal mounds of five types of giant cookies, easily seven inches in diameter. As Charlotte headed toward the cookies, Mary Ruth recovered them with a flour sack towel. "I made some smaller ones for us to have later."

"We'll need them sooner rather than later," Charlotte said.

Mary Ruth squinted at her. "Why will we need them sooner?"

"For the séance. We're having a séance this afternoon." Charlotte said it as though she wouldn't tolerate dissention.

"A séance?" Mary Ruth clearly thought Charlotte was making a joke. "You don't have a séance in the middle of the afternoon. Don't you have them at night?"

"She's giving us the early-bird special."

Francine chuckled to herself. Charlotte was a true senior when it came to knowing about every early-bird special available.

Alice blew on a stray piece of hair that hung down by her eyes. "Why on earth are we having a séance?"

Charlotte dug both fists into her hips. "For someone who had Attend a Séance on her Sixty List, you don't sound very enthused. I arranged this for you."

Mary Ruth's expression was one of realization. "That explains why Marcy disappeared. She's gone to get Merlina."

Alice's mouth went taut. "Don't think that I don't appreciate your help, Charlotte. It's just that when I got around to being part of a séance, I thought it'd be with someone I trusted a little more than the Great Merlina."

"You haven't even met the Great Merlina yet."

"The fact that she's related to Marcy does not inspire confidence."

"This is where I get out," Jonathan said. He gave Francine a kiss. "Have fun. I'll call you later when I get home." He snatched one of the big cookies Mary Ruth had hidden under the flour towel and went upstairs.

Francine sighed and watched him go up to get his things. "Where's Joy?" she asked Charlotte.

"She's back at the Covered Bridge Festival doing 'color pieces.' Channel Six sent a truck and cameraman after the station got a look at the footage of the rescue. She did a segment on the noon news about it, but the truck wasn't here yet. They want her to do a live segment from the Roseville Bridge for *The News at Five*. Say, Jonathan's not leaving, is he? Joy was counting on interviewing him."

"Oh, I'm confident he'll be leaving now."

The doorbell rang. "I'll get it," Mary Ruth said and scurried off as though she were glad to have something else to do right then.

They could hear the front door open, and then they heard Marcy announce in a loud voice, "The Great Merlina has arrived!"

"Wait no longer," Charlotte said.

The procession of Marcy, the Great Merlina, and Mary Ruth entered the kitchen, with Marcy swinging open the door and holding it for Merlina. Francine hadn't gotten a good look at her earlier because she'd been in shadows within the tent, but she was pretty sure Merlina hadn't been dressed in a midnight-blue gypsy dress that went all the way to the floor. The dress had a dramatic flair, with outer sleeves that covered the arms to the wrists and inner sleeves that fell away from her forearms like petals drooping from a spent tulip. A square neckline settled across her chest with medieval-looking embroidery that was repeated at Merlina's chunky waist. The same pattern ran down the front two folds of the dress to her shoes. Francine thought the shoes looked like thick, scuffed gray leather boots. Merlina wore an ornate gold necklace with multiple gold bracelets around her wrists. "I am here," Merlina said. "Are we ready to contact the spirit world?"

"We would be," Mary Ruth intoned, "except we have a batch of apple-cinnamon scones almost ready to come out of the oven."

"The spirits will not be willing to come if all parties are not going to be attentive." Merlina narrowed her eyes at Mary Ruth. "We'll wait." She threw her arms out to the sides, punctuating the word *wait* as though thunder would roll when she said it. Without pausing for anyone's permission, Merlina put a boot on one of the bottom rungs of a stool. "Does anyone have tea?"

"I'm sure we must have tea somewhere," Charlotte said, anxious to please. "Don't we?"

Mary Ruth pointed to a long narrow cabinet next to the refrigerator. "In there, I think."

Charlotte rummaged through the cabinet. "How about English breakfast?" She held out a box to show Merlina, who sniffed.

"Not much of a selection."

Francine choked back the retort she started to make. Instead, she said, "I might have some herbal tea in my purse. Let me check."

"Thank you," Merlina said. She took her foot off the stool and dramatically paced across the kitchen toward the dining room. Marcy, Mary Ruth, and Charlotte followed, along with Francine, who'd grabbed her purse and was rifling through it.

"This will do nicely," Merlina announced, placing her hands on the long, old-fashioned cherry dining room table that Francine was sure was a well-preserved antique. "The spirits love to convene around old things. It makes them comfortable."

"Then they'll love us," Mary Ruth said dryly.

Now that Francine was closer to Merlina, she noticed the dress smelled of mothballs. She briefly wondered how the spirits felt about mothballs. Merlina's complexion was dark, like she was descended from Mediterranean stock. *Perhaps the dress is authentic,* she thought. *Maybe Merlina does come from gypsy blood.*

The women returned to the kitchen. Mary Ruth told her volunteer staff they could go. Francine made tea and Charlotte persuaded Mary Ruth to surrender a few of the smaller oatmeal raisin walnut cookies. The women split the cookies and sat with their cups of tea back at the dining room table. Finally Mary Ruth and Alice got the scones out of the oven. As they joined the others, the scent of apples and cinnamon wafted in with them, making everyone's mouth water.

Merlina issued instructions to no one in particular. "Please douse the lights and lower the shade on the window." Marcy got up and made the room darker. "I can feel an older energy in this room," Merlina intoned, glancing furtively around as though she could see ghosts darting in and out.

"If it's on my part," Mary Ruth said, wiping her brow with the bottom of the apron she was still wearing, "there's not much energy left. I don't know that I'm up to a séance."

"You have to participate," Charlotte insisted. "All five of us do."

"Not me," Marcy said. "I'm only here to help." Which only made Francine more suspicious this was a setup.

"I meant Joy," Charlotte said.

Eerie music started to play from somewhere in the room and the little hairs on the back of Francine's neck went up. Then she realized that Marcy had brought along a portable music system.

"Everyone stop talking!" the Great Merlina said. "It's time to begin the séance!" She flapped the inner sleeves of her costume like birds' wings as she waved the others silent.

"But Joy isn't here yet!" Alice said.

The doorbell rang just then and before Mary Ruth could get out to the front room to open it, the women heard Joy's high-pitched voice exclaim, "I'm here, I'm here!"

"I knew that would happen," Merlina said without a beat.

But Merlina lost control as everyone except her and Marcy rushed to the front room to greet Joy.

"Did you see my report on the news at noon?" Joy said.

"We've been too busy, but we did DVR it," Marcy said.

The rest of the group was behind her. "We were going to watch it when we finished the scones," Alice said, "but then the Great Merlina showed up."

Joy's eyes registered confusion. "The Great Merlina?"

"For the séance," Charlotte said.

"We are about to start," Merlina loudly pronounced from the dining room.

"Let's get this over with," Francine muttered to the group.

"I heard that," the Great Merlina called.

Charlotte ushered them back into the dining room. "This will be fun. We've never done a séance before."

"Nor have we necessarily wanted to do one," Mary Ruth said. "It was way down on Alice's list, and now she's not sure she wants to do it."

Charlotte got huffy. "It's too late now. And let me remind you I hired her out of my own pocketbook to do this."

Francine wondered about that. It was unusual for Charlotte to spend money on anything other than books or meals out. She'd grown rather used to it. Charlotte's husband had died many years ago, and although he was a lawyer and made good money, his death had come unexpectedly early in life. Charlotte rarely commented about her finances, so Francine had no way to judge. Still, it was out of character. *So why is Charlotte so anxious to do this?*

It wasn't long before they were all seated at the table. Marcy lit a single candle in an ornate gold candlestick in the center of the table. Mary Ruth insisted on setting it on top of a plastic placemat in case it dripped. Merlina groused but didn't object.

They were just settled again when the timer in the kitchen buzzed. "I'm sorry," Alice said, getting up. "I must have hit the button twice when I took the scones out of the oven earlier."

"Apple-cinnamon?" Joy asked. Mary Ruth nodded. "I could tell by the amazing aroma. Can you spare one? I barely had time to down a bottle of water for lunch."

"I'm glad you can smell them," Alice said, heading into the kitchen. "It's been a bad fall for my allergies. I can only get a whiff when I'm standing close."

Francine did feel sorry for Alice. Her nose was perpetually clogged. It was sad to think she could only catch a whiff of the wonderful cinnamon and apple scent haunting the room like a ghost.

The timer continued to beep, then it went silent with a choked half beep. "Please return immediately," Merlina called. "Hopefully we can continue with no further interruptions!"

"We're going to have some cookies and scones after the séance," Mary Ruth assured Joy. "I'm putting Francine in charge of making coffee to go with them."

Charlotte waited four seconds before she became impatient. "Could we please just get started?"

"Coming, coming." Alice trudged into the dining room.

"Alice," Joy said, "you don't sound excited, considering this was on your Sixty List."

"Will everyone please stop saying that? I'm just on edge about it. Don't we all feel that way about half the items on our list? They seem exciting and daring when you first write them down, but then you're not sure you really want to do them when you get close to the time. That's the way I feel now."

The Great Merlina motioned everyone to sit. "Please. Nothing bad is going to happen. No one will come away possessed or anything. We are just seeking to contact the spirit world for guidance. Are we all agreed?" She didn't wait for agreement or disagreement. "Then let's join hands."

EIGHT

Marcy started up the eerie music again. She was the only one not in the circle. She dimmed the lights until the only source of light was the candle.

"Hear us, oh great spirits from beyond!" Merlina intoned, eyes closed. "We come seeking your guidance."

There was a momentary bit of silence, and Merlina opened her eyes a slit. She looked at the other women. They were all staring at her. She hissed under her breath, "I forgot to ask, who are we looking to contact?"

No one said anything. "Alice, we're doing this for you," Charlotte whispered. She was sitting next to her, so she gave Alice's hand a squeeze. "Is there anyone you want to contact?"

Alice's eyes widened. "I haven't had time to think this through. Can I have a minute, please?"

Merlina tapped her foot loud enough for everyone to hear. "While the connection to the spirit world is open," she said through gritted teeth, "we need to move."

"I have someone I'd like to contact," Francine volunteered. "That will give Alice time to think. I'd like to contact Doc Wheat."

Joy wrinkled her nose. "Who? I don't think I've ever heard you mention him before. Is it a relative?"

"No. Well, not that I know of. But he's the person who originally owned the property William was on, the one next to the Roseville Bridge. Supposedly he buried his wealth on the land."

"Oh Doc Wheat!!!" Merlina called out with a shaky voice. "You who once lived in this area! Come to us now! We seek your wisdom …" She let her voice fall off as she finished the last word.

All the women held their breaths. Except for Merlina, they glanced at each other wondering what would happen next. As nothing did, they let their breaths out. Merlina opened one eye. "He seems to be unavailable."

"Well, isn't that a bummer!" Mary Ruth said. "The only person we want to contact and he isn't there. Where is he?"

"I don't know where he is. I only know he's not available." She closed her eyes again. She cleared her throat. "Oh spirit of Doc Wheat!! We need your presence! There are people here who seek your knowledge."

Again there was anticipation. Merlina huffed a little. "This is unexpected. I almost always have success, especially when we're so close to where he lived."

"I agree," Mary Ruth said. "This close we ought to have a better connection. Are you trying to contact him in 4G? Maybe 3G is too slow."

Merlina ignored Mary Ruth. "Are there any other spirits here who could help us? Someone who knows Doc Wheat?"

For the third time, silence settled into the room.

Merlina's shoulders started to sway back and forth. Her head lolled back. She moaned as though she were struggling with something. Then she jerked forward and slumped on the table, the side of her head lightly hitting the wooden top.

The women stared at her. Francine, who was seated adjacent, prodded her on arm. "Are you all right?"

Marcy rushed to her side. "Shhhh. She's in touch with a spirit. Let's wait to see who it is."

Alice sat up. "I just thought of someone I'd like to contact. I'd like to talk to my husband's mistress, Jake Maehler's mother. I'd like to know why she thought it was a good idea to seduce my husband, and why she didn't tell him about his child. And I'd like to know if she thinks I should take him back. Heaven knows, I want to, but I'd just like to hear why this whole thing happened in the first place before I—"

Alice didn't get any further. Merlina sat up and stared directly into Francine's eyes. "It's burning," she said. "Burning. Now. And you're responsible."

"What?" Francine could see that Merlina wasn't really looking at her. Her dark eyes were vacant. Open, but vacant.

Merlina turned away momentarily to look at Charlotte. "And you know why."

"Why what?" Charlotte asked.

"Why it's burning."

"No, I don't."

Marcy got up in Merlina's face. "Who are you?"

No response. "I said, who are you?" she repeated.

Mary Ruth put her hands on the table and pushed herself up. "This is nonsense. I'm going to get some water to drink."

Merlina swung her head toward Francine again. "In the end, that was what I wanted too, the water. And he gave it to me. But it had more in it than I thought."

Francine tilted her head to the side. She thought of the vial William had been carrying when they found him on the creek bank. "William? Are you William?"

Merlina gave no response.

"You can't be William. William's in a coma."

"Unless he's passed away since you saw him last," Charlotte offered.

"Well, that's a happy thought," Mary Ruth snapped.

"At least I'm trying to be helpful."

"What's burning?" Francine asked Merlina.

No response.

Francine gripped her by the shoulders. She got more emphatic. "What's burning?"

Merlina's eyes rolled back in head. She pitched forward toward the table, but Francine had hold of her and stopped her from crashing onto it. Marcy grabbed Merlina and the woman began to shake uncontrollably. Between Francine and Marcy they lowered Merlina to the floor, where she settled into fetal position. Her shaking faded until it finally stopped.

Joy's cell phone went off. Her ringtone was the "March of the Storm Troopers" from *Star Wars*, so the noise was disconcerting. Joy answered it, running into the front room so as not to disturb the others.

"What just happened here?" Francine demanded from Marcy. "Is this a normal occurrence during a séance?"

"I don't know." Marcy sounded frightened. "I've only been through a couple of them with her. This is the first time she's reacted so violently."

"I hope she's going to be all right."

Joy re-entered the room clutching her cell phone. "I know what's burning. The station just called me about it. I have to get over there."

"Over where?" Charlotte asked.

"Roseville Bridge. Roseville Bridge is engulfed in flames and it looks like it's going to be a total loss."

There was a collective gasp from the women. For a moment, no one knew exactly what to do. Then Joy said, "I have to go get my purse. Does anyone know how to get there from here? I'm not sure I can find my way back."

Charlotte threw up her hands. "Wait! Why don't you just call the Channel Six news van? Aren't they here?"

"Good idea. I forgot!" She disappeared again into the other room with the cell phone.

"We should go, too," Charlotte said. "You know the way there, Francine. You can drive."

Francine's voice caught in her throat. She wasn't sure how to take any of this. Was Merlina faking it? Francine didn't believe in séances and ghosts and spirits inhabiting people. But if Merlina was a fake, she was doing a good job of being convincing. She was still passed out on the floor.

Marcy patted Merlina on the cheeks. "Wake up, wake up!" She turned to Mary Ruth, who had crossed her arms as though she didn't believe any of this. "Are there any smelling salts in this house?"

"Kosher or regular?"

Marcy narrowed her eyes. "You know what I mean. Help me out here. Please."

Mary Ruth gave an exaggerated sigh. "I'll go look."

Charlotte pulled on Francine's arm. "We need to go. Seriously. Sheriff Stockton will be there. He probably needs our help."

Francine was not convinced. "I seriously doubt that."

Mary Ruth re-entered through the kitchen doorway. "No smelling salts, but I did find some ammonia. Will that work?"

"Worth a try," Marcy said. "Thank you."

Mary Ruth knelt down next to Marcy. She unscrewed the cap on a white quart-sized bottle of household ammonia. Marcy propped up Merlina's head and reached for the bottle. She shoved it under Merlina's nose.

It took a moment for Merlina to breathe it in. Then her head kicked back like she'd been hit with an undercut. "What? What?"

Marcy continued to cradle Merlina's head. She handed the bottle back to Mary Ruth. "You're okay. You were in a trance."

"Did I connect with someone?"

"I'll say you did," Charlotte exclaimed. "It was a wrong number, but you got a live one. Or dead one, I guess. At any rate, we heard from the spirit world."

A horn blared from outside. Joy rushed in, holding her phone aloft. "Excuse me, excuse me! I'm glad Merlina is fine, but the station is here and I need to get going." She turned to Francine. "You're bringing the others, aren't you?"

Francine felt so confused. "I guess. Let me find my keys." She rifled through her purse, which was still lying open from when she searched for the tea bags. She found the keys to Jonathan's truck, but of course, he would have taken that. "The key to the Prius has to be in here," she said.

"If she can't find her keys, can I ride in the news van with you?" Charlotte asked Joy. "You'll want to interview me. After all, I'm supposed to know who did it."

"No," Mary Ruth corrected, "you're supposed to know *why*. Francine's supposed to know *who*."

"Who did what?" Merlina asked. She tried to stand.

Marcy helped her up. "We can fill you in on the way."

"We don't all have to go," Alice said.

Merlina shook her head, trying to snap out of her trance. "Where are we going?"

"Roseville Bridge," Marcy responded. "It's burning down."

Francine rattled her key chain. "I only have a Prius. I can't take everyone."

"We can take two cars," Marcy said. "I'll follow you."

"Why are *you* going?" Alice said.

"I'm going because my star client is going to do a live remote from a spot where history is being made for the second time. This is the biggest story in covered bridge history since the Bridgeton Bridge got torched."

"She's right about that," Charlotte said. "2005, if I remember correctly."

"I don't need to go," Alice said. "Sounds depressing. I'll stay back and drizzle the scones."

Charlotte put her arm through Alice's. "I think you should be there," she said under her breath, "to encourage Joy. I'm betting that handsome Sheriff Stockton will be there."

———

The Channel Six news van drove speedily, leaving them in the dust. The women drove in tandem—Francine with Charlotte, Alice and Mary Ruth in her Prius, and Marcy with Merlina in her Malibu. They made their way to Coxville Road, but couldn't get within a quarter mile of the Roseville Bridge before they were stopped by police. Smoke billowed in the sky above them. Swirling red and blue lights surrounded the immediate vicinity. Beyond that, close to the bridge, they could see firefighters moving about in the dirty haze. They moved slowly in their bulky firesuits as they handled the hoses spewing water toward the inferno. It seemed to be a futile effort.

A sheriff's deputy forced them to park on the grass off the side of the road. A pumper truck edged by them, heading for the fire. Francine figured there wouldn't be any fire hydrants nearby, but she hoped they could pull water from the creek. She knew some fire departments had special devices that could do that. The bridge was too remote from Rosedale, which was the closest town.

Joy got out of the news van and forced her way around the blockade, trying to get closer to the fire. She held her iPhone aloft as though it were a microphone. "But I'm a reporter," she insisted.

The deputy was a man with wide shoulders and a thick neck. It was clear he wouldn't budge. Finally she dug around in her purse and located her station ID. She flashed it at him. "See! Channel Six news. Now please let us through. That's my cameraman behind us."

"Doesn't matter who you are, you're going to have to do your broadcast from back here."

"But if you'll just let me get a little closer … Maybe you can let me through to the Rock Run Café? I could set up in their parking lot. I'd be out of the way."

The deputy shook his head. He used his night stick to draw an imaginary line from the barricades through where they stood. He didn't say anything, just walked back to where other emergency personnel had gathered.

The women clustered helplessly at the invisible barrier the deputy had drawn. Joy stamped her a foot on the grassy landing. "I bet they wouldn't treat Barbara Walters this way." They watched as smoke and soot raced from the lick of the flames and swirled away into the sky.

"No, they probably wouldn't," said a male voice. They tried to locate where the voice had come from. Then they noticed an older man pushing through the crowd.

Detective Stockton took off his cowboy hat and nodded at the women. "Lieutenant!" he called, returning the hat to his head. The officer returned to the barricaded area.

"Yes, Detective."

"Please escort these women over to the Rock Run. Allow the Channel Six van to get through. We're setting up an area in the parking lot for the press."

The deputy saluted, clearly unhappy with the order. "This way, ladies."

Joy waved to the truck to weave its way through. She sidled up to Detective Stockton. "Thank you, Roy," she said quietly.

He tipped his hat to her. "Be careful now."

NINE

THE SEVEN WOMEN TRUDGED behind the deputy a quarter mile to the Rock Run parking lot. Charlotte clung to Francine's arm as they traversed the uneven shoulder of the road. When the women had made it to the blacktop, the deputy pointed to the staging area where one of the stations from Terre Haute had a camera set up. Joy's crew in the Channel Six van hadn't been able to go much faster than the women, and they arrived simultaneously. The crew began to set up.

Joy checked her cell phone. "Good news," she said. "The Internet signal stretches out to here. I need to do some fact checking on this bridge." She began typing things into her phone.

Charlotte still held onto Francine, her left arm intertwined with Francine's right. Francine felt unnerved by the dancing flames of the burning bridge, which felt almost hypnotic. The bridge was like a skeleton now, the covering having been eaten away by the fire and dropped into the creek bed below. Steam billowed above the creek as the hot boards met the cold water. The fire department had trucks on both sides of the bridge, the men and women keeping the fire from spreading over the creek bank and into the cornfield. At this time in October, the withered stalks were brown and parched. They could go up like tinder if the fire reached them.

Francine remembered that the cornfield belonged to Zedediah Matthew, but was formerly Doc Wheat's. The horse barn owner had told Jonathan it was 300 acres. She wondered if it was all farmland. Surely with Big Raccoon Creek running through it there must be wooded areas. If Doc Wheat hid a treasure in it, it would be hard to find.

She would have thought that after so many decades since Doc Wheat owned it, the legend of this treasure would have died out. Maybe it had. Maybe her cousin William had been there for a completely different reason. But what?

"Have you heard from Dolly?" Charlotte asked, yanking Francine out of her thoughts.

"No. Jonathan and I just saw her earlier today. Why would she call me?"

Charlotte shuffled her feet a little, eyes on the ground. "I was thinking maybe his condition had changed. You know, based on the séance."

She thought back to the séance. Had William's spirit been reaching out to her? She shook her head at the idea. It was crazy. She didn't believe in such things. "The fact that I haven't heard from Dolly discounts the very notion that anything has happened to him." Francine checked to see if Merlina was within hearing distance, and was glad she wasn't. Merlina had made a sweep around the bulge of bystanders and stood at the creek bank, staring into the distance. "I know you want to believe in her," Francine continued, "but I remain skeptical."

The mention of Dolly tugged at her memory, though. She had promised to look for William's car, a mission she still hadn't completed.

The smells of burnt wood doused by water filled the air like sad remnants of a Girl Scout campfire when the last of the s'mores had been consumed. Acrid smoke stubbornly clung to the air. Francine could taste the rawness of it in her throat when the wind blew it right at her.

The news crew completed their setup and gave Joy the cue to begin. They were apparently doing it live, because Joy fielded some questions before she gave her report. Unlike her missteps earlier in the day when it had been so cold, Joy nailed this report from start to finish. She wrapped it up with a summary of the last time a bridge had burned down, the Bridgeton Bridge. "But unlike that bridge, which had a large number of festival events surrounding it and was rebuilt within a couple of years, the Roseville Bridge has no significance attached to it. It may go the way of the Jeffries Ford Bridge, which was destroyed in 2002 and replaced with a conventional bridge. Time will tell. I'm Joy McQueen, RTV-6 News." She held her pose, her tiny frame against the backdrop of the smoldering hulk of the bridge until the cameraman said, "And we're out."

Marcy was ecstatic. "Great job! Will they be coming back to you?"

Joy looked at her watch. "They said to be ready in another half hour for the opening of *News at Five*."

"This is giving you terrific exposure."

Detective Stockton made his way through the crowd, which parted for him. He came to the press area where Joy stood talking to Marcy. He leaned in to say something as though it were for her alone, but his voice was loud enough that Francine heard it. "Would you ask the camera crew to do a slow pan of crowd? I'd like for them to capture as many of the faces that are here as possible."

"I guess they can do that. Why?"

"I know," Charlotte volunteered. "Arsonists usually are at the scene of the fires they start because they want to see their handi-work."

Stockton eyed her. "I guess we can't put anything over on you, can we?" He gave her a crooked smile. "We appreciate your station's coop-eration. There are only two stations here, yours and TWTO from Terre Haute. I have one of my men filming it, too, but you can't cover everything. The more footage we have, the better. For the very reason Mrs. Reinhardt stated."

He took off again.

Charlotte stood a little taller. "He knows who I am."

"So do members of any police force after they meet you," Mary Ruth said. "And not always for reasons you'd like to believe."

Alice huffed. "You know what follows the five o'clock news, don't you? The six o'clock news. If Joy has the lead story at five, she'll be doing it at six too. Maybe even eleven."

Everyone realized what she was saying. Mary Ruth groaned. "We could be here a long time," she said.

"Yes," Alice replied, "and we don't have the luxury of time. Even with the food already prepped, we need to get back. I want to put my feet up and relax. Maybe fall asleep at a decent hour."

"You mean like eight o'clock?" Charlotte asked.

"Don't start on me, Charlotte. You'd fall asleep as early as I do if you didn't take those long afternoon naps."

"We should tell Joy," Francine said.

"Tell me what?" They discovered Joy standing right outside their little circle. Marcy was with her.

Francine took the lead. "Tell you that we are so proud of what you are doing, but we can't stay until the station finishes having you file reports. You could be here until after eleven."

Joy grimaced. "I hadn't thought of that. I don't even want to stay until then."

"You'll have to," Marcy said. "That's the nature of the news business."

"I know." She turned to Mary Ruth. "I understand that you need to go."

"We're going to leave you in Marcy's hands, and those of your news crew," Francine said, deliberating including Marcy so they wouldn't have to deal with her. "You'll have company and a way back to Rockville."

The women hugged Joy goodbye and returned to the car. As they got there, they found Merlina standing there. Her dark eyes seemed preoccupied. "I'd like to go with you," she said in a flat voice.

Alice glanced from Francine to Mary Ruth to Charlotte. "I don't know," she said. "This is a small car. We don't have a lot of room."

"Nonsense," Charlotte said. "The car has five seat belts. We'll make it."

"What about your aunt?" Francine asked.

"I'll text her and let her know I'm with you."

"There's no cell service!" they all said at once.

"Then I'll send her an email."

Francine didn't like this turn of events because of the one-more-thing she needed to do, even if the Roseville Bridge had burnt down and they needed to get back to Rockville to get ready for the next day. She certainly didn't want to be carting around someone she didn't trust when she did it. But she didn't have a choice. "We may not be going back to Rockville right away. We need to try to find my cousin William's car."

The dismay was evident from everyone's reaction except Charlotte's. "Do we have to?" Alice whined.

"It won't take long. Or shouldn't. The car should be somewhere around here."

Francine unlocked the Prius, and they all got in. Alice sat up front with Francine, leaving Charlotte, Merlina, and Mary Ruth in the back seat. Francine got on the phone and called OnStar. It didn't take but a few minutes for Francine to convince the OnStar people she was Dolly, but she'd had to go into more of the story than she wanted to. They gave in and provided directions, guiding her as she drove there. She had been correct in that it was only minutes away, on a road the OnStar people gave a county road number but which she knew locally as Wheat Farm Road.

The car would not have been easy to locate without navigational help. They drove down the chip-and-seal road until they passed a gravel driveway on their left. Francine put her foot on the brake just after they'd gone past. She realized what she was looking at.

"Why are we stopping?" asked Charlotte.

"This is Doc Wheat's farm. I suddenly realized the name of the road has nothing to do with the grain." She gave a short laugh. "I told you I was only around here as a child. How funny that I thought this led to a wheat farm." She studied the driveway, which had been carved out of a thick forest. There was no mailbox to indicate whose place it was, but she knew anyway. *Must go to the post office to preserve his anonymity*, she thought.

The OnStar person seemed to be waiting for her, so she moved on. He guided them about a hundred feet where they turned onto a bumpy bare-ground road on their right. The road descended into a hollow, turned to the right again, and went into a strand of trees. Hidden in that strand they found William's blue Lucerne. Francine pulled up behind it. The OnStar people offered to unlock the vehicle, but she assured them she had the key. She felt guilty about having lied she was Dolly, and she found herself trying to prove she was the owner.

They probably didn't care one way or the other.

She also assured them the group was perfectly safe. Which she thought was true. They were surrounded by a forest of maple trees whose leaves had turned a flaming red color. Beautiful. But it was also secluded. She was glad to be in a group. She unlocked the doors to her car and got out. She glanced around. She saw no one.

Charlotte was the next one out of the car. She stabbed her cane into the ground as an anchor and leveraged herself out of the back seat. Merlina got out next, then Alice and Mary Ruth. Merlina walked back along the road but stopped short of the enclave. Alice and Mary Ruth hung around Francine's car, while Francine and Charlotte circled William's.

William's vehicle looked undisturbed. Francine unlocked the car and scouted around the front seat for anything that would indicate why he'd been there, why this particular location.

"Find anything?" Charlotte asked.

"Nothing. Looks like William keeps a very neat car."

Charlotte opened the passenger door. "It might be detailed on a regular basis. What's that smell?"

Francine sniffed. The inside smelled like one of those artificial scents used to cover up disagreeable odors. "Raspberry death," she said, and laughed. "That's what my son Chad calls it."

Mary Ruth cleared her throat like she needed to get their attention. Francine jerked her head up, hitting it on the roof. "Oww!" she said out loud. She pulled her head out of the car.

A man in a red plaid shirt and worn jeans stood at the entrance to the copse of trees studying the women. He seemed surprised to see them, but she wasn't sure if it was them, William's car, or that there were now two cars back here. She wondered if this was the first time he'd noticed William's car, and if it was his land they were on or someone else's. No matter. They were trespassers.

He seemed to make a decision. He waved and walked toward them. Francine noted that when he came to Merlina, he nodded at her as though he knew her.

His smile was wide and friendly. However, the heavy build, bushy beard, and his height, which Francine estimated to be six-two, gave him a rugged mountain man appearance. He didn't give off signals that led Francine to believe he was anything but curious. As he neared the car, she could see that his eyes were a medium brown, like hers, and that his beard, which had looked dark from a distance, was speckled with flecks of gray.

"Hello," he said. "I've seen the owner of that vehicle, and you don't look like him."

Francine has not expected him to speak so properly. "He's my cousin," she said, surprised. "Do you know him?"

"Not well. I've explained to him that I'm a private person and don't like him sneaking around my property, but he still did it. I've had to run him off a few times."

Francine felt a tinge of fear. There was no question in her mind it was Zedediah Matthew. She wished she'd kept the OnStar people hanging on the phone. She checked the inside of William's car for a button that would hail them, but she didn't see it. She forced herself to turn and face him and make sure he was unarmed.

"You don't need to be afraid of me. I'm not going to hurt you. What happened to William? And do you know anything about the smoke and sirens coming from over there?" He pointed in the direction they'd come.

"He fell down the embankment at the Roseville Bridge and now he's in the hospital. That was earlier today. We just came from Roseville Bridge as it was burning to the ground." She spoke of the two events as though they were related; she hoped they weren't.

"Is William going to be all right?"

"He has a concussion. The doctors are concerned."

The mountain man shook his head. "I'm sorry to hear that," he said, but Francine wasn't clear which part of the news he was sorry to hear about. He extended his hand to her through the open window. "I'm Zedediah Matthew."

Francine chilled a bit in the intense shade. But her manners, not to mention her curiosity, kicked in. He was being hospitable; it behooved her to return that cordiality. She shook his hand. "Francine McNamara. William's wife, Dolly, is at the hospital with him, and I told her I'd go look for the car. These are my friends." She introduced everyone. She could tell they were uneasy, too, but they came up to meet him.

"Francine McNamara," he repeated. He peered into her eyes like he was looking for confirmation of something. "I thought you looked familiar. You and your friends. You've been on television, haven't you? Weren't you the Skinny-Dipping Grandmas?"

Charlotte stood up taller. "We still are."

Francine gave a short laugh, but his knowledge only made her edgier. "Guilty as charged. You have a good memory, though. It's been several months since we were featured on *Good Morning America*."

"But your friend Joy is on the show regularly. She talks about your group."

"That's true." Francine found it difficult to believe this man watched *Good Morning America*, but she had no idea how else he would recognize her. "Mr. Matthew, I'm sorry if William has bothered you in the past. I don't know why he would do that, but . . . ."

"Please call me Zed. And I know why he did it. Same reason a lot of others have done it." But he didn't elaborate.

Francine was stymied. Did she want to pursue what William and the others had been searching for? Check that. Of course she wanted to pursue it. It was an almost unspoken dare that she ask.

But she didn't want to play games with him. "We're sorry to have disturbed you this afternoon. We'll just take his car and leave."

"That's fine." He backed away from the women. "I'll just head on back to the house. Good luck on completing your Sixty Lists."

The fact that he could remember the name they gave their bucket lists stopped her. One of her items was to take chances more often, and for some reason it came to mind. But before she could say anything, Charlotte butted in. "What do you think William and the others were looking for?"

He regarded her. "Charlotte. You're the one who figured out who killed Friederich Guttmann. I'm not surprised you would ask. But the answer I have isn't a simple one to explain." He let that hang there a moment and then asked, "May I invite you all back to my house to discuss this over a cup of tea?"

Francine hesitated, but Charlotte was all over this. "Of course. I could use a good cup of tea."

Francine decided to be the voice of reason. "May we have a moment?" Without waiting for an answer, she took Charlotte by the arm and led her off to the side of the car, as far as she thought necessary to be out of earshot. He seemed friendly enough, but the idea that he'd run William—and presumably others—off his property made her nervous about being alone with him.

The other women took Francine's hint and they gathered in a circle.

"Charlotte," Francine said, "I'm not sure this is a good idea."

She seemed astounded at their cluelessness. "How else are we going to get to the bottom of this if we don't question him now? You think we'll have another chance? And we have safety in numbers."

Alice fingered her cross pendant, a clear sign she was on edge. "Not necessarily. He could feed us poison and kill us all at once."

Mary Ruth put her hands in her jacket pocket. "I'm torn between thinking you sound like Charlotte with her conspiracy theories and thinking you are one hundred percent correct." She hesitated. "If we go in, I'm not eating anything, just in case."

Merlina stepped in and joined their circle. "I know Zed. Not well, but well enough to trust what he says. I think it's safe."

Everyone looked to Francine.

"Your call," said Mary Ruth. "He's courting you, not us. You can tell that by the way he directs his comments to you. And you drove."

Zed called over to them. "It's an invitation. Admittedly, I look dangerous, but that's a deliberate choice. I'm actually very considerate, especially when I invite someone into my house. If it makes you feel easier, call your husband and tell him where you are. I wouldn't suggest someone do that and be a bad host, would I?"

Mary Ruth poked Francine in the arm. "See, what did I tell you? He wasn't talking to the rest of us."

"Wait a minute," Alice said. "How is he getting a signal out here if we weren't able to get one at the Roseville Bridge? This location is every bit as remote."

Francine checked her phone for a signal. It was surprisingly strong. "He must have some kind of signal booster on his property." She didn't know how such things worked, but she could believe Zed could figure it out. She was grateful they apparently had the same carrier. "You really think it's okay for us to stay?" Even as she said it, she was already reminding herself she could check #42 (Take More Chances) off her list if they had tea with him.

"Of course it's fine," said Charlotte. "We should go in and cross-examine him. If it makes you feel better, call Jonathan."

Surely he wouldn't tell me to call Jonathan if there were any danger. "Give me just a minute."

She called Jonathan, catching him at the office. She briefed him on the situation. "So he's been a gentleman?" Jonathan asked.

"Yes."

"And it's you, Charlotte, Mary Ruth, and Alice?"

"And Merlina."

"Who?"

"The medium Charlotte hired."

"What's she doing there?"

Francine began to stutter out an explanation, but even to her it sounded confusing.

"Never mind," Jonathan said. "I'm not sure I want to know. Shouldn't a medium be able to sense if there were danger coming?"

"Be serious."

"What does Charlotte think? Or is she even giving you a choice?"

"She's lobbying heavily for us to go in."

"Do you think you're in danger?"

She took a deep breath. "No, I don't. He seems to want to make a connection with me. I don't think he would hurt me or any of us if he were trying to do that."

Jonathan was silent for a moment. "I trust your judgment. Plus, I know what you're like when you're investigating a mystery. In some ways, you're as bad as Charlotte. Just be careful. At the first inkling of any danger, promise me you'll get out of there. And keep your cell phone handy."

"I will. I'll call you as soon as we're done, so you'll know."

"I'm calling you in a half hour if I don't hear from you."

"Good idea. It'll help us wrap up the conversation if it goes too long."

"Do you want me to head back to Rockville? You know I will if you need me."

"Let's keep that an option for now. I'll talk to you soon." Francine disconnected. "Okay," she told the others. "Let's have tea." The women moved toward Zed, hanging together as a group. Francine clutched her purse containing her cell phone.

Zed was talking to Merlina. Though the conversation seemed cordial, there was some point of contention between them. Francine wondered if they had made the decision to accept his invitation too quickly.

But Merlina apparently knows him, she thought. *She wouldn't go in if there was any danger.*

Just then, he caught sight of them approaching. He smiled. "Good. I'm glad you trust me. I think we have much to discuss." His words were clearly directed at her. But he included the others as he added, "Let's go in and have tea."

Have tea while the Roseville Bridge burns. It felt bizarre to think of it that way, even weirder to find herself starting toward Zed to do it. The women moved with her. Francine clutched her purse containing her cell phone.

TEN

Francine wondered how they could have a lot to discuss when she'd only just met him. They walked the long gravel driveway back to his house. Even Charlotte didn't complain, though she hung onto Francine as they walked. *Good thing we're all wearing the shoes we've been preparing food in*, Francine thought. They were comfortable and allowed for better navigation on the slick gravel. The driveway drenched by the rains earlier in the week still hadn't dried out.

The driveway curved to the right, but before it did, they passed under a stately wooden arch. A sign beneath it grandly proclaimed MATTHEW 1844 RANCH. Francine wondered if it had really been around since 1844. It was possible. Indiana became a state in 1816, and land was being claimed and deeded in all parts of the state. She almost said something, but Zed was quite a ways in front of them.

It wasn't long before they'd lost sight of Wheat Farm Road altogether. The late afternoon sun danced in and out of the towering trees. As they approached the house, the trees thinned out and the sun drenched her in a long spell of sunshine. It made her feel warm. All the women seemed to enjoy it.

Zed's house was a log cabin. "The original part of the house was constructed in the late 1800s," he said, "but it's been added to since then. It's now a three-bedroom, two-bath ranch home. I've tried to modernize it but still stay true to the first owner's vision." He held the door open for them.

As Francine entered she noticed cameras under the eaves of the house. *He must have a security system*, she thought. But she decided not to mention it.

She felt surprisingly calm as she followed the other women into the home.

What could Zed possibly know of the original owner's vision? she wondered once she got inside. They didn't file house plans with the county back then. She was pretty sure while the original owner might recognize the ambiance, that would be about it. The interior resembled a hunter's lodge, with knotty pine paneling that gave the house a slight woody scent. More noticeable were the mounted game heads, which she found a bit gruesome. The feature that most startled her was a taxidermied young buck standing majestically in the back of the room. It has a small crown of antlers and looked like it was ready to take on all challengers, despite its youth. She approached it, repulsed and yet fascinated. Charlotte stuck to her side.

"I see you've noticed Bucky."

Francine ran her hands over the deer's beautiful coat. "I've never been this close to a wild animal before."

Charlotte tentatively touched the antlers. "He's not that wild anymore."

Francine thought back to the shots that drove William out of the woods and hit the bridge near where she had been standing. Zed only said that he'd heard shots and expressed a vague sympathy for

William's condition. He hadn't denied being the one to do it; of course, they hadn't asked him, either. She said, "You're a hunter."

"Have been all my life, but I don't do much of it anymore. I find the chill of the morning and the requirement of holding still for long periods of time tough on the old joints." He smiled. "I can tell the prey makes you uncomfortable. Let's go into the kitchen for that tea I promised you."

Zed's kitchen was light and inviting. Located at the back of the house, it had large windows which allowed the afternoon sun to warm the room. Zed indicated they should sit at the square, eat-in kitchen table. Though it was not large, they could all sit there if they crowded together.

To Francine's surprise, two loaves of some kind of quick bread lay on a cooling rack on the counter, almost as though Zed had expected company. The smell of dates was strong and her mouth began watering almost immediately. They'd skipped the cookies and scones after the séance due to the fire news, and it was getting toward suppertime.

"You're a baker?" Mary Ruth asked, spotting the bread.

Zed smiled. "I am. I find recipes to be rather like formulas. If you follow them exactly, you'll get the same results. It's scientific. At the same time, baking is an art form because the conditions vary every time you make something, and sometimes you have to make substitutions in ingredients. I imagine you feel the same way."

Mary Ruth chuckled. "No. That feels more like an Alton Brown explanation. But I do like to experiment and make up new recipes."

"There's a bread knife in the knife block. Would you do me the favor of slicing it up while I prepare tea? It's date-nut bread."

Zed made tea the old-fashioned way, with loose, black tea he placed in two Brown Betty teapots, each holding enough for several cups. While he put the kettle onto boil, Mary Ruth expertly sliced up the first loaf. Zed showed her where the dishes were, and she put a slice on each of six plates. She distributed them at the table.

For some reason Francine remembered the mythological story about Persephone and the six pomegranate seeds she'd eaten when in the Underworld with Hades. The story ended badly, with Persephone forced to live in the Underworld for six months, making the world go into winter. Francine put it out of her mind. Zed was no Hades and she was no Persephone. And she would most certainly not eat six slices of date-nut bread. Though, if the bread were as good as it smelled, she would be tempted.

Francine looked out the windows at a long and wide backyard. While the entrance to the house had been nothing more than a narrow driveway dominated by the woods, the back was grassy all the way to where the cornfield began. From there, the cornfield looked like it went on forever. The yard was dominated by an ancient greenhouse and two gardens. One garden was clearly for vegetables, since she recognized the cool-weather plants that still looked good, like spinach and broccoli. Droopy tomato plants stung by the recent frost were dying. Tall, withered cornstalks, likely the remnants of his sweet corn harvest, were still in the ground.

"Is that an herb garden?" Francine asked of the second, smaller garden. "The bush looks like sage and the leggy plants look like basil, but I don't recognize the others."

"Very astute of you," Zed replied. The kettle came to a boil at that moment and he poured the water into the Brown Bettys. As it steeped, he said, "I put that in. The vegetable garden came with the property when I purchased it from Doc Wheat's estate after he died."

Francine was accustomed to the wonderful baked goods Mary Ruth made, and most people's didn't compare. But the date-nut bread had smelled tempting from the moment they'd walked in the kitchen, and now that Mary Ruth had set a piece in front of them, she had to exercise willpower not to wolf it down. She picked off a corner and popped it into her mouth. It was melt-in-your-mouth good. It had a rich, buttery taste she had not expected, which she let linger on her tongue. Mary Ruth could not have made better.

Everyone but Charlotte nibbled nervously on the date-nut bread. Charlotte devoured hers in a few bites and greedily eyed the remainder of the loaf. But she seemed to decide otherwise. She looked at the old-style greenhouse. "The greenhouse must have come with the property too?"

Zed gave her a wry smile. "It looks like it, doesn't it? I haven't kept it up as well as I should. It still produces marvelously, though. I keep telling myself I should tear it down and replace it with one of those modern shelter-like structures with plastic windows, but I can't bring myself to lose that bit of history. If the Historical Society ever saw it, it'd probably be declared a historic building."

"How old is it?"

He poured tea for all of them, using a strainer to catch the loose tea bits. "I'm guessing it was built in 1930, about the time the Depression took hold. After we finish our tea, I'd be happy to show it to you."

They all agreed they'd like to see it.

Zed had managed to relax Francine with his hospitality. The kitchen and the conversation felt so friendly she almost wanted it to last into the evening. But they needed to get back to Rockville, so she felt compelled to move things along. "You were saying about William…?"

"Yes. William has been here many times before, several in just the past year or so. He seems to be obsessed with the legend of the Doc Wheat fortune. Are you familiar with it?"

"I've heard his name a couple of times. My family's farm was near here, but I grew up in southern Indiana, near Evansville. My mom and dad moved there when I was young. My father didn't like farm work and my mom couldn't persuade him otherwise. He got a job in the Whirlpool factory. Grandpa's farm was sold not long after he died."

Zed nodded as if he were already familiar with her history. "Doc Wheat was an eccentric farmer who purchased this land back in 1921. During the Depression he developed an interest in herbalism, studying native plants for their healing powers. He became convinced that just about any disease could be cured by finding the right combination of plants. At one time his home remedies were popular and shipped all over the world. He gave himself the title 'Doc Wheat.' But the birth of modern pharmacy put him out of business." He indicated Francine's teacup, which she hadn't touched. The others were already half through theirs. "Don't let your tea get cold. It's a special blend I make. The base is Oolong I order off the Internet, but I like to tinker."

She sipped the tea. Like the bread, it had some extraordinary qualities. She could taste a peach-like sweetness to it, but it had a hidden bite that wasn't quite revealed until the finish. For some reason she thought of tarragon. She almost laughed at her own description; she sounded like Mary Ruth describing a wine. She wanted to ask Zed more about it, but she reminded herself it was more important for him to continue the story. "So what was William looking for, Doc Wheat's formulas?"

Zed leaned forward as if confiding a secret to them. "More likely he was looking for the fortune. Rumors were rampant at the time that he'd made a lot of money from his formulations. Now, I don't know about any fortune, but I do know Doc Wheat didn't trust banks. Probably a result of the Depression. Anyway, even before he died people were sneaking onto his land digging around for buried treasure."

The women hung on his every word. Charlotte asked, "Did anyone find it?"

"No one found anything."

Francine popped the last of her date-nut bread in her mouth. Again, she appreciated the mouth feel of the bread and the richness of the dates and nuts. But then she realized it had the same hidden bite at the end, like the tea. She wondered what it was.

Charlotte continued her questioning. "Then why would William think there was a fortune?"

Zed finished his bread in three bites and brushed the crumbs off his beard. "I love dates," he said. "Part of the reason was Doc himself. He fueled the rumors even as he ran people off his land. Claimed he had a treasure no one would ever find. When Doc died in the 1960s, he left no heirs and I bought the land. Paid a pretty penny for it too."

"What do you think of the legend, then, if you haven't found the fortune, and you live here?"

"A fortune is not the same as a treasure. I'd hazard to guess whatever his 'treasure' was, it wasn't the kind people expected."

Charlotte put her teacup down. "It seems odd for a person to believe strongly in a rumor like that without some kind of impetus."

"Have Francine ask William about that next time she sees him." Zed leaned back in his chair and appraised Francine. "You definitely come from Miles blood," he told her. "You favor your mother."

"How did you know …? Oh, wait. I told you William and I were cousins."

"You did, but from the time I saw you on *Good Morning America* and they said your name, I knew who you were. I hoped we'd meet."

"I don't mean to be pushy," Mary Ruth said. "It's been lovely to meet you, Zed, and I give you props for your date-nut bread. But if we're going to see the greenhouse and get back to Rockville, we'd probably better get on with that."

Zed scooted his chair back from the table. "Of course," he said. "I understand you especially have work to do for tomorrow." They all stood, and Mary Ruth began to gather up the cups and dishes. "Just leave it all," he said, waving her off. "I'll clean up later. It's a pleasure to have such polite guests for a change."

Zed opened the back door and led them across the yard to the greenhouse. The length of the black-roofed building faced south and had large leaded glass windows, one of which was cracked and needed to be replaced. The building also needed to be scraped and given a new coat of forest green paint, but structurally it looked fine. "I use the greenhouse to start plants for the vegetable garden over there," he said, pointing, "and so I can have some vegetables and herbs during the winter." He tried to turn the knob on the door but found it locked. "Forgot the key. Wait here, and I'll be right back."

The minute he was back in the house, Charlotte murmured to the group, "So what do you think?"

Alice scratched her head. "He seems nice enough. I hadn't expected tea and bread from a man with his reputation."

They all nodded in agreement. Francine turned to Merlina, who was still dressed in her medium outfit. "You said you know him. Is this how he has acted towards you in the past?"

She shrugged her shoulders. "Yes and no. He's never been unkind, but he's never been this friendly, either."

"So how do you know him?" Charlotte asked.

Before she could answer, Zed opened the back door and returned holding the key. He unlocked the greenhouse and turned on the overhead light, holding the door for them.

Francine was impressed with how well-organized the greenhouse was. Baskets of flowers hung near the windows, and eight long rows of tables held mostly starter plants, although there were some larger plants in pots. "I brought the flowers inside when we had the first frost a few nights ago," he said. "I haven't moved them back out, and I may not. I like having the color in here."

"They're beautiful," Francine said. She and the others strolled through the greenhouse, walking up and down each aisle. Francine found that Zed was following her, which caused the remainder of their group to shift to other aisles. They chattered among themselves under their breaths, so it was hard to hear.

Some of the rows had tiny plants Zed must have started recently from seed. Francine recognized beans and tomatoes and others, but she stopped at a row in the middle containing things she didn't. "What are these?" she asked.

"Native plants that don't survive the winter. I grow them in here during the cold months so I have access to them. They do surprisingly well in a greenhouse. I'll start more in late winter from seed and transplant them to the third garden in the spring."

"The third garden?"

He winked at her. "Yes, the third garden. Doc Wheat's garden. It's not easy to find. I presume it was the source of Doc's famous remedies. Biologically, it's an incredible assembly of native plants, some of which I don't think exist anywhere but here. It's why I've kept it up. The interest in native species is starting to bloom again—forgive the pun—and I tell myself that one day I'll get in touch with some of the state biologists to let them take samples and redistribute them across the state."

"Where is the garden?"

He shifted his eyes toward a corner of the greenhouse where a cover was thrown over what look to be an all-terrain vehicle. "We'd have to take the ATV."

Francine had no intention of getting on an ATV with a virtual stranger. "We probably don't have time today, then."

He seemed amused by that. "Probably not. But I hope that you'll come back so I can show it to you. You'd love the place. It's hidden away in a small canyon and fed by a spring that sprays into the air like a tiny geyser."

Francine pictured it in her mind. "I'll do that. Thank you for inviting me back." She found herself still checking out the corner where the ATV was. There was an antique curio cabinet that contained several shelves of mason jars. Though she couldn't be sure, they did not appear to have anything in them. The jars were lined up except for one row in the front where a single jar was missing. The cabinet had a keyhole, and she wondered if it were locked. But why would Zed keep empty jars?

Zed touched her on the arm and indicated they should go outside. The move felt a little off to Francine, but she went along with it. They stood outside the greenhouse, just to the side of the open door. Francine thought she could probably be seen by the women inside, but not Zed. He was too far to the right of the door.

Zed slipped Francine a small book he took out of his jacket. "Please put this in your purse, Francine. Did you know I knew your grandmother Ellie?"

Francine was surprised. With his still-dark hair and his beard hiding aging in his face, Zed looked to be a few years younger than her, hardly old enough to call her grandmother by her first name. "You did?"

"It's a long story how I got this diary, but I'll skip that for now. Suffice it to say it's hers. I had always meant to give it to your mother, but when your family moved to Evansville I lost touch. The reason I'd hoped to meet you was I wanted to give it to you."

Francine was stunned by the appearance of this second diary, but she tried not to show it. She checked the women in the greenhouse. They were in a semicircle examining what Zed had described as native plants and hadn't seemed to notice that neither she nor Zed were inside. She glanced down at the delicate diary in her hands. It was similar to the one William had had in his possession, except this one had a purple fabric cover with the heart graphic embroidered in it. It had a square lock holding it closed like the first diary. It was not locked, however, and she opened the cover. The binding had split from the spine. She flipped to the first page. Francine had many of her grandmother's handwritten recipe cards, and this, too, was definitely in her grandmother's handwriting. "You've read it then?" Francine asked him.

He nodded. "Many times. You'll think it rude of me perhaps, to have read a young lady's diary. But it has some wonderful historical bits of information in it. For instance, she tells the story of her mother's love affair, the one that took a turn for the worse at the Roseville Bridge."

Francine took in a sharp breath. Though her grandmother had died when Francine was still a teen, the story of her grandmother's mother had never been accurately told to anyone as far as Francine knew. The family story was made up of rumor and innuendo. "She wrote down the details?"

"Yes, as her mother told the story to her. I find it an interesting coincidence that you were at the bridge earlier today. What were you doing there?"

Zed knew I was at the bridge? Does that mean he fired on me? Though she had no intention of telling him the truth about why she was there, she was saved from having to create a lie because at that moment her cell phone rang. The women heard it and noticed them standing on the outside.

"We'll be back in in a moment," he told them and pulled the door to the greenhouse closed. "Who's on the phone?" he asked.

Francine looked at the number. "My husband, Jonathan."

"Good," he said, smiling. "Answer it, and be sure to tell him I've been a proper host."

She tried to regain her composure, but her fingers couldn't seem to push the green button to answer the phone. She stabbed at it twice. The phone continued to ring. She connected on the third try. She forced herself to relax, even as she saw the panicked look on the women's faces inside the greenhouse. They were all uncertain how to react to having the door closed on them. "Jonathan?" she said into the phone.

"Yeah, it's me," he said. "I told you I would call back in a half hour if I didn't hear from you. You're still okay, right?"

"Yes, we're still at Zedediah's," she said.

"And everything is okay?"

The women were staring at her from inside. She didn't know exactly what to say, but Zed was so near to her she decided to play along with him for now. Other than close the door, he hadn't made a threatening move. She motioned to her phone so they knew she was on it.

"He's been a good host. He just handed me my grandmother's diary."

"It's different from the one William had on him?"

"Yes."

Jonathan paused. "I guess it would have to be."

"I think Zed and we are just about finished," she said, giving Zed a quick smile to indicate she meant to leave soon. "He's just wrapping up a tour of his greenhouse, and then we'll be on our way. Shall we plan to meet in Rockville, then?"

"Is that a hint, or do you just want him to think I'm coming your way?"

"A little of both."

"Call me when you've left."

"I will."

They said their good-byes and disconnected. Francine noticed the women were making their way toward the door. Francine put her hand on the knob. She hadn't seen Zed lock the door and hoped it would open to her touch.

He put her hand over hers. "You still don't trust me, do you?"

"Please let go of my hand."

"So you don't trust me." He took his hand away and held both of his up in a surrendering position. "The Roseville Bridge has secrets. I'm … protective of them. Perhaps one day you'll know and understand … I have something in the house that might convince you to trust me. I'll go get it. Here's the key to the greenhouse." He handed it to her and strode quickly into the house.

Francine opened the greenhouse door. It had been unlocked, as she thought. Relieved, she joined the other women inside.

Then she heard a *pop* coming from Zed's home. She looked back.

And saw the wall of the kitchen where they had been sitting minutes ago explode.

ELEVEN

FLAMES QUICKLY ENGULFED THE side of the house facing them. The house was plunged into a small inferno.

"Oh my God!!" Alice exclaimed.

They stared out the greenhouse windows in shock. It felt like an eon to Francine, but it was surely only moments before someone said, "Call 911!" It was Charlotte.

"What about Zed?" Alice asked. "Where did he go?"

Francine's feet started moving. She hurried outside, pointing. "He went back in the house. I think he might have been in the kitchen when it exploded. He was moving fast, though. He might have made it into another room."

The others followed. Charlotte grabbed at Francine's phone. "Aren't you going to call 911?" She managed to slip it out of Francine's possession. "What's your passcode? Have you changed it again?" She fumbled with the phone.

"I haven't. You just can't hold onto it. Let me do that." Francine juggled the phone away from Charlotte. She punched in 9-1-1, grateful the number was simple. Her hands were shaking too. Not much less than Charlotte's.

But there was nothing on the other end.

"I can't get a signal."

Mary Ruth wrung her hands. "What happened?"

"The signal booster must have been located in the house, and we've lost the connection."

"No, I mean what *happened*? What caused that *pop* sound, and then the fire?"

"How should I know?"

Francine felt someone prodding her from behind. She turned to find Alice swooping them forward with her arms.

"We need to get back to the car," she told Francine.

"Is it safe to go past the house?" Mary Ruth asked. "It's on fire, for heaven's sake. The trees could go up next."

"How else are we going to get out of here?"

"This way!" Merlina's voice sounded steady. They searched for where her voice had come. She was headed for the driveway, walking backward facing them, her hands beckoning them forward.

They followed. Merlina's costumed silhouette was framed by the fire. She looked like some kind of creature from a horror film. *But she's not afraid*, Francine thought. *And she's leading us to safety*.

Francine helped Charlotte along the gravel driveway. Merlina's path had them on the outer edge, as far from the house as they could get. Once they got past, they breathed a sigh of relief. But Merlina didn't slow down. "Keep coming," she urged them.

"Easy for her to say," Charlotte grumbled. "She's forty years younger." But the complaint was hollow. Francine had a good grip on her, and the two of them scurried around the bend of the driveway toward Wheat Farm Road.

Alice was two steps ahead, her pant legs swishing together. She turned her head. "We can use William's OnStar to call 911. It has satellite reception, I'm pretty sure."

"It does," Francine said. It was a great idea.

But when they got to the hidden copse, the only car there was Francine's Prius. William's Buick was gone.

"Where's the car?!?" Alice flung her arms wildly as she danced around looking for it. "Someone took the car!"

Merlina grabbed Alice and took control of the situation. "It's going to be all right. We all came in Francine's car; we can all leave in Francine's car."

Alice tried to pull away from her. "But how will we call the fire department? What happened back there? What will happen to us?"

Francine fed off Merlina's calm and not Alice's hysterics. She dug around in her purse for the key to the car. "We'll be just fine. Zed's house won't be. We need to head back to the Rock Run to get help." She offered up a silent prayer for Zed. She hoped he survived. He might have been strange, he might have been dangerous, he might even have been guilty of what happened to William. But she wanted to hear him out. How did he know her grandmother? Why was he trying to make a connection with her? Was his version of the Doc Wheat legend true? And was he lying when he said he'd never found Doc Wheat's fortune?

Francine found the key and unlocked the car. They piled in, each in the seats they'd had before. Francine wound back to Wheat Farm Road and they took it toward CR 350W.

Only a minute down the road they saw rotating red lights ahead of them. Moments later they heard the piercing sound of a siren and saw a fire truck rushing toward them. Wheat Farm Road was narrow.

Francine pulled to the side. The fire truck, a pumper truck emblazoned Rosedale Volunteer Fire Department whistled past.

She let out a breath. "I guess we don't have to worry about calling the fire in."

"Makes me wonder who called it in, though," Charlotte said. "There are no neighbors for miles."

"Maybe it was Zed," Mary Ruth said. "I hope so. He was a good amateur baker."

Francine found herself answering grimly. "Let's not hope that's his epitaph."

The women were silent. Francine didn't move. Finally, Charlotte said, "So, are we going?"

"I was thinking maybe we should go back and tell them what we saw," Francine said.

"The firemen will be too busy to deal with us," Mary Ruth said.

A sheriff's car, lights flashing and siren wailing, sped past them.

Charlotte's head swiveled as she watched it go by. "That was Joy's favorite detective in that car!"

"It did look like him," Francine said. "He wears that distinctive Stetson. Maybe that's a sign we should go back."

"No!" said Alice. "I don't want to go back!"

"If this were a John Wayne movie, someone would slap her," Charlotte muttered in the front seat.

Two more sheriff's cars went blazing past.

"Alice, I think we should go back." Francine said it gently.

"I'm beginning to think you're all voyeurs," she retorted.

Just then, the Channel Six news van raced by.

"Now that's the sign we should go back," Charlotte said. "Joy and her crew are in hot pursuit of the story. We should give her the exclusive."

Francine groaned. "Really, Charlotte. *Hot* pursuit?"

"I do what I can," she answered.

"I think it's all well and good that you want to give her a story," Mary Ruth said, "but let's not forget that I have a business to run tomorrow. I need to get back to Rockville. I need a good night's sleep. *And* I have to get up early and do some baking. That's a caterer's life."

Marcy's SUV came barreling down the road next. She passed Francine's car and left it in the dust.

"There's your answer," Merlina said, as though she had divined it. "You can borrow Aunt Marcy's car, and she can ride home with us."

No one objected as Francine did a three-point turn and headed back to Zed's house.

Before they reached the scene of the fire, they encountered a blockade being set in place. A sheriff's car straddled both lanes of the narrow road, lights flashing, preventing anyone from getting past. That included the Channel Six van, which was pulled to the side of the road, and Marcy's car, which was behind it. Marcy was out of the car and arguing with the deputy, a tall, thin young man who looked like he needed to grow into his sheriff's outfit. There was no sign of the Channel Six crew.

The young deputy wielded a flashlight. It was then Francine realized the sun was getting low in the sky and she checked her watch. It was nearly six thirty. The deputy used his flashlight to indicate that Francine should turn around and head in the direction she'd just come.

She couldn't see the fire because of the trees, but the smoke drifting through the air was convincing evidence of the battle the firemen were waging down the driveway and to the right.

Francine wondered about the Rosedale Volunteer Fire Department. This was probably out of their league, especially coming on the heels of the Roseville Bridge fire. She hadn't seen a pond or any kind of water near the house, which was too bad. They would need a bigger source of water to battle the blaze. She wagered more emergency vehicles from throughout the county would soon be on their way here.

She rolled down her window as the deputy walked up to the car.

"We need for you to move your car, ma'am. You can't get through, and we need to keep this access clear for additional emergency personnel. Please turn around."

Francine thought fast. "Where's the Channel Six crew? We're looking for our friend Joy McQueen. We have some important information for her."

"We've set up a second barrier for the press that's a little closer to the scene."

"Can we go down there?"

He shook his head.

"Already tried," said Marcy.

"What if I told you the important information I have for her?"

"Unless you have important information for either the fire department or the sheriff's department, and I doubt that, you need to turn around and go back."

Francine opened her mouth to say something, but just then Mary Ruth leaned up from the back seat and put her hand on Francine's shoulder. "Be careful what you tell him. We don't want to end up at headquarters being questioned. That would only delay getting me back to Rockville."

Though Mary Ruth had clearly not intended it, the deputy heard every word. "Do I understand you ladies know something about this fire?"

Choruses of "yes" and "no" sounded once, then twice, with some of the voices changing their response. The deputy stared suspiciously. "So which is it?"

Charlotte cleared her throat. Everyone looked at her. "Some of us know something, and some of us don't."

"Which ones of you know something, and what is it that you know?"

"I don't know anything," Mary Ruth said. "In fact, I barely know these people." She sat on the passenger side of the back seat. She opened the door and got out. Marcy loomed behind the deputy. Mary Ruth pointed at her. "But her, I know. She's my publicist. She's getting ready to take me home."

Marcy looked more like she was getting ready to make a run for it toward the fire, where Joy was presumably broadcasting. But that got her attention.

"I'm your publicist?" Then, in a more affirmative tone, "I'm her publicist." She used her thumb to point to herself. "Yep. That would be me."

"And you are preparing to take me back to Rockville."

Now she frowned.

"Because," Mary Ruth continued, "we need to finish strategizing on how we are going to meet the demand for our corn fritter donuts in the morning."

"I thought I recognized you," the deputy said. "You're the caterer, one of the Skinny-Dipping Grandmas." He bent over and peered into the car. He examined their faces. "In fact, you're all Skinny-Dipping Grandmas."

"Not quite," Merlina said. "I'm not old enough to be a Skinny-Dipping Grandma. Though I aspire to be some day."

"So," Charlotte said, "with the exception of Mary Ruth and Marcy, who were just leaving, the rest of us have knowledge of how that fire started."

"Don't throw me in that group," Alice said. "You're on your own." She got out of the car and joined Mary Ruth and Marcy. "I'm her business partner. I don't know anything, either."

The deputy looked confused, but in the end, Mary Ruth, Alice, and Marcy were allowed to get into the SUV and leave. The deputy called for Detective Stockton, who walked back from the scene of the fire in about five minutes. Francine and Charlotte were still in the car. Stockton and the deputy stepped away and had a few words.

Stockton walked up to the car. "So, do I understand that you ladies started the day at the Roseville Bridge, where a man was shot at, and which burned down this afternoon, and now you have firsthand knowledge of this second fire of the day?"

"We get around," said Charlotte.

"Yes, you do."

Before they could say any more, additional emergency vehicles came screaming to a stop on Wheat Farm Road. In the space of ten minutes, Francine counted three fire trucks from neighboring departments, two additional sheriff's cars, and a state police car.

The fire trucks were directed around the blockade. The deputies left their vehicles and were sent to the scene for assignments. The state policeman walked with a swagger, ignored Stockton completely, and headed down the driveway toward the fire, exuding self-importance.

"Well," said Charlotte, "I sense tension."

Stockton returned to the car. "You can get out now."

They both started to get out.

"One at a time, please. I want to interview you independently." He pulled a notepad out of his front pocket.

Charlotte was the first one out, which was fine with Francine. She hoped Charlotte would wear him out and when it got to her, she would be able to avoid divulging any of the personal details Zed had revealed—especially the appearance of the second diary, which Charlotte didn't know about yet.

When it was finally her turn, Stockton didn't make Charlotte get back in the car, but he told her she needed to be quiet. Francine focused on what happened after Zed went back in the house. She told of the popping noise, which only she had heard since the others had been behind the closed door to the greenhouse. She said the fire started immediately after.

"What color was the fire?" Stockton asked.

"Color? I don't know."

"It was a blue fire," Charlotte said. "Definitely blue."

"I told you to be quiet," Stockton said.

Francine crossed her arms. "What does color have to do with anything?"

"It reveals what accelerant might have been used by the arsonist," Charlotte said. "Blue would indicate gasoline."

"Is that true?" Francine asked Stockton.

"We don't know yet that it was arson. We haven't gotten that far yet."

"For heaven's sake, Roy, you'll never get anywhere with Joy McQueen if you're going to be that tight-lipped," Charlotte said.

Stockton seemed bemused by her statement. "What makes you think I need to get anywhere with Ms. McQueen?"

Charlotte rolled her eyes at him. "Be that way, then. But what else do you think it would be but arson? First the bridge, now this house. And Francine just testified there was a *pop*. I'm willing to bet you'll find evidence that the fire was unleashed by remote control."

"For the moment, the fires are of undetermined origin, and it is only a coincidence they happened on the same day and so close together. I would recommend you keep yourselves out of trouble by not speculating."

"And I bet you'd like for us to keep this information to ourselves too."

"In fact, I'd like for you not to discuss that you were here at all. Do you think you can do that, for the moment?"

"Depends," Charlotte answered. "For example, suppose that we agree to keep quiet in exchange for a free-flow of information."

"It won't be a free-flow. I can guarantee that. But let's say that I'll let you in on what I know, when I can reveal it."

Charlotte shook her head. "I don't think that will work, Roy. If we're going to help you break this case, we're going to need to know sooner rather than later. And keeping us informed will simply mean you'll get to visit Ms. McQueen more often."

Stockton appeared to consider her words, but Francine thought he was just humoring her. "Well, there's that," he said eventually.

He let them go.

Dusk had settled in as they left the scene. Francine turned on the light inside the car and checked her cell phone. Still no cell reception, as expected. "I bet Jonathan is frantic," she said. "I was supposed to call when we left."

"Then we need to get back to civilization as soon as possible."

Before she gave up staring at the phone trying to will it to connect with the network, three bars lit up. She saw her phone was receiving a message.

Meet me tomorrow in Bridgeton.

Francine looked at who it was from. She took in a sharp breathe. Charlotte fed off her reaction. "What?" she asked.

Francine didn't answered. She immediately typed back.

You're alive?

Yes.

Bridgeton will be packed with people.

Perfect place to hide in plain sight. Come alone.

Francine took two seconds to think about that.

Can't promise that. I need a cover too. When?

Afternoon. Can you bring clothes? I need to disappear.

How will I find you?

I will find you.

Then the number of bars faded like a light being turned off at a switch.

TWELVE

FRANCINE DIDN'T WANT TO tell Charlotte whom she'd texted with and what their conversation was about, but there was really no way around it. Charlotte had witnessed her doing something, and she couldn't bear to lie to her best friend. Although she had in the past. But only when she felt she had to do so to avoid hurt feelings or when she did so for her own privacy's sake. Charlotte could be a very prying person.

"He's alive?"

Francine didn't look over at Charlotte because she was driving back to Rockville in the fading light on country roads, but she could detect the amazement in her voice.

"I don't know how else I would have gotten a text. How he got the cell signal to go on and off like he did is a mystery to me, but for those brief moments, we were texting and interacting. So he must be alive."

"And he wants to meet us at Bridgeton tomorrow?"

"No, he wants to meet *me* at Bridgeton tomorrow. I only said I wouldn't come alone."

"Who else are you going to bring along? You said this is a mystery to you. Who else do you know who solves mysteries?"

Francine let that pass.

I need to disappear, he'd written. Why?

"Hold on to my cell phone," she told Charlotte. "When you see that we're in range to receive calls, let me know. I need to get hold of Jonathan."

Francine slowed as she went by the Rock Run Café, which was full of people. The charred remains of the Roseville Bridge were off to her right. She saw that the area was draped with crime scene tape. Gawkers skittered across the busy county road from the Rock Run to where they could view the bridge and then back, which is why she had to go slow. "Good thing this area has street lights," she said.

When they reached US 41, Charlotte announced cell coverage was back. The phone buzzed angrily in Charlotte's hand. "Text coming in," she said. "It's from Jonathan. He says, 'Where are you? Call me right away.'"

Francine pulled over to the side. Charlotte gave her the phone. Francine called Jonathan.

He sounded frantic. "Are you okay?"

"Yes. I'm fine. Have you heard about the Roseville Bridge?"

"It's impossible to escape it. It's all over the news. Joy seems to be everywhere."

"Well, we now have a second case of arson. Zed's house."

"And you were just there."

"We were there when it happened. We were out in the greenhouse." Francine told him the story. "And now Detective Stockton thinks we are somehow involved, just because we were at the bridge this morning when William came running out of the cornfield and then ended up in a coma, and then subsequently the bridge burned down, and then we were at Zed's house when the other fire started."

"I could see how he would think that," Jonathan said dryly.

"You're not helping."

"So how can I help?"

"For starters, you can come back to Rockville. I need you." She told him about Zed still being alive and wanting to meet her in Bridgeton. She didn't mention the clothes or the fact that Zed needed to disappear, not in front of Charlotte. Not yet. She wanted to think about that.

He came back with a low whistle. "Why meet you?"

"That's what I'd like to find out."

"Do you feel safe tonight?"

Did she? She knew the house in Rockville had a security alarm system. If Jonathan wasn't there she would share a room with Charlotte so she wouldn't be alone. *Am I a target?* She didn't think so. After all, she didn't know anything. The people who seemed to know something, like Zed or William, were the targets.

"Yes, I'll be fine."

"As long as you feel safe, I'll finish my work here and be there first thing in the morning. Before eight o'clock. Tell Mary Ruth I'll be there in time for breakfast."

"You'll be disappointed. She's not fixing anything special. We've all got plenty of work to do just getting her dessert booth ready."

He said he'd still be there in time for breakfast. They hung up.

"I've been thinking," Charlotte said. "Shouldn't we look for your cousin William's car?"

"Charlotte, we've been up since six o'clock this morning, and since then I've had a photo shoot, witnessed my cousin fall down a creek bank and into a coma, been interviewed by the police, helped

Mary Ruth at the festival, visited my cousin in the hospital in Clinton, seen the Roseville Bridge burn, seen Zed's house burn, and been interviewed by the police a second time."

"You left out the séance and the fact you told Dolly you would find William's car, which you did and then lost it again."

"The point is, I'm kind of tired. That would make a thirty-year-old tired, and we're way past that."

"I'm only saying it won't look good to wait until morning since you lost the car."

Francine had to agree Charlotte had a point, even though she knew Charlotte was not interested in the car for the sake of her relationship with Dolly. She found the number for the OnStar people. "What am I going to tell them, that I've lost the car again?"

"I'm sure it's nothing they haven't seen before."

Francine steeled herself for the embarrassment she would feel, then called the number. She explained the situation.

"Give me a moment to look up that information." The voice went offline for fifteen seconds or so, then came back on. "Let me just ask you a couple of questions. Did you call about three hours ago for help in locating it?"

In Francine's opinion, the male voice on the other end was neutral. He didn't express skepticism, but neither did he sound like he was buying her story.

Charlotte, however, took offense. "You don't sound like you believe her. Don't you get calls from people who lose their vehicles more than once? I should tell you we're elderly. We lose things all the time."

"I didn't say—"

"You ever meet a group of retirees at the mall for lunch? Afterwards, we're all wandering around the parking lot looking for our cars. It's like a scene out of *The Walking Dead*, except we're not dead yet. This isn't a whole lot different."

"Except we lost it on a country road in the middle of nowhere," Francine whispered to her.

"What?" the male voice said. "I didn't catch that."

"I said, this car has a history of getting lost. It's always wandering off."

There was a pause on the other end of the line. "I've located it."

"Where is it?"

The OnStar rep gave Francine directions. "I know where that is," she said. "Thanks." She closed out the call, restarted the car, and drove north.

"You know where it is?" Charlotte asked.

"Yes, and we're headed there now."

"Where is it?"

"At William and Dolly's house in Montezuma."

"How'd it get there?"

"That's what I'm hoping to find out."

———

A short time later they drove the long, narrow, maple-tree-lined drive into William and Dolly's estate outside of the tiny town of Montezuma. The setting sun was now obliterated by dark clouds, and a wind had picked up. Francine sensed a storm was brewing. With it came the feeling what they were doing was somehow illegal. As the house came into view, Charlotte took in a sharp breath.

Francine was already creeping along in the Prius, but now she stomped on the brakes. "What is it?"

"The house," Charlotte said, "looks like something out of *The Munsters*."

Francine took a second look. She'd never thought of it in those terms, but then she'd almost always been there in the daylight. They were about a hundred yards from it. The Victorian house had a three-story tower on one end and a two-story addition on the other. It had been successfully designed to look like it'd been built at the turn of the century. Outside spotlights lit the front, but because the house was in a wooded area, shadows covered much of the upper story windows, giving it a foreboding look. The front porch light highlighted ivy growing up the side of the house as though it were going to devour the place.

"It's not that creepy," Francine insisted, her voice a little unsteady.

"Yes it is. It looks exactly like the kind of home a funeral director would own."

"He's not a funeral director. He owns a string of assisted-living facilities."

"Same category. Let's find the car."

The driveway wound around the back. Security lights came on as they approached the detached two-car garage. The light blue Lucerne was parked in the middle of the driveway about twenty feet from the garage doors, which were closed.

"How do you suppose it got here?" Charlotte asked.

Francine pulled up behind it. "Dolly said her sister was coming up from Memphis. Maybe she retrieved it since I hadn't gotten the job done yet."

"Was she by herself? Someone had to have driven her there."

Francine said nothing and peered out the car windows, hoping to see signs of life in the house, but all the windows were dark.

"Why wasn't it pulled into the garage? Surely there was a garage-door opener in the Buick."

"I don't know."

"It doesn't look to me like anyone's home," Charlotte said impatiently.

Francine studied the house. There were no lights on anywhere. It did look unoccupied. "I'm going to ring the doorbell first."

Charlotte opened her door. "Go ahead. I'm going to crack this baby open."

"I'm not sure we should do this. However it happened, the car found its way home."

"Quit waffling and get the keys out."

"Just a minute." Francine dug through her purse. She didn't think of herself as the kind of person who kept a lot of stuff in her purse, but it still took her a good twenty seconds to find William's key. She tried not to think about how it would look if they got caught searching the car when she handed it over to Charlotte.

Charlotte eased herself out of the Prius. She unlocked all the doors to the Buick with a double-click. She made her way to the driver's door and scooted in.

Francine finally got out of the Prius and joined Charlotte. Together they checked the front and back seats, took everything out of the glove compartment, and probed the pockets on the back of the front seats. They found William's car registration, the Buick manual for the Lucerne, his car insurance information, and trash. William apparently frequented Burger King. The only odd thing was a sheet of notebook paper from William's company, Warm Memories Retirement Communities. William had written the number 17 on it. Francine recognized William's neat block lettering. She tucked it in her pocket.

Charlotte still had the key. She held it up. "Let's check the trunk."

The idea of opening the trunk put Francine just a little on edge. Big things could be hidden in a trunk. *Like dead bodies*, she thought. But she shook it off. *Just Charlotte's influence.* Everything with her played out like a mystery novel. Still, she held her breath as Charlotte pushed the button on the remote entry and the trunk popped open.

There was no dead body. For that Francine was grateful. But there were a pair of muddy boots, a small hand shovel, a bigger shovel, and a flashlight with extra batteries. Both of the shovels had dirt on them.

Francine moved the shovels and the boots out of the way so she could make certain there was nothing behind them. A quart mason jar, the type she'd seen in the curio cabinet in the greenhouse at Zed's house, sat behind them. Francine lifted it from the truck and held it up, examining it from all sides. Clear liquid sloshed slightly.

"What's that?" Charlotte asked. "Hooch?"

Francine rotated the glass container in her hand. "Water?" She unscrewed the cap, looked inside, and took a sniff. "Yes, I'd have to say water." She held it out to Charlotte, who also sniffed it.

"Has a kind of metallic smell," Charlotte said.

"It reminds me of the water I used to drink at my grandmother's house. We pulled it straight out of a well she had on her property. Hard as rocks. I felt like I could never get my hair clean when I showered at her place."

"Are you going to taste it?"

Francine held it up, looking at it through the bottom of the jar and rotating it again. "I don't think so. We don't know where it came from or if William added anything to it. Or even if it is water."

Charlotte reached out her hand and Francine let her take the jar. For a moment, she thought Charlotte might take a swig out of it, but then her friend seemed to think better of the idea. "You remember that William had a vial of something when he came running out of the woods," Charlotte said.

"Dolly had one in her purse too. I saw it when I visited William in the hospital."

"You didn't tell me that."

"So far it hadn't come up in the conversation." Francine began to rearrange the trunk so it looked like it did before.

Charlotte clutched the jar. "You're not going to put it back in there, are you? Without testing it?"

Francine thought a moment. With William in the hospital, would anyone really notice it was gone? Dolly might. "I don't feel right taking it. When will we have the opportunity to put it back? If Dolly knows it was here, then she discovered we have it, it would look bad." She pried the container out of Charlotte's hand and put it back where it came from.

Charlotte pushed out her lower lip.

"Look, I would love to test it to determine it is indeed water and not some kind of accelerant used to start fires. But if I'm proved wrong ... well, I don't want to go there." She was relieved there weren't matches or gasoline or anything to indicate William might have wanted to set a fire. Not that William could have set the fire at Zed's house or at the bridge. As far as she knew, he was still in the coma.

"Chicken."

But there were the shovels and the dirt in the truck. "Do these make William look like a treasure hunter?"

Charlotte waggled her eyebrows. "Finally, you come around. I love the way you're thinking now," she said. "However, let's play devil's advocate. At this point the evidence is circumstantial. Tasty, but circumstantial. Shovels and dirt just mean he was digging. He could have been planting trees at one of his nursing homes."

Francine shook her head. "Not William. Dolly maybe."

Francine rooted around the trunk some more. She pulled on a flap on the left-hand side that looked like it might be used to trap reusable grocery bags. At least, that's what she would have used it for. But something black was in it. She pulled out small tablet computer with a keyboard cover attached.

"What have we here?" Charlotte asked. "A hidden laptop?"

Francine contemplated whether she should boot it up. "It's a tablet, not a laptop. But it was definitely hidden." She rotated it around in her hands, thinking about it some more, then blew out a breath. She put it back.

"We have to take that!" Charlotte hissed. "He must have had it hidden back here for a reason."

"He could have had it back here to keep it hidden for perfectly innocent reasons. For example, so it wouldn't get stolen out of the car."

"But think what could be in it!"

"I have, and I don't think we have the right to invade that kind of privacy."

"Coward. We can't leave both the mystery water and the secret laptop back here. What kind of investigators would we be?"

"Petty larcenists is what we'd be. We are not licensed investigators. And even then, I bet it would be illegal."

"Go ahead," Charlotte said, "stand on principle. You'll find yourself wishing you'd have taken it."

Francine put a fist on her hip. "I doubt it."

Charlotte suddenly pointed toward the back of the heavily wooded property. "Did you see something?"

"Where?"

"Back there in the woods. I'm sure it was something or someone moving among the trees."

They both stared in that direction. Francine definitely didn't want to be caught snooping in William's trunk. She searched the yard for a few moments. "I don't see anything. It was probably some form of wildlife."

"Then it was some kind of wildlife that resembled a human."

"I don't see anything there now. And you couldn't have gotten that good of a look at it."

"He could still be back there, hiding behind a tree. Some of those trunks are big enough to hide a grizzly bear."

"There are no grizzly bears in this area."

"Bigfoot, then."

Francine gave her a look. "Let's get out of here."

They returned to the Prius. Charlotte opened the door and worked herself into the passenger seat. "I still wonder how the car got here."

"Me too," Francine said after Charlotte was buckled in. "Me too."

THIRTEEN

FRANCINE, CHARLOTTE, AND JOY made sandwiches and joined Mary Ruth and Alice in the large family room at the back of the mansion to eat a late supper. Marcy had come and retrieved Merlina, so they were back to their own group again. The room had a big-screen television on one side that Francine estimated to be at least a sixty-inch model. On the other side of the room was a Ping-Pong table, a Ms. Pac-Man video arcade game, and a floor-to-ceiling bookcase full of board games. The women sat in front of the TV on a sofa and two easy chairs that had white L.L.Bean slipcovers on them. They put their food on the coffee table in front of the sofa.

Joy said she had arrived at the mansion immediately ahead of them. "Once the news team back at the station agreed they had enough recorded material and they didn't need me live for the eleven o'clock news, I was able to leave. I told them I could either be live tonight for *News at Eleven* and dead tomorrow for *Good Morning America*, but not alive for both. Guess which one they chose?"

"How did the six o'clock news go?" Francine asked.

"We were just about to watch it," Mary Ruth said. She doled out crudités with a dilled yogurt dip leftover from when she and Alice had eaten. "I set up the DVR to record it when Merlina, Alice, and I got back."

Joy, who was slouched on an easy chair, sat up and stretched. "Needless to say, the tone for tomorrow's report at the Roseville Bridge will be much different than it was for this morning's, given that the bridge is a burned-out mess. The photo shoot may not come up at all, but I still need you all there just in case."

Alice yawned. "Well, I for one am not going to be sorry if you can't find a good segue from the tragedy of the bridge going up in flames to the sexy photos Francine and Jonathan were doing at the bridge."

"You can't throw Jonathan and me under the bus! You all took photos like that too."

"Says who?" asked Mary Ruth. She fiddled with the remote control, but nothing seemed to be happening on the television. "We didn't do ours at the Roseville Bridge."

"Just a minute," Charlotte said. "We have to think of how this will reflect on Joy. They count on her to get happy news stories about us senior citizens, and I think the sexy calendar idea with all of us involved has the potential to rival the skinny-dipping situation."

"The very fact that anyone thinks the public will find it fascinating probably means they won't. Who can predict what's going to become newsworthy next? Pinup calendars by older women have been done before."

Charlotte's voice got a little louder. "It has been a good five years or more since those ladies in England did it. That was the last time. This bridge burning down could be just the ticket. Francine and

Jonathan's photo session yesterday contained perhaps the very last photos to be taken in the bridge."

Francine wondered why Charlotte kept supporting the idea of the calendar being in the press. "The burning of the bridge needs to be the focus of Joy's report, Charlotte. If the Bridgeton Bridge incident from 2005 is any indication, they'll need to raise a lot of funds to rebuild it. That's the better story."

"You're right, Francine," Charlotte said, seemingly struck by the idea. "A national focus on raising money may be exactly what's needed here."

Francine got suspicious whenever Charlotte switched sides on an argument too swiftly.

Mary Ruth handed the remote disgustedly to Joy. "I can't figure out what I'm doing wrong."

"Why do you think I can fix it?"

"Because you're the media person. And because you've got Toby in the basement copying all the video footage you shot this morning so I don't have him to fix it."

Charlotte mulled that. "He's copying it so you can give it to Roy in the morning, isn't he?"

Joy huffed. "Roy asked for it. Don't make a big deal out of this."

Charlotte put her hands up. "I'm just sayin'."

Joy studied the remote. She pressed two buttons and the news anchor who had been frozen on the screen came to life. "There you go. Let's see how it came off and then I think I may be off to bed." She began to fast-forward through the newscast for her segment.

Mary Ruth returned to her spot on the sofa. "You might as well know I'm not going to the Roseville Bridge. Alice can go if she wants, but I have to stay back and get the cinnamon rolls baked and cooled and iced. They need to be fresh and ready to sell first thing. And we all remember the disaster the *last* time I appeared on *Good Morning America*."

"I hardly think it was a disaster," Charlotte said. "So you fell into the pool and had to be rescued by Francine. Look at all the good that came out of it."

"Nonetheless, I'm glad it's behind me and don't see the need to relive it. Besides, this is business. I trust I can have everyone's help again tomorrow after you come back from doing Joy's *GMA* report?"

They nodded. Joy stopped fast-forwarding and hit the play button. "This is before Zedediah Matthew's house went up in flames. Watch how I changed their focus when they asked about why we were there."

They sat through the segment. Joy's report was a capsule summary about the two incidents at the bridge. On a tight close-up of her, she described William's being chased out of the cornfield by gunshots they believed to be from a rifle, his fall into the creek, Jonathan's stopping him from drowning, and that he remained in a coma. Her report was accompanied by video she'd shot herself and supplemented by footage the station had obtained of the Clinton hospital William was in. Then the cameraman pulled back and the remains of the Roseville Bridge came into view. In the background, the firemen battled the blaze, but there was no question the bridge was a total loss.

As the segment concluded, the female anchor asked, "You were a live witness to the incident. Tell us how you came to be at the Roseville Bridge so early this morning."

"The Covered Bridge Festival, of course. But we've just received a report that a house not far from here is also on fire and may be a total loss as well. The police haven't yet said whether arson was involved or not. We're heading there next. We're in contact with the

Parke County Sheriff's Department about all these incidents and will keep you informed as the investigations unfold."

Apparently there'd been no good way to turn the conversation back to Joy's reason for being at Roseville Bridge because the anchors thanked her for the report and moved on to the weatherman, who was sitting in a chair beside them. He was the new, handsome face of the weather team and he smiled brightly with teeth that surely had been artificially whitened. Joy turned off the television.

After Francine, Charlotte, and Joy finished their meal, Mary Ruth pulled out some cookies. "We can all have one cookie for dessert, but no more than that. I'm saving everything else for tomorrow morning."

Before long the women trudged off to bed. Though it was only nine o'clock, everyone needed to be up early. Mary Ruth would be up at four o'clock to pull stock out of the freezer and organize tasks for the morning. Alice was getting up at four thirty, and the rest of the women planned to stagger their showers starting at five o'clock. Joy said they needed to be out at the Roseville Bridge by seven o'clock.

The other women made their way up the staircase, but Charlotte seemed to be having trouble getting up the first step. Francine slowed her climb to wait for Charlotte. "What's going on? Is your knee bothering you again?"

Charlotte put a finger to her lips and indicated she should keep quiet. Francine wondered what was going through her mind.

When they could hear doors closing, Charlotte motioned Francine to come back down the stairs with her, which she did. "Toby," she whispered.

"What about him?"

"The photos you took of the bridge this morning, of the image carved in the beam. This would be a good time to have Toby analyze them."

Francine felt exhausted. She couldn't believe Charlotte wasn't as well. "Why is this the perfect time?"

"Because Toby's alone, he's already working on something, and we won't have to let anyone else know what we're doing."

Francine would have like to have excluded *Charlotte* from anything Toby might discover, but she'd remembered the photos and wouldn't likely let go of the idea. Plus, there was also the matter of the second diary, hidden in her purse. Knowing what the carved image looked like might help her when she met Zedediah the next day at Bridgeton. Charlotte didn't need to know that was the deciding factor.

The basement stairs turned out to be quite narrow. Francine went first, clutching the handrail. She made sure Charlotte was steady behind her. When she reached the bottom of the stairs, she was glad to see the basement was more than a cellar. At some point it had been built out. It had an open recreation room to the right and a bedroom with an adjoining bathroom to the left. Francine could see a light coming from under the bedroom door. She knocked. "Toby, it's Francine and Charlotte."

Toby opened the door. He had on an orange tank top that read, *Sun's out, guns out,* and blue cargo shorts that covered his knees. The tattoos on his arms were on display, but what struck Francine was how much progress he'd made on losing weight. He had lost his beer gut and was gaining definition in his muscles. "Shouldn't you be in bed?" he asked. "I thought we were all getting up early?"

"We needed your help on something," Charlotte said from behind Francine, still negotiating the final stair. "We—that is, Francine—took photos on the bridge this morning that we need some kind of enhancement of in order to be able to see."

"You mean you need them lightened?"

"And maybe blown up, although I wouldn't use that phrase around Sheriff Roy right now." Charlotte chuckled at her own joke.

"Who? Never mind, c'mon in."

He opened the door to let them in. The room was narrow and small—no more than a bed, desk, and two chairs crowded together across from the door and a closet on the wall adjacent to the door. Toby's laptop sat on the desk. There was barely any leg room between the desk and the bed. Toby squeezed into the desk chair.

His laptop was an Apple computer with a large screen, and it was open to some video game that involved a lot of gunplay. He shrunk the game into a corner of the laptop. "I'm sorry there's only one other chair in the room," he said. "One of you can sit on the bed if you want."

The bed's comforter lay on the floor, revealing a plain white blanket. "I'll take the bed," Charlotte said.

Francine sat in the other chair and handed her phone to Toby. He opened the photo app. "I assume you're talking about the most recent photos taken today? These dark ones?"

She nodded. "Can you get to them?"

"I'll just email them to myself."

"Will it take long?"

"Shouldn't."

While he was waiting for the photos to go through the email, he said, "So these photos were taken at the Roseville Bridge?"

"Right where we were standing when we got shot at," Charlotte said. "I made Francine look to see if there were anything significant about the spot."

141

"And you found this carved into the beam?"

Francine nodded. "We did."

The emails came in. Toby made the whole thing seem effortless. He pulled up the photos one at a time. "These all look the same."

"They're at slightly different angles. I wanted to make sure I got it."

He shrugged. He picked one and kept enlarging the photo, almost to the point of distortion. Francine had recognized the image well before then.

"It's the heart on the diaries," Francine said. "Much cruder because it's hand carved into the wood, but I'm sure that's it."

"Yes!" Charlotte said. "Wait. Did you say dia*ries*, as in plural?"

Francine tried to put a confused look on her face rather than the sheepish one she was sure had appeared at first. "Did I say diaries? I meant diary. I'm just tired."

Charlotte's narrow-eyed frown suggested she was not convinced. Francine hoped she would not have to explain herself later.

Toby continued to play with the image. "You can see how dusty this is, and how it distorts if I blow it up larger. Now I want you to look at this." He moved the photo up. There was something below the heart.

"Can you make it any sharper?" Charlotte asked.

"Only if I reduce the magnification." He made two clicks with a button on the keyboard and the image was a little more focused. "I think it's because of where it was located on the beam. It was a little more protected and collected more dust. Plus, the image is just smaller altogether."

Charlotte jabbed at the screen with her finger. "It's a key."

Both Francine and Toby leaned toward the screen and knocked heads. Francine's glasses were jammed into her face. "Oww!" She pulled away, removing the glasses and rubbing the bridge of her nose where the impact had been felt.

"I'm sorry," Toby said. He rubbed his temple where the corner of her glasses had made contact.

Charlotte continued to point the screen. "It's an old-fashioned key, the kind you'd find that fits a door as old as this mansion is."

Francine put her glasses back on and inched a little closer to the screen, wary of where Toby was. "I can believe that. But I haven't seen that image before."

"Have you had a chance to look at the diary yet?" Charlotte asked.

"Well, no, not much."

"Then how can you be sure?"

Francine shook her head. "I can't."

"Is there anything else below the key?" Charlotte asked Toby.

"Maybe." He reached over and used the cursor to move the key image up to the top of the screen. "There's this carving, but unlike the heart, it's linear, and I think it must be letters."

The three of them guessed at each individual letter.

"It's so fuzzy I feel like I need to clean my glasses," Charlotte said.

"You do need to clean them," Francine replied, "but that's not necessarily the problem here."

Charlotte pulled off her glasses and squinted at them to check their condition. She put them back on. "It's like we've reached the end of the eye chart, where the letters are teeny-tiny and you're making wild stabs at what the letters might be, and the doctor finally decides you're finished."

"Except in this case we can guess that there are words," Francine said, "and spaces between the words. I think there are four words altogether and the first has three letters."

Toby got out a sheet of paper. "I agree. And then this must be a space, and the second word is three letters as well."

Fifteen minutes later Francine was satisfied they had a reasonable solution to puzzle. "So, do we agree it's probably, 'you are to mine'?"

Toby yawned. "Except it doesn't make much sense."

Charlotte stared at the screen. "Can you put the heart graphic and the key graphic and the words altogether, like it would be on the beam?"

Toby seemed exasperated. "I can, but that was exactly the first photo." He went back to it. "The heart graphic is clear, you can barely make out the key, and the words are so faint that we would have missed them if we hadn't spent time blowing it up and looking at each quadrant of the photo."

"But let's look at is as a whole," she insisted. "Heart, key, you are to mine."

Francine got it right away. "In a sense, 'You are the key to my heart.'"

The three of them looked at each other. "Does that mean anything?" Toby asked her.

Francine closed her eyes for a moment. She was very tired, but sometimes when her mind was weary it went places and made connections it wouldn't normally have made. "If we extrapolate what we know, that this is the bridge where the coachman and my great-grandmother made love the first time, we could guess—since the heart has the same design that's on the diary—that either the coachman or my great-grandmother carved it into the wood."

"Or both," Toby added.

Charlotte was more circumspect. "It was done more than ninety years ago? Seems hard to believe it could have lasted that long."

Francine thought about that. "It was protected, obviously. Hard to see, hard to get to, and I bet it was no easy task to carve. It might not have been done all at once. It might have been done over a period of time."

"What did you say happened to the coachman?" Toby asked.

"He was fired immediately."

"Then he would have had time to do this in his misery."

Charlotte pointed to the heart. "A man would never have created this heart. Look at the little doily loops that surround it. I have to believe a man would have just drawn a heart."

"Maybe not if he'd seen the image before," Toby said.

"We don't know when it was carved," Francine said.

The three sat back in their chairs.

Charlotte tapped her fingers together. "We still don't know that it had any significance. The heart figure ties your great-grandmother to this carving, but it's just a love note. Lovers carve similar things in trees, spray paint them on ghetto walls..."

"But people don't get shot for standing next to them, though," Francine said.

Toby snickered. "Depends on the ghetto."

"Too bad this wasn't taken with a really high-resolution camera. Maybe there's something more there we can't see."

"There are the squiggly lines," Toby said.

Silence filled the room for a moment while the two women processed what Toby had said.

Charlotte tried to take control of Toby's mouse. "What squiggly lines?"

He wrested the mouse from her. He moved the photo up where they could see something below the printing they'd been examining. Two wavy lines stacked on top of each other came into view.

"Water," Francine said. "It's the universal sign for water."

"I thought it was just an end mark," Toby said. "You know, like 'end of message.'"

"Under other circumstances I might agree with you," Charlotte said. "But I think this is a subtle link. Key plus water plus love."

He turned to her. "Then you know what it means."

"No," Francine said. "It's just another clue."

The two let Toby return to his video game.

"Do you think it has anything to do with the mason jar and the two vials?" Charlotte asked after Toby had closed his door and they were on their way to the stairs.

"I doubt it. That was probably carved a long time ago into the beam. The vials and the mason jar are from today."

It was a long, steep climb up the basement stairs and then up the second staircase to the room they were sharing.

"I can't believe they didn't build this thing with an elevator," Charlotte grumbled.

"It was 1899, for heaven's sake."

"I mean when they renovated it."

"It probably would have ruined the character of the house to try to fit one in."

"It has every other modern convenience. Did you get a look at the media room they created in the fifth bedroom? The television screen is so big it covers the wall. And the smell of popcorn was so strong I bet they own stock in Orville Redenbacher's popcorn company. If there had been a bowl of kettle corn in front of me, I would have done a face plant right in the middle of it."

"You do that anyway whenever we have kettle corn," Francine remarked. "Doesn't matter where." She took Charlotte's arm and helped her up the final stair. They made their way down the hall.

"Well, maybe I do like kettle corn a bit more than I should," Charlotte said.

When they closed the door behind them, Francine decided to stop Charlotte's complaining by asking a question that had been gnawing at her. "What's going on in that devious mind of yours about this calendar?"

Charlotte gave her a forced innocent look. "Whatever do you mean? You act like it wasn't my idea. It has all along been mine."

"It was on your Sixty List to be a sexy pinup girl. Then you shifted it to where we were all a part of it and pushed us to do the photos, not just you."

"It's been a freeing experience for everyone to deal with their sexuality, especially as older women. We don't have the same bodies we used to, but that shouldn't keep us from taking care of what we do have and not being afraid to express our needs. Isn't that what you said on *The Doctor Oz Show*?"

"Yes. No. I mean, you're taking the words out of context. I didn't say anything about sexuality."

"You didn't have to. The camera did."

"What's that supposed to mean?"

"I mean, you were on *Dr. Oz* because you looked good in a wet sundress. It wasn't just a physical thing the public was clamoring for. They thought you looked sexy. And Dr. Oz brought the subject up."

"You'll recall, I deflected it. A lady does not talk about such subjects."

"Which made the audience hoot even more. Your face turned red."

"But I refused to talk about it anymore. It was like they wanted lurid details. Well, they have no business knowing how often Jonathan and I do it or how we do it. Dr. Oz respected that and didn't bring it up again."

"Only because they went to commercial right after you said that."

Francine pressed her lips into a line. She regrouped. "Here's what I think. I think you have plans for this calendar."

Charlotte avoided eye contact. "You're just letting the Hendricks County visitors bureau remark influence your thinking."

"I'm still wondering if this isn't something sneaky you're doing without our permission. You practically bullied me into getting my photo done in the first few weeks of October. If you'd just let it rest until later, I wouldn't have been forced to do anything in the early morning during the Covered Bridge Festival and Joy wouldn't be tap dancing around it on *Good Morning America*."

"This is not the first time, nor will it be the last time, that Joy will be pressured to reveal things we're doing on our bucket lists."

"I'm just saying I suspect this is working to some kind of nefarious advantage you are hiding from us."

Charlotte huffed. "I love it when you use words like *nefarious*, even when they don't apply to my motive. I am only helping others get through their Sixty Lists, just like you are. What about tonight's séance? Didn't I help Alice check that off her list? I arranged for that whole thing to happen. And boy, did it turn out spooky. It would have been better if Merlina's head had spun around once or twice, but you can't fault that creepy 'and you're responsible' line she said to you. She practically spat in your face."

"She also said that you, Charlotte, know why."

"I'm glad you brought that up. I've been meaning to talk to you about it. Do you think she means I know the motive or that I will figure it out? I am pretty good at figuring out these kinds of things."

Francine knew she'd inadvertently let the conversion drift in a different direction, but she figured at this point Charlotte had to know she was watching her like a hawk. If she tried to do anything with the calendar like let it slip into the public realm, they'd put a stop to it. "I do not put a whole lot of stock in Merlina's ability to conduct a séance or believe that she really did contact the spirit world."

"We'll see. At any rate, I depend on you to focus our investigation. You're the logical one; I'm the creative one. Together we make a great sleuthing team."

Francine yawned. She was physically tired and tired of conversation as well. "Let's just go to bed." They each made a trip to the bathroom down the hall, changed into nightgowns, and eventually climbed into the queen-sized bed that was high up off the floor. She made sure the little wooden stepstool was on Charlotte's side so she could get the height necessary to get in. Francine fluffed a pillow and pulled it behind her head, propping herself up. "I'm wondering if Mary Ruth will let you near the food booth tomorrow."

Charlotte took off her white-framed glasses and set them on the dresser. "She might. Her business promises to be even more popular than it was today. Think of all those customers who didn't get her corn fritter donuts. And after tomorrow's *GMA* report we'll be back in the news big-time, which will help drive business the rest of the week."

"Maybe you're right, but if you get any flak from her, I'd like you to scoot out and do a little investigation at the Rockville Public Library."

Charlotte put her hands on the mattress to stabilize herself and took the two steps up that enabled her to get a leg into the bed. She pushed and pulled herself into sleeping position. "What do you have in mind?"

"Find out what you can about Doc Wheat."

"You keep bringing him up. What for?"

"You heard the story from Zed. Doc Wheat owned the property before Zed bought it. He said Doc was the original herbalist medicine man. Claimed he could cure all kinds of illnesses. He made a fortune some people still believe is buried on his land. Zed intimated that William believed it, and so have others. It's why he's gotten the reputation he has for being unfriendly. He's had to drive fortune hunters off his land."

"You seem to know all about him. What do you want me to track down?"

"For one thing, find out if Zed is telling the truth, if he's gotten in trouble for chasing people off his land."

"How am I supposed to track down these rumors?"

Francine frowned in exasperation. "Like you always do, Charlotte. Nose around. Ask questions. You can start at the Rockville Library. It's just down the street."

"It is?"

"Didn't you see it when we drove by the Methodist Church, the one with the hot pink windows? It was right next to it."

"The Carnegie building?"

"Yes. What else did you think would be in a Carnegie building?"

"In Brownsburg, it housed the Chamber of Commerce for a while. In Plainfield, it's the headquarters for a fraternity. In Carmel, it's a restaurant," Charlotte argued.

"But in Danville, it's still the library. And in most little towns it still is. What's happened to your powers of observation?"

"They are tired and are ready for sleep." Charlotte flopped over on her side. "What time do we have to be out at the site of the Roseville Bridge tomorrow?"

"O-Dark Thirty. Not to worry. I've set the alarm."

Charlotte chuckled. "Good night, Francine."

Francine lay in the dark and waited for Charlotte to fall asleep. Next to her, she clutched the two diaries she'd taken possession of that day: the one Jonathan had taken from William and forgot to turn into the police, and the second one Zed had given her. Although she hadn't lied about being very tired, her curiosity about her great-grandmother and how that history connected her and Zed would keep her from falling asleep.

FOURTEEN

CHARLOTTE DRIFTED OFF TO sleep quickly, which was fortunate. The storm Francine had thought was building earlier in the evening finally let loose. She could hear the rain beating on the roof and hoped it would not wake Charlotte. When Charlotte's breathing became regular and easy, she slid out of bed, clutching the diaries to her breast with one arm, her robe with the other. She tiptoed out of the room.

The hallway was dark, but a nightlight near the bathroom provided enough light to navigate. Francine didn't want to take the stairs, which had a habit of creaking, so she headed to the opposite end where the media room was located. The door was open and there was light from a piece of electronic equipment. The thought of Jonathan and knowing he would be there in the morning comforted her. She closed the door behind her and turned on the overhead light.

The room was flooded in light. Francine had to squint until her eyes adjusted. The media room was a glorified in-home theater. It felt awkward to sit in one of the plush, rocking-chair theater seats and read, but that's what she intended to do. She set the two diaries on an arm of the chair and pulled on the robe, which helped her get comfortable. The house had cooled down for the evening. Francine hadn't brought slippers, so she tucked her feet under her and draped the bottom of her robe to cover her calves. Finally settled, she lifted the first book. Below the heart graphic was a square latch that held it closed. The latch could be locked but wasn't. Francine pressed the middle of the square and the latch came free. She opened the book to the first page.

The line in the middle of the first page stated that it was the diary of Ellie Miles. The date below that simply said 1928 and Francine wondered if the diary had been a Christmas present, because the book started on January 1. The pages were delicate after so many years of existence and she found she had to turn them carefully because they tore easily.

The first entry was long. It was like her grandmother had been waiting for a long time to write and it had a pent-up urgency to it. Francine wondered if the woman had been going over the words in her mind well before she put pen to paper because they flowed across the page uninterrupted by any scratch outs or additions caretted above the text. The first entry was when Ellie was twenty-three. Ellie was not innocent—at least in *knowledge* of the ways of men and women if not in *practice*—because the first entry began with her mother's confession to her that she was not the daughter of the man she believed was her father.

Mother says Father was not her first love in every sense of the word. At first I wasn't sure what she meant, and we sat looking at each other. But then I realized she had no intention of going further, but only to let the gravity of the words sink in. My hand flew to my mouth when I comprehended why she had stopped there. In truth, I had wondered about this at times. I look a little like Mum, but nothing like Father. I had not fully anticipated that there was a truth behind this until that moment. I asked her what happened to my real father, but instead she told me this story, that she'd had a forbidden lover. The man was her carriage driver. He was handsome, she said, and only a few years older than she. He'd made it clear he fancied her, and that had led to some cautions from her father, who did not want to see her marry beneath her station. She believed her driver had been threatened by her father, likely in physical terms. He never spoke of it, though, and the secret passion they had for each other continued unabated. She said it was painful to only look at him, to not be able to surrender to his embrace.

When she told me this, I could feel the fire she had inside her for him. She said they never acted on their feelings because they were never left alone. She regretted that she never had the chance to be reckless. And then she smiled.

I asked how it happened.

One time at dusk, she replied, he'd had to drive her from her father's office in Rockville to their home outside Rosedale. It had been an emergency. Her father had been training her to be his secretary in the law office, but one of his clients had had a severe accident and wanted to see Father alone. He'd not wanted to leave her in the office, but neither was it well-mannered to bring her with him. He sent them home but demanded the driver return immediately for him.

So they'd come home via the Roseville Bridge. It was near dark and there was intermittent rain. The driver had held up in the bridge for a heavy downpour to pass. Mother said the beating of her heart pounded in her ears and she didn't hear him get off the buckboard and drop onto the floor of the bridge. But then he was outside the carriage door and asking if she minded if they stayed out of the rain for a short while, and she opened the door and pulled his lips to hers. It took no time at all before she learned how feverish love could be. She said she thought she might lose her mind when he touched her in certain places and brought her more pleasure than she'd ever known. She learned how it felt to have a man inside her and how it could be painful and yet deliciously so.

Did you get away with it? I asked her.

The rain was strong during the time they spent in the bridge, and they hoped it might excuse the time they were late in get-ting home. But she said her face betrayed her. Her mother sus-pected what had happened the instant they reached the house and he let her out of the carriage. She'd tried to straighten up her clothes and her hair, and he'd done his best to maintain a detached air, but the driver was discharged that night after he'd brought my father home. By sunrise he was gone, and within days there was a new driver, older and with a family.

Did you ever see him again? I asked Mother.

We'll save that for another time, she told me.

The entry ended. Francine quickly flipped the page. The diary had begun with a life-altering event and Francine couldn't imagine what would come next. But the next entry was about the anger her great-grandmother faced from her family, and not too many entries later there was the disgrace the family felt when she was found to be with child. A marriage was hastily arranged with a suitable widower whose wife had died at an early age. They'd had no children, and so the widower was apparently pleased to have one child who could be born with his last name and, most importantly, a fertile wife.

Francine continued to scan through the diary. Her quick scan didn't bring to light any additional information about the handsome driver, only details leading up to the birth of her grandmother, at which point the diary ended. Francine felt sad as she closed it for now.

What she had learned was that her own grandmother had been a love child whose birth had been resolved by a forced marriage. She considered what that meant. For one, it might mean that she and William were more distantly related that she thought. Her grandmother Ellie and William's grandfather Earnest were siblings, but only half. At least, she presumed that. The diary's end hadn't covered a large part of her great-grandmother's life. Did she ever find her lover again? Did she remain tightly bound in the arranged marriage, or did her tendencies toward being the black sheep of the family continue? *There must be more to the story*, she thought, looking at the second diary.

It was the last thought Francine had before she awakened suddenly hours later. She looked at the time. Three thirty in the morning! Mary Ruth would be up in a half hour, and she needed to get up an hour or so after that. She hurried back to the room.

Moving stealthily along the corridor, she wondered how these two diaries had suddenly appeared. How was William in possession of one, and Zed the other? What had happened to the rest of the diaries, and who had them?

Zed had indicated that there was a connection between him and Francine. There were lots of possibilities there. As she thought about it, what made the most sense was that Zed was probably a descendent of the carriage driver and wanted to learn more about relatives that were connected to him by blood but not by name. If so, she wondered how he'd uncovered the truth. Perhaps his great-grandfather had been more forthcoming than her great-grandmother.

So then, what was William's fascination with Zed? Did he understand there was some familial connection to Zed, or was he simply interested in the treasures that may have been buried on Doc Wheat's property? That was certainly Zed's position.

Yet Zed wanted to reveal more to her. He was risking a lot to meet her at Bridgeton. Though she knew Mary Ruth needed her at the food booth, she desperately wanted to fulfill her promise to Zed to meet him. If he was to keep hidden "in plain sight," afternoon was the best since it would be very busy then. Depending on how crazy business was at Mary Ruth's—and it held the promise to be much worse than it had been today—she might be able to get away if they ran out of food again. She didn't particularly wish that on Mary Ruth, but on the other hand it would solve her problem. It might even bring Mary Ruth more notoriety, which could only help her in the long run.

If they survived the mob scene a second day. They had been lucky the way everything turned out, although she suspected this time there would be more attention from the police.

Francine tiptoed back to the bedroom and opened the door, which creaked slightly. Charlotte was snoring loudly, covering the sound. Francine snickered a bit, slipped off her robe, and laid it aside the chair where she'd originally dropped it last night before going to bed. She slid back the covers and carefully climbed into bed, the diaries tucked under her pillow. In the morning she would put them back in her purse.

Charlotte's snoring stopped in mid-snort as Francine settled in. Charlotte had been facing away from Francine's side of the bed, but now she stirred a bit. "Francine, is that you?" she asked, the sleepiness heavy in her voice.

"Yes. I had to go to the bathroom. Go back to sleep."

"Okay." In a moment or two she was snoring again.

Francine knew she needed sleep, but she couldn't stop thinking about the mysteries that had been presented her. Finally, when her mind was settled and she thought she'd be able to drift off, Charlotte got up and went to the bathroom. By the time her cell phone rang at five thirty, Francine wasn't sure she'd even gotten three hours of sleep.

"Is it that time already?" Charlotte grumbled.

"I'm afraid it is," Francine said, "and I'm betting Mary Ruth truly got up at four o'clock as she said she would and has a lot of stuff for us to do."

"I have no idea why someone would want to be in a profession that requires being up with the hoot owls."

"She's good at it, and she makes people happy. Lots of people wish they had jobs like that. Besides, I'm sure you get used to it." Francine, resolved to get out of bed, scooted her legs toward the side. Without thinking, she simultaneously dragged her hand out from under her pillow. One of the diaries flew out of the bed and hit the floor with a clunk.

Charlotte sat up with a jolt. "What was that?"

"Nothing." Francine scooted out of the high bed, scooped up the diary, and tried to hide it back under the pillow. As she did, she looked over at Charlotte. Her friend had already seized her white framed glasses off the nightstand and was watching her intently. Which only proved Charlotte could move quickly when she wanted to.

"If it's nothing, then what did you just shove under the pillow?"

"Personal. It's personal."

Charlotte reached her hand over to Francine's side of the bed and placed it on the pillow. "Really, Francine. There is nothing that is going to make me want to see what's under there more than telling me it's personal. How personal?"

Francine knew that denying it at this point would only make it worse. On the other hand, Charlotte only knew of the first diary. She could keep the second a secret by admitting to the first. "It's my grandmother's diary, the one William had."

"When did you have time to read it? What does it say?"

Francine sat on the edge of bed. "It details the reason my great-grandmother was considered the black sheep."

"Hot dog!" Charlotte exclaimed. "Are the details lurid?"

"It's a steamy confession, given the time period. It's when my grandmother learned the truth that the father she knew was not her biological father."

Charlotte took off her glasses and looked Francine in the eyes. "I'm surprised they didn't make your great-grandmother wear a scarlet letter."

"The diary recounts the story from her infatuation with the carriage driver—the feeling was mutual—through the incident at Roseville Bridge and to the birth of the baby. That's the last interesting story."

"I wonder if your grandmother had other diaries that covered more of her life."

"I wonder that too." She especially wondered what other knowledge Zed wanted to share with her in Bridgeton. But she had no time to focus on that now. "Why don't you get into the shower first? I'll go down and see how Mary Ruth is coming along and if she needs anything before we have to leave for the bridge. Or what used to be the bridge."

Charlotte brightened. "That's right. We need to look our best for *Good Morning America*."

Francine checked herself out in a mirror that hung over an antique dresser by the door. "I'm not sure I have a 'best' in me this morning. It's going to take a lot of makeup to cover the bags under these eyes."

FIFTEEN

FRANCINE HELPED CHARLOTTE DOWN from the bed. She made sure her friend was stable and in the bathroom before re-hiding the second diary and leaving the first for Charlotte to find. Then she headed downstairs. She wore her slippers and the lightweight white robe she'd thrown on a chair not too many hours ago. The yeasty smell of cinnamon rolls permeated the house.

As she neared the kitchen, she was surprised to hear the voices of the other three women gabbing in the kitchen and the noise of food being prepared. She swung open the kitchen door to the find Alice at the stove scrambling some eggs, Mary Ruth at the oven with the door open stirring some kind of potatoes on a baking sheet, and Joy at the central island nibbling on a cinnamon roll while making notes on white index cards. She had her tablet open to a search engine page.

The three looked up when Francine entered the room. "Good morning," Alice said brightly. "Did you sleep well? Where's Charlotte?"

"Charlotte's in the shower. I slept well except for this nightmare where we had a séance, the Roseville Bridge burned down, and we're scheduled to be on television this morning."

"Bad news," replied Alice. "All that really happened. Are you hungry? The rest of us are, and we're getting ready to eat. We've made plenty."

"That's good. I forgot to tell you that Jonathan will be here for breakfast." Her hand flew to her mouth. "Oh no! I also forgot to let Jonathan know we would be out to the bridge by seven o'clock! He wasn't planning to show up until around eight."

Mary Ruth waved her off. "No problem. As Alice said, we have plenty. He can heat up any leftovers. Plus we have baked goods. Lots of baked goods."

"With any luck, we'll be back by eight o'clock," Alice said.

Francine looked out the window at the day that was dawning. The rainstorm that had blown up during the night was gone. There wasn't a cloud in the sky. Stars were visible in the western half of the sky. In the eastern half, rosy streaks formed on the horizon. She hoped it would be a good day. Sunshine would help for sure.

She crossed her arms as she studied the amount of work that had been accomplished. And Joy was dressed and ready for the day. "I thought we were going to stagger our showers starting at five thirty," she said to Joy.

"Who could sleep with all this work to do?" Joy said. "I got up with Mary Ruth at four o'clock. I really need to be on my game by airtime, although I'm told there'll be no *Good Morning America* report. They weren't interested. It'll be local only."

Francine peered into the skillet full of eggs Alice had just taken off the heat. Even given that Jonathan was coming, it seemed like a lot. "Is Cox's Army coming over for breakfast?"

Mary Ruth pulled the baking sheet out of the oven and placed it on the top of the stove. "You forget that Toby's here. Our trainer has him on a high-protein, low-fat diet."

"He's looking pretty buff. I noticed it yesterday. The low-fat part has got to be difficult considering all the tasty stuff we're making."

"Being disciplined about sampling is the hardest part of being a caterer. You have to know the food tastes good but you have to watch the calorie content. Fortunately for Toby, he's young, and now that he's exercising, he burns calories like your presence burns bridges."

Before Francine could respond, Toby burst through the back door to the kitchen carrying a stack of bulk vegetable oil containers. One of them he placed to the side. Whereas the others were white, the one he separated had a yellow tinge to it. "I'm starved. Cleaning out the food truck after yesterday's corn fritter donut stampede wasn't easy. Is breakfast ready yet? I feel like we've been up for hours."

"We have been," Alice answered. "And don't pretend I didn't see you sneak one of the apple-cinnamon scones I made yesterday."

Toby winked at her. "Whoever said I was pure? I'll burn it off just being on my feet all day trying to pacify customers." He placed the bucket and the plastic containers in the far corner of the kitchen. He went over to where Francine stood next to Alice and also peered into the skillet. "The eggs look pale. You made them with mostly egg whites, didn't you? So I needed to get some fat in my diet with the scone."

"The eggs are as prescribed by our trainer." Mary Ruth scooped heaping spoonfuls of breakfast potatoes into a large bowl. "You'll get some healthy fat with these potatoes. I've baked them with olive oil and spices. Where did you get the yellowish container you brought in? I don't buy that brand of oil."

"Are you sure? Because two of the four full containers out there are the same brand. They're all the same anyway." He said it in a teasing manner.

Mary Ruth's mouth straightened. "You know better than that. I'm particular about all the ingredients. I'll have to talk to the supplier out here. Alice, don't use those today unless you have to."

"Right now I just want to eat," Toby said. "Are we at the bar or the table?"

Joy finished writing a note on an index card and placed it with a small pile of other cards. She got off the bar stool. "The table. Sorry I'm a bit behind in setting it. I'll get right on it."

"Shall I go up and see how Charlotte is coming?" Francine asked.

"Yes," Joy answered, pulling forks, knives, and spoons out of drawer. "If she's out of the shower, just have her come down. She can get ready after that. I don't know that I'll need all of you for today's segment, but I'll need the moral support. Plus, this is going to be tricky."

"In what way?"

"I'm trying to stick to the bridge and what a tragedy it is to lose another covered bridge like the one at Bridgeton or Jeffries Ford. If it even gets rebuilt, it'll no longer be historic. The problem is that the anchors may try to swing this to the reason we were there yesterday morning. My counter will be to bring up yesterday's events—your cousin William being in a coma and the fire at Zedediah's house that may or may not be arson. Those don't leave much room for joviality in the story."

Joy disappeared into the formal dining room.

Francine felt sad about everything. Nothing was going right for any of them. She left the kitchen and headed toward the staircase, only to find Charlotte with her robe pulled tight and her wig askew negotiating the stairs, both feet on a stair step before progressing down to the next one. "How are you feeling this morning, Charlotte?"

"Like I just performed a high wire act. I mounted the bed to sit down and put on my slippers, but I fell back and rolled into the center of it. It held me captive like a sausage in a pig in the blanket. I fought just to get to the edge of the bed and then practically had to rappel to the floor."

"You should have called for me."

Charlotte finally reached the bottom of the stairs. "Nah. I've already accomplished more than I do most days. It's made me hungry."

"That's good. I was coming to get you for breakfast."

"Breakfast is served!" called Mary Ruth from the dining room.

But Francine's cell phone rang at that moment. Surprised because of the early hour, she studied the caller ID. It was Dolly.

"Go on," she told Charlotte, shooing her into the dining room. Charlotte didn't move, though, and Francine let her stay. Her life was too interesting right now to expect Charlotte to pretend it wasn't. "Hello?"

"This is Gloria. I'm Dolly's sister." The voice sounded like much like Dolly's, but it was raw with emotion. "I'm calling to let you know William died last night."

The news hit Francine hard. "I'm so sorry," she said in a rush. "I don't know what to say. How did it happen? How's Dolly doing?"

Charlotte took her by the arm and indicated a nearby upholstered chair for her to sit in. Francine sat.

"Dolly is devastated, as you can imagine. He was doing well and no one expected this."

"Did the doctors give a reason?"

"All they can tell us is that anytime someone goes into a coma like he did, there's injury to the brain. William's case didn't look dire, and they thought there was a good chance he would recover, but basically, he didn't."

Francine had known going in that recovery from brain injuries was difficult. She felt like the doctors had been honest. In the hospital they'd never ruled out death. But she wondered why William had tilted from having a decent prognosis to death.

Francine looked at her watch. Much as she wanted to support Joy, she felt it was her duty to support Dolly. "I can be there in less than an hour," she offered.

"That's kind of you, but Dolly needs time alone. It's been a difficult night and she's had no sleep. Why don't I call you back later in the day? That might be a better time for you to visit."

"I understand. But if she needs anything before then, please call me."

"I will, thank you." Gloria disconnected. Francine set the phone in her lap.

"William?" Charlotte asked.

Francine nodded blankly.

"I'm sorry."

"Me too." Francine recounted the little she knew surrounding William's death.

Charlotte held Francine's hand. "Brain injuries are serious things."

"I know. Even if a patient comes out of a coma, sometimes the recovery process takes years. William's life could have been marked with terrible symptoms or unbearable pain. I don't want to sound Pollyannaish, but sad as it is, it might have been better for him this way."

Charlotte thought a moment and her eyes went wide. "The séance," she said. "At one point you asked if the spirit Merlina had contacted was William. It might have been."

Francine felt a brief moment of anger. "Don't go there. I don't believe for a moment Merlina contacted the dead. And besides, the séance was in the afternoon. Dolly's sister said he died last night."

"Maybe he was already in the state between life and death."

"You hired her. How can you believe in this?"

"Hiring Merlina was supposed to help Alice. It just didn't go at all as I expected."

Mary Ruth bustled out from the dining room. "Let's move it. We need to get breakfast going." She took one look at Francine and turned to Charlotte. "What happened?"

"William died."

"Oh no."

———

Intellectually Francine knew breakfast would be delicious, but she found herself staring at the portions Mary Ruth placed on her plate. She stuck a fork in the eggs but couldn't bring them to her mouth. She set the fork back down. She looked up and found Charlotte watching her.

"You have to eat, Francine."

"I know. It just ... too many things are happening at once, and it makes me sad. Being shot at, the two fires, William's coma, and now his death. I don't know what to make of it."

"None of us do," Joy said. "But we have to go on."

"The scones came out very well, Alice," Mary Ruth said. Francine could tell it was a deliberate attempt to change the subject. "Has everyone tried one?"

The rest of the women murmured about how good they were. Francine was glad that Mary Ruth had cut them into more normal serving sizes, not like the ones she would serve from the food stand. She took a nibble. It tasted wonderful, with a rich buttery taste that lingered on her tongue after the perfect blend of cinnamon and apples had faded. "It *is* good," she said, and the nibble inspired her to eat more. Eventually she finished the scone and followed it up by eating a bit of the scrambled eggs and breakfast potatoes on her plate, followed by a small sample of a warm cinnamon roll. The food made her feel better.

Joy looked at her watch. "It's now almost six fifteen. We need to be at the bridge and ready to go no later than seven o'clock, and it takes us twenty minutes to get there from here. Can everyone be ready in fifteen minutes?"

"I haven't even been in the shower yet," Francine said, "so no, I can't be ready in fifteen minutes. Why don't you hitch a ride with the news van? We'll be there in plenty of time. You know they won't get to this until the second hour." There was a great amount of grumbling, but everyone moved in a rush.

Toby said he would take care of getting the dishes in the dishwasher and shooed the women out of the kitchen after they'd brought their plates from the table. "I've already showered and I'm ready for the day. Plus, I won't be on camera. It's the rest of you who need to be ready for showtime."

Francine was surprised. Mary Ruth wasn't going and she'd assumed neither would Toby. "I didn't know you were planning to be there."

Toby shrugged and worked on getting the leftover eggs and potatoes into containers. "I'm driving you. It was Grandma's idea. She said she would feel better knowing I was there."

Francine took a quick shower, dried her hair, and did the best she could putting on some makeup to cover the lines in her face and the bags under her eyes. She kept thinking about William. It bothered her that William's death had been so abrupt and that the fire to the bridge had come on the heels of his accident there, not to mention the fire at Zed's house. Were all of these really linked, or was it just circumstance?

She was certain William couldn't have had anything to do with the fire at Zed's house, but what about Dolly? Dolly had made a threat to go after whoever had shot at William, but surely she'd been at the hospital with William and had nothing to do with the fire. And Zed couldn't have had anything to do with William's death without half a dozen people at the hospital noticing him.

She came out of the bathroom to find Charlotte had changed clothes and was doing her best to speed read through the first of Francine's grandmother's diaries. She'd hoped to satisfy Charlotte with the first while keeping the second hidden. Plus, letting Charlotte read the first diary would go a long way to securing her cooperation at Bridgeton, which Francine suspected she would need.

A half hour later the women met their deadline and assembled in the hall. They shrugged on coats because of the cold. "We don't look bad," Alice said, checking out her sporty new Columbia winter coat in the gold-framed hall mirror. "Let's move."

Toby drove. The sun was up but not high enough to produce a lot of light. The cameraman from Channel Six was there. He was setting up a portable light stand powered through his truck while Joy looked over her notecards. Toby parked in the Rock Run parking lot. They made their way down to where Channel Six was, immediately behind the orange barrels blocking access to the burned out bridge. Yellow police tape was strung across the barrels. A Sheriff's Department officer sat in a squad car, watching the action. Two other stations were there with large broadcast trucks, one from Terre Haute and another from Indianapolis.

Joy inserted and earpiece and took the microphone. Both tested fine and she was ready to go for a seven-thirty segment. It turned out to be for the station's local broadcast and involved Joy alone.

However, the anchors used it to set up for a longer segment fifteen minutes later. The cameraman strategically placed the women and a Toby in the background of the shot, making it look like there were still gawkers at the scene.

Joy recapped the tragic events of yesterday. Francine couldn't hear what they were saying, but soon Joy singled her out of the crowd and motioned her forward. Francine's eyes went wide. Joy's arm went firmly behind her shoulder to keep her in place in front of the camera. "This is Francine McNamara," Joy said, introducing her. "Her cousin William is the one who was in a coma but passed away last night. First of all, on behalf of the entire WRTV news team, we are terribly sorry about what happened. We understand that it was unexpected. Can you tell us anything about why he had a turn for the worst?"

A lot of things went through Francine's mind, most of all resentment that she would be asked such a question at this time. The only thing that made it bearable was that she knew Joy was only acting on what was coming out of Indianapolis. "I'm sorry," she said. "I don't have any more to add."

Joy nodded as though she was receiving instructions through the earphone. She spoke into the camera. "I understand we have a crew from our affiliate in Terre Haute who will be updating us from Union Hospital where they will be talking to the doctors." Then she turned to Francine with the microphone. "Do you think there's a connection between the incident involving him and the fact that someone set fire to the bridge?" she asked.

"I've given it some thought," Francine said, almost, but not quite, making it up on the spot. "The two things come close together in time but seem very different. Someone shooting at William would appear to be related to him being somewhere he shouldn't, but the act of arson seems deliberately evil."

"What can you tell us about the other fire yesterday? We understand you witnessed it. Could the two be related?"

"I'll leave that for the police."

"Why do you think your cousin was here?" Joy continued.

Francine was way out of her comfort zone. "I don't know. William and I weren't that close anymore. I hadn't seen him in several years."

Joy hesitated. She covered the ear containing the earpiece with her hand, as though she wanted to be sure of the next question. She looked as though she had something distasteful in her mouth. "Can you remind our viewers what were you doing here at the Roseville Bridge so early yesterday?"

Francine knew Joy couldn't avoid the question, coming live from the *GMA* hosts. "As you know, Joy, our bridge club has developed some notoriety for our bucket list items. We were here working on one of them. But I really think the focus in Parke County needs to be on finding the person who set fire to this historic bridge to prevent any further incidents, and then determining how to replace the bridge as they did in Bridgeton so many years ago."

And with that, Francine stepped back into the group with Toby, Alice, and Charlotte.

Joy wrapped up her segment, made sure her mic was off, and then handed it and the earpiece back to the cameraman before huddling with the rest of the women. "You handled that beautifully," she told Francine. "I think you have a future in public relations."

Francine laughed nervously. "I learned how to do it from a pro."

"There wasn't a whole lot more they could say at that point. I was proud of you."

"I'm just glad it's over."

Charlotte pulled at Francine's sleeve. "What makes you think it's over? Mark my words, until the arsonist is caught, this story won't go away, and until William's death is resolved, neither will the questions about why we happened to be here that morning."

They all stood quietly for a moment, contemplating Charlotte's warning. Toby was the first to speak. "We need to get back to Rockville. There might already be a line of people waiting. I bet it'll be a good morning for cinnamon rolls and coffee."

Alice chuckled. "And we have to watch out for those crazy corn fritter donut addicts."

Francine and the others took steps toward the car, but Charlotte remained rooted in place. She had a faraway look in her eyes, like something had suddenly occurred to her.

Francine wanted to ask but knew it would only lead to more standing around. If she remembered, she would ask her about it in the car when they were on their way. "C'mon," she said, "we need to go." She took Charlotte by the arm and helped her across the bumpy roadside terrain to the car.

SIXTEEN

By the time the others returned, Jonathan and Mary Ruth were at the food booth getting it ready to open at nine o'clock. Jonathan was wearing a black flannel shirt and blue jeans, which Francine thought made him look ruggedly handsome. Handsome or not, Mary Ruth had him working and the others joined them soon.

The weatherman had warned that the clear skies would drop the temperature overnight and it would struggle to get warm until the sun got high in the sky. In Indiana, the warmest temperatures were never at noon but rather later in the day, more toward four o'clock when there had been several good hours of sunshine. And so it was that everyone, including Jonathan but excluding Charlotte, was bundled in layers underneath pink Mary Ruth's Catering aprons, answering calls for hot coffee, cocoa, tea, and Mary Ruth's cinnamon rolls, which were selling almost as fast as Toby could get them out of the box. He'd been given the task of carrying supplies from the pickup truck to the food booth and unloading them for Jonathan, who placed them in a warming oven while trying to keep up with the brewing of coffee and tea. Francine was working on the cocoas individually and pouring tea and coffee while Joy, who was the chief saleswoman, called out what was needed from the open sales window. That left Mary Ruth and Alice to the task of preparing the corn fritter donuts, which had become the sensation of the festival. The dough had been refrigerated overnight, but now it needed to be shaped into balls and dropped into the fryer until each had achieved that perfect golden brown color. Then they would be cooled slightly on a rack, dipped in the honey-cinnamon glaze, and served warm.

Like the day before, Mary Ruth could not keep up with the demand, even with the addition of Jonathan, whose presence allowed Alice to help with the donuts. The process was a tedious one.

Joy bustled back and picked up a tray of the donuts Mary Ruth had just set out. "Every one of these is already sold," she said. "Can you speed it up?"

"Not without more hands." She looked around. "Toby, get those cinnamon rolls unloaded as fast as you can. Joy needs your help up front."

"There's no room for all of the rolls," Toby complained. "I can't stack the boxes more than three high without the rolls on the bottom being flattened, and I know you won't allow that. I have to bring them in as needed. Where's Charlotte?"

"Off doing detective work," answered Francine. Also, she needed Charlotte to get the clothes Zed had requested, since she and Jonathan were tied up.

"Detective work?" Mary Ruth sputtered. "I thought that's what Detective Stockton was in charge of. Don't tell me he needs her help. He looks experienced enough to me."

"You didn't give her any tasks to do. As usual, I might add. So she decided to follow up on a few loose ends."

"You sound like you approved of this."

"There are a few unanswered questions the two of us have about why William may have been out on Zed's property."

"How is that connected with the fire?"

"We don't know that it is. But Charlotte said she had a theory. And since the events occurred one after the other with the fire at the bridge in between, we have to consider the possibility that all three are related." This was in spite of what she'd said on the morning news show.

The minute timer beeped and Mary Ruth yanked two baskets of corn fritter donuts out of the fryer, sliding the front of the baskets onto a wire notch that held them above the fryer so the grease could drain off back into it. She shook them impatiently. "Well, how long will it be until she gets back? I've changed my mind about her. I can find plenty of tasks now for her to do."

Francine looked at her watch. It was only nine thirty. The Fabulous Sweet Shoppe had opened a half hour ago, the same time as the library, which had been Charlotte's first stop. She had no idea how easily obtainable information would be on Doc Wheat. She'd hoped since he was a local legend, there'd be a book on him Charlotte could check out, enabling her to move onto the Dollar General store, where she could buy clothes for Zed and maybe some food, too, to take to him at Bridgeton. With the way sales were moving here, Francine guessed they'd be sold out by early afternoon and could get over to Bridgeton while it was still daylight.

"I can call her and see where she is," Francine said.

"Don't make it long," Joy said, heading back toward a box of cinnamon rolls. "I need you to pour a half dozen coffees, one large, and two large cocoas."

Francine rushed to get those done, set them up for Joy, and then call Charlotte. From the whispery voice Charlotte used when she answered the phone, she knew Charlotte had to be in the library.

"There's just hardly anything on Doc Wheat," she said. "The Local History section has some books that go back into the late forties and early fifties, but they don't have more than a couple of pages on him, and it's all the same stuff Zed told you. I asked and the librarian said there were no books written about Wheat. Oh, and she said to say how sorry she is about William. He was a regular at the library."

The thought grabbed Francine. "He was a regular?"

"I'm already ahead of you there. I asked all sorts of questions about any research he'd done or what kind of books he read. It seems he was a history buff. Loved biographies, especially anything local. And get this. Supposedly he was *writing* a book about the history of area, starting back when settlers first moved into Parke County."

"Had anyone seen this book?"

"Not in print. Here's the kicker. He had a laptop computer he'd bring in and work on. Don't you wish you'd taken that laptop out of his car now?"

Francine had to admit if she'd known that, she might have been more tempted.

Charlotte continued, "The librarian said he had interviewed a lot of local people about what stories had been passed down to them. And genealogy. He was always taking pictures in graveyards."

"Sounds macabre."

Mary Ruth tapped Francine on the shoulder, making her jump. "Is that Charlotte?" Francine nodded. "How fast can she get over here?"

"I'll check," Francine told her, then watched Mary Ruth hustle back to the donut station.

Now Francine whispered like Charlotte. "We need you over here. The line's getting longer and longer and we can't keep up. Mary Ruth even asked for you."

"Humph," Charlotte sniffed. "It's about time she recognized I'm as good as the rest of you at helping."

"Don't get a big head. She only said she could find a lot of tasks for you to do."

"I could come back now. I've gotten just about all I can get here. But what about that other project, the one at Dollar General?"

Francine turned her back to Mary Ruth and the others and her voice got even softer. "Don't worry about that one. We're going crazy. I can send Jonathan out to run that errand as soon as things calm down here."

She closed out the phone call and turned around to find Mary Ruth talking to a customer. "No, we're not going to have any of the flourless chocolate cake available until lunchtime. That kind of chocolate is for lunch, not breakfast. But if you want, I can ice your cinnamon roll with the same chocolate frosting we use on the cake."

That seemed to be enough to satisfy the customer. Mary Ruth slapped some frosting on his cinnamon roll, and he walked away with it and one of the warm, rich cocoas Francine had crafted and handed to Joy. Making the cocoa she likened to preparing one of her oft-requested hard lemonades during the summer. Hand mixing was required and the beverage went down smoothly. She wondered if that was a food truck idea waiting to happen. After all, lemon shakeups, elephant ears, and funnel cakes were a staple of the food trucks you could find at county fairs across Indiana. What if you kicked up the lemonade a notch?

She pushed the thought from her mind as she began work on another cocoa. She was five behind. Jonathan looked like he was having a little better luck keeping up with the coffee urns. He had tipped one up to drain it and had a filter with fresh coffee grounds waiting to go in. "This is nuts!" he said.

"Charlotte will be here soon," Francine announced. "Perhaps you should have let Charlotte help from the start. At some point you've got to forgive her."

"I'm *not* still holding a grudge against her because of the health department incident, despite what everyone thinks," Mary Ruth confided. She checked a dozen donuts on a cooling rack, determined they were okay, and passed them off to Alice for drizzling with the honey-cinnamon glaze. "It's become a way of defining our relationship. I do care about her, but she's always putting herself first, and this is my way of reminding her that doing so can have negative consequences for other people."

"She doesn't always put herself first, though sometimes it seems that way. What about last night? She helped Alice check the séance off her Sixty List."

"Mark my words, it will turn out she had an ulterior motive for doing that."

"That's uncharitable of you."

Mary Ruth put another batch of the corn fritter donuts into the fryer and hit the timer. Toby came forward from the back. He was carrying two bulk vegetable oil containers. "I need you to look at this," he said.

"Cover my station," she ordered Francine and Alice. "I'll just be gone for a moment."

"We can stay right here." He handed her the white container. "Hold this."

She took it from him. "Okay."

"Get a feel for its weight."

She moved it up and down with her arms. "Feels normal."

"Now try this one." He handed her one that had a yellowish tint to it. Francine recognized it as one they'd seen last night when Mary Ruth had declared it an inferior brand.

Mary Ruth's expression changed the moment he handed it to her. "It's so much lighter."

"Makes me wonder what's in it."

Francine overfilled a coffee while watching the two of them. She mopped up the mess with a bar towel. "Have you opened any of the containers yet today?"

"I haven't," Mary Ruth answered. "Alice always changes out the grease. Alice?"

"I did that last night, so we should be good today. Why?"

Francine popped lids on the remaining coffees she'd poured and handed them up to Joy. "Jonathan, would you be a dear and help Toby take those containers back out and check them to make sure they have grease in them?"

Jonathan looked puzzled. "Why?"

"Because I've been around Charlotte too long. Earlier this morning she said we wouldn't be safe until the arsonist was caught. If she were here, her suspicious mind would link the different densities of those two containers and conclude one of them may be an accelerant."

The look on Toby's face told Francine he didn't understand. "An accelerant?"

"Like gasoline. Like an arsonist would use."

Jonathan and Toby hurried to the back to check.

"It's probably nothing," Francine said. She began another hot cocoa, trying to keep up with the number of orders she had in front of her. Mary Ruth went back to frying donuts.

Toby was back in fifteen seconds. He held up two fingers. "Two of them. Both the off-brand. They smelled like gasoline. What does it mean?"

Francine considered what to do. "It means we need to be on guard. And I think we should advise Detective Stockton right away."

"That won't be difficult," Alice said. "He's in line."

Everyone glanced toward the long line. Stockton was wearing a black Stetson this morning instead of the white one he'd been wearing yesterday. He had on his brown Parke County sheriff's uniform, and people were telling him to cut in line ahead of them. He was advancing quickly, doffing his hat at each person letting him advance.

Francine got a kick out of the expression on Joy's face when she heard him order a corn fritter donut, coffee, and the latest news report on the Skinny-Dipping Grandmas. She seemed ready to give him the withering glance she'd been using on the people who'd recognized her from the newscasts and made sarcastic remarks. But when she saw who it was, she broke out in a wide grin. "Coming right up," she said. "Do you need any clues to go with that?"

"I was going to ask for a bit of your time, but I see that you're pretty busy."

Suddenly Charlotte was standing next to Stockton. Francine had been so absorbed in the interaction between he and Joy she hadn't seen her come up. "Lucky for both of you, it's time for her break," Charlotte said. "I'm here to take her place. Just let me get back there."

For a change, Mary Ruth didn't object. And when she asked Charlotte to use wax paper sheets instead of her fingers when transferring the food to the plates, neither did Charlotte.

Detective Stockton came in from the back to confer with Mary Ruth. He removed his hat as he entered. "It does smell like gasoline," he told her. "We've searched the rest of your supplies and your grandson assures us everything else looks normal to him. I'm taking the two containers with me when I leave. But that won't be until I finish my donut and coffee."

"Do you really think someone is trying to blow us up?"

"It's either that or they're trying to frame you." He bit into the donut.

"It's the former," Charlotte said. "Think about it. Alice would have opened the container. She has bad allergies. She wouldn't have noticed the smell."

Francine tensed when she realized how true it was. *Had they come that close to being blown up?* Maybe Alice would have noticed the weight of the gasoline versus the weight of the oil. But maybe not. At any rate, it implied that someone knew a lot about their little group. *We're on TV regularly*, she thought. *How much about our lives have we revealed to anyone who wants to know?*

"You need to be on guard," Stockton said. "Joy, could I talk to you, please?"

The two of them disappeared out the back door.

Despite the scariness of what could have happened, the group continued to wait on customers. Charlotte was no Joy when it came to serving people with a smile, but she was surprisingly effective in staying on task. "Here you go," was about all Charlotte said as she rang up the order, took the money, and dispensed the food.

"She could at least say 'thank you' or something," Alice muttered to Francine.

"Have you noticed the line is moving faster, though?" Francine said. "Let's not get too critical. When Joy comes back, we may actually catch up. How are we moving faster?"

"It's because we have to," Alice said. She was no longer drizzling the glaze but dunking the donuts in it. "We're doing whatever it takes."

Joy came through the back door of the booth with Detective Stockton. She retrieved another corn fritter donut from the case and gave it to him.

"I just received a phone call," he said to the group, "and given the circumstances, I think you should know about it."

Charlotte handed the wax paper sheet she was using to handle the food to Joy. "The guy with the goatee wants a dozen cinnamon rolls. With chocolate frosting. I don't know what to make of that. I've gotten more requests for chocolate iced cinnamon rolls. I didn't even know that was an option."

Mary Ruth studiously avoided answering her question.

"Anyway, that'll use up the last box we have up front. Toby will have to bring more from the back." She moved quickly to where Stockton was standing.

"A few more orders like that and we'll be completely wiped out of cinnamon rolls," Toby said.

"Then we'll just sell them cookies," Joy said with a smile. She moved to the sales position. "Any coffee to go with those cinnamon rolls?" she asked the man with the goatee.

"This will only take a minute," Stockton said, then his deep, rumbling voice went so soft only the women around him could hear it. "You may have heard rumors that we did not locate a body in the fire on Zedediah Matthew's property. Based on what we heard from your eyewitness testimony, we had expected to. Now, after a thorough search, we're convinced he got out alive."

"That's good, isn't it?" Mary Ruth asked. "I can tell you that man knew how to bake. Although it was based on a small sample size."

"Yes, it's good that he's alive. But I think you know that William Falkes is not. So we want to talk to Zed Matthews. He's now wanted for questioning in regards to Mr. Falkes's death."

"On charges of Involuntary Manslaughter?" Charlotte guessed.

"At this point we only want to talk to him."

"Why are you telling this to us and not others?" Francine asked.

"We believe he may try to contact one of you. We want you to keep us informed." He looked at her as he said it.

Francine picked up on his gaze. "What possible reason could he have for trying to contact one of us?"

"We'd rather not say."

She gulped, wondering if they'd somehow intercepted his text to her. She knew it was possible, though she didn't understand how they could have found it so quickly among the millions of texts that must have occurred in the area with the Covered Bridge Festival going on. "Is there a reason for us to be concerned?"

"He's a dangerous man. And quite possibly desperate. Everything in his house went up in smoke last night. He'll need resources from somewhere."

Francine thought about this. The police must already be monitoring things like bank accounts trying to locate him. Zed certainly indicated last night he didn't want to be found. What would it look like if she was caught helping him? On the other hand, he wasn't guilty of anything yet.

She glanced at Charlotte, hoping to caution her not to say anything.

But Charlotte had a mischievous smile on her face. "Don't worry, detective," she assured him. "We'll let you know if he tries anything."

SEVENTEEN

"WELL, THAT WAS DISTURBING," Francine whispered to Charlotte after Detective Stockton had left and they were back to serving customers.

"I find it more disturbing that Stockton's first name is Roy. That would mean, as a couple ..."

"... they would be Roy and Joy." Francine glowered at Charlotte. "I've already thought of that. And it's not the most disturbing thing."

"Lighten up."

"What are we going to do about Zed?" Francine could hear the anxiety in her own voice. William's death rankled her for many reasons, including reminding her that she was now involved in another murder case.

"I think we should meet him as planned. If my estimates are correct, we will run out of food right after the lunch crowd. Again. That will give us plenty of time to get to Bridgeton in the middle of the afternoon."

Mary Ruth threw away the last empty box of cinnamon rolls. "Out of cinnamon rolls!" she called up to Joy. "How many scones are left?"

"They were gone a half hour ago. I just got an order for a dozen corn fritter donuts. Can you fill it?"

"Yes, but I'm on my last batch. I've got maybe thirty more to glaze."

"What's left?"

"We still have ten dozen cookies and six flourless chocolate cakes I can cut into pieces. They're the only things left in inventory." Mary Ruth let out a sigh but didn't appear shaken.

"I still have coffee!" Jonathan said. "Sell coffee!"

Francine turned to Mary Ruth. "You seem remarkably calm considering how little you have left and that we're just approaching lunch hour."

"Six hot cocoas!" Joy announced.

"Remember, yesterday afternoon Marcy convinced me that shortage is not a bad thing."

"How can it not be a bad thing? Customers are grumbling about it. They're leaving unsatisfied!"

"It makes them want to come back. It's special. Do you remember how the guys used to drive all the way over to St. Louis to buy Coors beer when we were in our early twenties? It was only distributed west of the Mississippi. It had an allure. Marcy says this shortage can have exactly the same effect."

"You really have hired her, haven't you? You weren't just kidding yesterday at Zed's."

"For the duration of the festival, yes. And maybe a little after."

Francine looked out over the crowd standing in line. They were anxious. "I don't know. Looks more like they're standing in a bread line to me."

Jonathan wiped his hands on a towel that was coffee-stained. "You don't remember bread lines. We're not that old."

"Heard about them."

"Have you noticed the orders they've been placing are getting bigger and bigger?" Mary Ruth said. "They're hoarding."

Francine chuckled. "They can't possibly eat them all before they go stale. Are they freezing them for later?"

Jonathan laughed. "Maybe there's a black market for them."

Joy butted in. "I don't care what they're doing with them. We've got to get the orders filled until we run out! Francine, can't you work faster on those hot cocoas?"

Francine set out the six cocoas she was working on and sprayed whipped cream in each one. Then she snapped a lid over the tops. "Hot cocoas up!"

Charlotte, working beside Joy, packaged up a dozen of the whole grain cinnamon-raisin cookies, using bakery sheets to handle them. "Two more coffees!" Charlotte called. "Do you have the other two coffees ready that I asked for?"

"Oh, dear, I'm sorry, I took them to fill an order I had," said Joy. "I thought they were mine."

"Four more coffees!" Charlotte grumbled.

"I'll get them," Jonathan said.

"I'll make more while you pour those," Mary Ruth said. "I'm out of things to do anyway, now that we're not scrambling to make more confections to sell today."

Francine was still worried. "Does the crowd know we're going to run out?"

"Marcy's out there re-directing those in the back of the line to other vendors."

"Wait!" Alice said suspiciously. "Are the other vendors paying Marcy for that service? They should!"

"I didn't ask," Mary Ruth admitted. "I'm more concerned that they not become unruly. I think Marcy's goal is to defuse a bad situation and keep the Mary Ruth mystique alive, so I think she's pitching them to come back earlier tomorrow while suggesting they find somewhere else to eat right now."

Joy used a spatula to put several pieces of the chocolate cake on paper plates and passed them over the counter, taking in money for them. "We've seen an increase in police presence in the area in the last fifteen minutes."

Charlotte snatched up the four coffees Francine had prepared before Joy could get her hands on them. "Well, no wonder the cops are hanging around. There's no attraction stronger in the universe than between cops and donuts."

"That's politically incorrect, even coming from you, Charlotte," Mary Ruth said, spooning coffee grounds into a coffee urn. "I bet Detective Judson back in Brownsburg doesn't eat donuts. I saw him at the pool this summer with his family, and he's got abs."

"Diet is the killer part," Toby said, coming in from the back. "I'd have abs if food didn't taste so good." He turned to his grandmother. "Detective Stockton said we need to be sure we lock up tight when you close for the day and put some kind of security system on the door if you have one. They patrol the areas, but with so many vendors, it's difficult to keep an eye on every booth."

"I just sold the last dozen corn fritter donuts," Charlotte said. "Batten down the hatches and prepare for storms!"

"Relax," said Mary Ruth. "What can we do but sell what we have? There's always tomorrow."

Maybe Marcy's not such a bad influence after all, Francine thought.

———

Not more than fifteen minutes later they were totally out of food. They could have continued to sell hot cocoas and coffee, but the crowd wasn't very interested in those without the treats, so they decided to close up for the day. While there were many disappointed customers, most left quietly to find other places to eat. It was close to one o'clock by the time they got locked up, remembering Detective Stockton's warning to double-check everything. They bought sandwiches from a vendor across the street from them, who was so excited by their presence that he had his picture taken with Mary Ruth holding a sandwich. Then they headed back to have lunch at the mansion. Francine quietly sent Jonathan to Dollar General to purchase some items for Zed.

Everyone was tired from being on their feet all morning. Francine kept a watch on the time while they sat quietly and ate lunch. When Mary Ruth's helpers started to arrive, Francine raised a question. "Can you spare Charlotte, Jonathan, and me for a couple of hours?" she asked. "We need to get to Bridgeton sometime this afternoon. We won't be gone very long, I promise."

"Oh, that sounds like fun," Joy said. "Why don't we all go? We can just work later tonight. I'd rather do that than spend all afternoon doing more prep work, and then sit around all evening too tired to do something."

Francine was caught off-guard by Joy's request. She hadn't anticipated having more company. It complicated matters. "I don't mean to make more work for you or take away your help," she told Mary Ruth.

Mary Ruth looked around at the ingredients she'd started to pile up. She grimaced. "I only have two helpers today. How long do you think you'll be gone?"

"No more than a couple of hours. We can't do much shopping."

Alice weighed in. "There's nothing really to shop for anyway. All of us have all the junk we need in our houses. Aren't we looking to downsize?"

There was general murmuring of agreement.

Joy seemed puzzled. "Then why would we go, if we aren't going to look at junky antiques or buy knickknacks we don't need? There isn't much else. With all the sampling we've been doing from Mary Ruth's sweets, we certainly don't need to try any of the high-fat fair food being hawked."

"We can people watch," said Charlotte. "It's one of the best places to watch people."

They could all agree on that, but Francine knew that wouldn't explain why she would be carrying around a bag of clothes and food once they got there.

"There's a reason Jonathan, Charlotte, and I need to go that has nothing to do with people watching," she said.

"We figured something was up," Joy said. "Even before your cousin passed away, you've been acting secretive, you and Charlotte. And now Jonathan's here. Why is it you suddenly need to go to Bridgeton?"

Francine saw no way out but to tell the truth. The story spilled out of her. "And he told me not to bring anyone with me. So even bringing Jonathan would violate what he asked. Having all of you there may keep him away."

Alice was aghast. "Why is it you want to meet with a man who may have killed your cousin?"

"There's some connection Zed has to me, and I don't know what it is. Yet. I know it has to do with the past. He tells me he's going to reveal it. I want to give him the benefit of the doubt. I think he was only chasing William off his property and didn't intend for him to get hurt. William's death has complicated matters, but I still want to find out what this connection is. Zed doesn't have much time before the police catch up to him, I think, so he's going to have to reveal it soon somehow. Meeting him in Bridgeton gives him that opportunity."

"Here's what we'll do," Joy said. "We'll all go together, but when we get to Bridgeton we'll hold back so that we can see you but we'll just melt into the crowd. He said he'd find you, right?"

"Fine help we're going to be if we're not by her side," Charlotte said.

They all looked at Charlotte.

She crossed her arms over her chest. "It's not like we can move quickly enough through a crowd to be of any help."

"I appreciate that you want to protect me," Francine said. "But he doesn't mean me any harm. I honestly believe that. He's gruff and he's probably guilty of something, but I don't feel personally threatened. What did you find out about him when you went sleuthing at the library?"

"He's threatened plenty of others," Charlotte answered. "The Parke County Register reported several run-ins he's had with the law. They're all the same. Someone was trespassing on his property, and he was within his rights to throw them off. Mostly it involved guns, though. The police didn't like that. He never wounded anyone, but he scared them."

Francine nodded. "I'm sure he scared them. That was my first impression of Zed. But he didn't hurt any one of them."

"At least not until William," Joy said.

"That may not have been intentional," Charlotte answered. "Anyway, the papers liked to print photos of him with the stories. He always looked like he's one of those survivalists you see on the Military Channel. I bet he could live in the wilderness and kill game animals with his bare hands."

Another observation Francine could agree with. "How old do you think he is? Did the papers say?"

She shook her head negatively. "On and off he's been in the papers for probably twenty-five years, and he looks about the same in all the photos."

"Twenty-five years? Really?"

"It's probably the bushy beard hiding all the wrinkles and the fact he has sunken eyes. If you get stuck with eyes like that, you're gonna look old even as young as forty, and I'm sure he's older than that."

"You think he's about our age? Early seventies?"

"Funny you should ask. I went back and checked the genealogy records they had for the county, and I couldn't find him anywhere. I went back to the 1920s."

"So he must've been born in another county," Joy said, like the answer was obvious, "or he'd be living in one of those nursing homes your cousin and his wife own."

The thought of William and Dolly and their nursing homes made Francine realize she hadn't heard from Dolly or her sister since this morning. She wondered how Dolly was doing. As busy as they'd been, she could have missed a phone call. She checked her cell. There were no calls. Nothing.

Jonathan came in carrying two full, distinctive yellow sacks from the store. They all stared at him. "What? A man can't do a little shopping?"

"They all know why I sent you," Francine said. "I couldn't help it. They all want to come to Bridgeton."

"Except me," Mary Ruth said, "though I'd like to. Now, I'm sorry to have to rush this along, but if you're going to go, you need to do it now. Go find Zed and then come back. I'll need you."

Soon they were in two cars headed for Bridgeton.

EIGHTEEN

THE ROADS FROM ROCKVILLE to Bridgeton were anything but straight. Francine felt she was on a mission to get there and get back, so she was driving a little faster than the posted speed limit. The sun had baked the interior of the car despite the cool weather. With her coat on, Francine was feeling a little nauseous. But apparently not as much as Charlotte.

"I'm gonna throw up! I'm gonna throw up!" Charlotte said, clamping her hand over her mouth like she was trying to hold it back.

"Should I pull over?" Francine asked. Charlotte didn't normally get carsick but she was making abnormal burping sounds. "I think there are some wet wipes in the console. Can you get them, Alice?" Alice sat in the middle of the back seat of Francine's car. Other than Charlotte, who was swaying in the front seat like a wounded seal ready to take her last dive into the deep, Alice was best positioned to get the wipes out.

Alice unbuckled her seat belt and scooted forward, flipping the top of the console up. "What good will that do? These thing are too tiny to mop up if she blows her lunch."

"Use them like you would a damp washcloth. Apply them to her forehead."

"I'm not leaning up here with no seat belt on, not with you going so fast around the curves."

"I don't know what you're talking about. If I go any slower we'll get to Bridgeton about the time we need to turn around and go back to do prep work for tomorrow's food." The roads from Rockville to Bridgeton were admittedly two-lane and full of curves, but Francine was taking them as slowly as she could.

Jonathan, who was driving his truck, had Toby with him. The truck hung back, almost like they sensed something was going on in Francine's car.

"Nothing is more nauseating than the smell of someone throwing up," said Alice. "If she throws up in here, I will too, and then I'll be wiped out for the rest of the day. No food for tomorrow."

Joy was playing with her phone in the back seat. "There's no cell reception out here, either, so I can't check navigation to see how much farther it is or whether we could go a different route."

Francine pointed all the air vents toward Charlotte. "There are no roads to Bridgeton that aren't winding like this. I've taken us about the only good route there is. Just hang on for ten more minutes, Charlotte, and we'll be there."

"Can you make the air cooler? That seems to help some." Charlotte burped again, a belch that came from down deep in her gut.

Joy sunk deeper into the down jacket she'd brought. "You might as well do it, Francine. My teeth are chattering in the cold but it's preferable to having Charlotte vomit."

Charlotte snatched the wipes out of Alice's hand and pasted them on her forehead. She leaned against the car door. "Ten minutes? You promise?"

"Ten more minutes until we reach the outskirts of Bridgeton," Francine said. They came to an intersection, and she followed another little hand-lettered sign that pointed the way. "Once we reach the traffic there we'll slow way down."

Joy sat up. "I just got a text! I just got a text! I don't know how, since my phone only shows one bar of reception, but it's there."

"What does it say?" Alice asked. "Have you sent out a plea for someone to meet us there with Dramamine?"

"I didn't think of that, but I can, if another text goes through. The Channel Six live remote team is out at Bridgeton! The station sent them out there to get some b-roll of the Covered Bridge Festival since they're already out here. They want me to do a segment by the Bridgeton Bridge since it was the one that was destroyed by arson years ago but has been rebuilt."

Francine weighed the consequences of that. "So in essence you're going to attract *more* attention to the fact that we're out here. That might scare Zed off."

"Everyone knows we're out at the Covered Bridge Festival," Joy said. "For heaven's sake, Mary Ruth is a headliner, especially the way she sells out of food. And with the two cases of arson and my reporting both locally and on *GMA*, it's not like we're incognito. Look at it this way, I can keep the attention focused elsewhere while you search for Zed."

"Just text them for a Dramamine," Charlotte pleaded.

Francine was relieved Charlotte managed to hold it together until they rolled into Bridgeton. There was a major slowdown of cars, and the locals were out in force with homemade parking signs trying to get them to parking spots. $3 PARKING THIS WAY! read one sign held by a woman in a wheelchair. The sign directed people down a dirt-packed road past her trailer home.

"Should we take that?" Alice pointed to the sign. "I know it'll be a long walk for Charlotte, but I want to get her out of the car."

Francine inched forward past the woman. "No, I'm not afraid of paying five dollars as we get closer. The uneven ground will be bad for Charlotte's ankles."

"I just hope there's a parking spot left in a five-dollar lot," Joy said. "Look at all the people!"

"I'll be okay." Charlotte mopped her forehead with the wipes. "It's better now that we've slowed way down. I have a giant headache, though."

People are meandering in front of the car like cattle and chickens in third world countries, Francine thought. *This is crazy.* She was tempted to beep her horn but no one else in front of her was doing it, and that was a good twenty cars. They just maneuvered around the people as they could.

"The fact we had rain last night and the drop-offs on the side of the road are still wet doesn't help." Alice had her face plastered against the window. She stared wide-eyed as Francine's front bumper passed just inches from a stubborn woman who refused to move to the right to let the car get by her.

Joy was still texting on her phone. "The Channel Six van is straight ahead. They're actually at the covered bridge. They say to just keep going and eventually you'll get through."

"Do they have any advice on parking?" Francine asked.

"Just a minute." Joy used two thumbs to tap out a message. A few seconds later she said, "They said there's a parking lot on the other side of the bridge that still has spaces in it. Five dollars."

"That's what I expected to pay."

The crowd wouldn't part like the Red Sea, and consequently it took fifteen minutes for them to make the torturous trip from the edge of Bridgeton to the actual site of the bridge. Jonathan was still behind them. When they arrived at the parking lot, Francine found a close spot but Jonathan had to drive farther down the lot. Alice jumped out and helped Charlotte from the car. "If you're going to vomit, do it out here."

Charlotte bent over and made a few gagging noises. Finally she straightened back up. "I'm trying, but it's not coming. I think maybe I'll be okay."

"Come with me," Alice said. "I'm going to find you some Dramamine." She looked at the others. "I'm not making the trip back to Rockville until this woman has medicine." She handed Charlotte's cane to her and shut the door.

Joy pointed to the Channel Six van. "I don't want to look like I'm trying to be a hotshot reporter or anything, but I need to get over to the crew and see what they're doing and if they need me. Since it looks like we're dividing up, where will we meet?"

Francine opened the trunk and pulled the bags of food and clothing that Jonathan had obtained earlier to give to Zed. "Is the news van going anywhere? Maybe we can use it as an anchor point."

"The van is right by the bridge on this end, which is where all the shops are. If you come back and find it gone, just meet where the van is now. The bridge won't go anywhere. At least I hope not."

Alice looped her arm in Charlotte's and they headed out toward the bridge area, where there were at least a few regular stores, not ones that only set up for the Covered Bridge Festival. "Maybe there will be a drug store or some sort of general store that has over-the-counter medication," she said.

"Good luck!" Francine called after them. Joy hadn't wasted any time and was already on her way toward the Channel Six van, leaving Francine to wait for Jonathan and Toby in the sea of cars.

"Where is everyone?" Jonathan asked. The suddenness startled Francine. He'd come up behind her.

"Where'd you come from?" she asked.

"We had to park three miles away," Toby exaggerated. "My Fitbit says I got ten thousand steps just finding you."

Jonathan scanned the area, amused. "What happened to your carload?"

"Charlotte got carsick. Alice took her to find Dramamine. Joy is over there with the Channel Six news crew." She pointed toward the Bridgeton Bridge.

"You know what Alice told my grandma?" Toby said. "Alice said where she and Joy used to be like sisters, she feels her sister has replaced her with a career."

Francine set the bags on the ground. "I think she's still getting used to the notoriety. It feels like she's had the job for a long time, but it's only been four months. I hope Alice will give her a little more time. We don't even know that this will last, given the fickle nature of the news business."

"True. And Grandma certainly appreciates the help she's getting from Alice."

"It looks like the two of them have bonded over the catering business. Maybe Joy and Alice are just excited about having second careers so late in life."

"You and Charlotte should be detectives!" Toby said. "That would be good second careers for you."

Jonathan vigorously shook his head. "I don't think so."

Francine picked up the bags. "Just keeping Charlotte out of trouble is enough of a job." She checked the bottom of the bags and saw a smear of mud. Then she looked at her shoes. They were muddy too. "We need to get up toward the road so my shoes don't attract any more mud."

"I think I'll go find Alice and Charlotte," Toby said. "See how they're doing."

Francine walked toward the road. "I know Zed told me to come alone, but I'm keeping Jonathan by my side. The two of you can do what you like. Just don't stray too far from the news van. That's our meeting point." Francine pointed him in the direction Alice and Charlotte had headed.

That left her and Jonathan. "So where are we going?" he asked.

"Zed didn't give me any instructions. He only said he'd find me. I thought we'd walk the main road from the bridge to the end of town where we drove in, and then back."

"The crowd's thick, so that should give him good cover."

Jonathan took one of the bags and together they watched where they stepped until they were out of the field that was serving as parking lot and onto the paved road. They were close to the Bridgeton Bridge. They could see Joy standing with a cameraman outside the van, which was parked in front of the bridge. The crowd that flowed around them on their way to walk through the bridge gave them second and third glances. A few people stopped to ask Joy for her autograph, which then caused more people to stop.

"It might be a good idea for us to put as much distance as possible between ourselves and Channel Six," Francine said.

She and Jonathan began to pick up the pace. Francine was torn between looking side to side in the hopes of seeing Zed and watching in front of her to make sure she didn't run into anyone. Or that no one ran into her.

"Do you think he'll be in disguise?" Jonathan asked.

"He'll certainly stand out if he isn't."

Vendors were stacked up along each side of the road like books in a bookcase, broken occasionally by pathways that led the crowds back to where even more crafters could be found. Jonathan seemed disgusted by the whole thing. "This is what I hate most about the Covered Bridge Festival. All this stuff is just … stuff."

Francine gazed at the sea of people coming toward them. "Have you ever seen this many people dressed in fall-themed sweatshirts?"

"Ugly sweatshirts. It's a fad."

"They're certainly ugly." Francine spotted one in a screaming orange color that had a giant jack-o'-lantern with eyes that indicated the pumpkin was drunk. The round face of the sizeable woman who wore it was reddish. It was possible she was soused, as well.

The smells of the festival that Francine had admired back in Rockville were less prominent here, perhaps because of the sheer size of the spectacle Bridgeton had become. What was usually a tiny center to the burg, anchored by a grain mill on Big Raccoon River when the county was new, swelled to a giant marketplace during the two weeks of the festival. The carnival atmosphere stretched as far as Francine could see on both sides of the only road going through Bridgeton. There were so many food smells colliding with each other that she couldn't distinguish any, so there was nothing to enjoy about it.

"What's a bamboo pillow, and why are they so big?" Jonathan asked.

"I don't know," Francine said, continuing on. A few moments later she realized Jonathan's curiosity had gotten the best of him, and he'd stopped back at a booth. Before she could turn around, someone put their arm around her. A man she didn't recognize clamped his hand over her mouth and steered her toward a nearby pathway, pulling her toward a vacant booth draped in black cloth where no one, especially Jonathan, would be able to see her.

NINETEEN

"IT'S ZED," THE MAN said through gritted teeth. "I'm not going to harm you. We just need to get out of sight."

Francine stomped on his foot and gave him a sharp elbow in the ribs. His hand unexpectedly came off her mouth. "No, we're not," she said. "If you want me to trust you, you're going to have to play this my way."

He nonetheless continued to pull her toward the booth. "The police are looking for me."

"They'll never see you here in the crowd. I don't even see any around."

"Trust me, they're here."

"Why should I trust you at all?"

"Because you stand to gain something people have searched for and never found."

"Doc Wheat's treasure?"

"In a manner of speaking."

"How is it yours to give?"

"Have you read your grandmother's diary that I gave you?"

"I barely got through the one that William had with him."

"You didn't read the one I gave you?"

"You don't know what my life was like yesterday. It was nonstop from morning to night. I get tired. I'm old, you know."

"You're one of the youngest old people I know."

He said it as though it should have some significance. She took it as a compliment. They stood beside the booth. He dropped his arm from her shoulder and took possession of the two bags containing food and clothing. It was clear to her he was not going to try to drag her inside. She took a step out of his reach.

This gave her a chance to examine him. The voice was craggy and sounded like Zed's. But he was clean-shaved, his hair was cut, and he smelled of Old Spice. He was still intimidating because of his size, but he no longer looked like a mountain man. He was dressed in khaki cargo pants and was wearing an oversized ugly brown sweatshirt with pumpkins, footballs, and spray of colored leaves.

"Nice sweatshirt," Francine said.

"Thanks. They're pretty easy to find around here."

Francine started to cross her arms over her chest, but stopped, preferring to keep them loose in case she needed to defend herself. "You're wanted for questioning in the death of my cousin William."

"And you expect me to turn myself in?"

"It would be the right thing to do."

He shook his head. "Wanted for questioning is the same thing as being wanted. I've been a nuisance to the people around here for a long time, and the authorities would love to get something on me. It would be Involuntary Manslaughter, but still chargeable."

"You don't feel any remorse?"

He shrugged. "I didn't kill him. He didn't die from being in the coma. He died because he was poisoned while he was in the coma."

The news startled Francine. "Can you prove that?"

"I don't have to. The coroner will."

"But you know who did it?"

"I am familiar with the work of the person who did. But that's not what I came here to talk about. So, you did read the first diary, then, the one William had?"

"I skimmed it last night."

"And?"

"My great-grandmother had a child out of wedlock."

"Which means?"

Francine knew people were streaming by them, but she couldn't see them. She was facing Zed, who was backed up against the black cloth separating the booths. She sensed there were not many behind her, and they moved quickly. She knew Jonathan would be looking for her. "I don't know what it means."

"Your grandmother and William's grandfather were only half brother and sister."

"We're still blood relatives."

"But only through her mother's side."

"What are you getting at?"

He seemed frustrated at her denseness. "*You* are the father's heir, not William. If you'd read the second diary, it would give you some inkling of the significance of what I just told you. Our conversation would have gone very differently, but ..." His voice trailed off.

"Okay, so give me a chance to read it. I'm sure I'll have questions for you by then."

"No doubt you will. But this is the last you'll see of me."

He was running from the law. "Are you going away?"

"In a manner of speaking." He seemed sad.

She threw him a questioning look.

"I've made a lot of mistakes in my life, but the worst was being smug. So certain I knew what I was doing. Now I wish I had that clarity, even knowing now how flawed I am."

He took a step forward.

She took one backward. Then she realized he was not advancing toward her but preparing to leave. "Earlier you talked about the secrets of the Roseville Bridge. It's gone now. What were they?"

"The diary should help you figure them out. In many ways it helps that the bridge is gone. I find it ironic. The person who wanted the secrets it contained has caused its destruction."

"You know who set the fire?"

"Shortly you'll have all the information you need to put together the mystery." He gave her a wry smile. "The only clarity I have left is the sense that it's time for me to go, to finish the task I should have taken care of ten years ago." He looked away from her, up into the nothingness of the air, and she could tell he was blinking back tears. "My life has no purpose without her."

Francine had simply become too confused with his vague references. "Who is this person you're talking about? Is it my grandmother?" She asked it even though her grandmother had been killed in a traffic accident much longer ago than ten years.

That brought his attention back to her. "Someone I treasured as much or more than her. I'm going to give you a hug. Will you let me? I won't hurt you. I could never hurt you."

For whatever reason she believed him. "Okay."

He embraced her and held her tight, as though it would be the last human interaction he would have. She felt his strength, then his gentleness, then his weariness. His body started to rack with what might have been sobs, but it stopped. He cleared his throat and spoke quietly. "Prove you are worthy of her. Find who killed William, and the truth should become evident to you."

From out of nowhere she heard Alice exclaim, "There she is!"

Francine turned to see Alice about a hundred yards away. *Where did Jonathan go?* Alice had three sheriff's men with her. They stood where the bare path intersected the main road, but they didn't remain still for long. The second after Alice finished identifying Francine they were in motion, running toward Zed. He turned and charged into the hanging black cloth, crashing into the vendor on the other side of it.

Zed ducked to the ground and crawled under the cloth, continuing to pull on it. The aluminum frame strained, but it wouldn't give. Francine wondered if he were trying to pull the entire construction down. Then she smelled popcorn burning and something else too. Something less recognizable. She looked closely and realized the cloth was smoldering. It began to throw up smoke. Something behind the cloth caught fire. Flames began to lick the bottom of the cloth. The deputies trying to get fight their way through the cloth backed away. They ran up the path toward the paved road but a voice yelled, "Fire!" Francine was certain it was Zed.

It was then she felt Jonathan's hand. "I'm here," he said. "I was searching the aisles looking for you when I heard Alice."

The crowd erupted into a frenzy. People stampeded away from the booth. She knew Jonathan was trying to hang on to her but her wrist was being twisted and she cried out in pain. He had to let go or risk breaking it.

Francine found herself swept up in a growing mass of bag-toting women and junk food–carrying men heading toward the bridge.

She spotted Joy and the Channel Six news van and tried to steer toward them, but the current of the crowd was too strong. She tried to fight her way out. As they neared the Bridgeton Bridge she caught a break and stumbled out of the crowd toward the river bank. Her momentum carried her forward, farther than she wanted to go. Soon she teetered on the bank, her feet tangled up in each other. At the last moment she was able to regain some balance and she managed her fall into the river so that she landed in a deep pocket of water.

The coldness of the water shocked her system. She gasped and stood up. Willing hands from bystanders helped her up the bank. When she finally reached terra firma, she found herself shivering in the chilly air and surrounded by a bank of cell phones, cameras, and the Channel Six news team recording the incident.

———

In the end, she was reunited with Jonathan, who found her towels so she could dry off. A vendor donated an authentic souvenir Covered Bridge Festival wool blanket for her to wrap up in, which she wore while being interviewed by Joy for a Channel Six news story.

Next, she had to talk to the sheriff's department. She told them about how Zed had grabbed her out of the crowd to talk to her. She did not, however, admit to having been there to meet with him. Feeling like she ought to throw them a bone for rescuing her, she did tell them about Zed's accusation that William had been poisoned.

They left to return to their temporary home in Rockville immediately after that. Francine insisted on going with Jonathan in his truck. Charlotte wanted to go with them, claiming she would have less motion sickness in the front seat of the truck. Joy joined the group in Jonathan's truck, which had a back seat. Alice and Toby took Francine's car, Alice driving.

"What is it about you and wet clothing that attracts such attention?" Charlotte asked. Francine sat between her and Jonathan in the front, still wrapped in the souvenir blanket trying to warming up.

"I'm glad you're doing better now that you've had some Dramamine," Francine said, "but that doesn't mean I'm going to honor that stupid question with a response."

Joy looked up from her cell phone. "The news van had set up a WiFi signal for me, but it's gone now. Honestly, there's no reliable cell service anywhere in this county." She sighed. "And you needn't be so nasty to Charlotte. I didn't ask any tough questions, you know. You're lucky it was me interviewing you so I only touched on the wet sundress incident last summer. If you hadn't taken off so much of your wet clothing while the camera was pointed at you, it wouldn't have come up. Déjà vu."

"The sweater and the jacket were heavy and wet and cold. They had to come off so drying off the rest of the clothes and wrapping up in the hideous blanket would have some effect."

Joy put the cell phone in her purse. "I thought you would be okay with it. I mean, you were so anxious to get those pinup photos I took of you and Jonathan …"

Charlotte started coughing. And coughing. Then she switched to gagging.

Francine looked at Charlotte with narrowed eyes. "I gather this is something you don't want discussed." She turned to Joy. "I don't know what you're talking about."

Joy got defensive. "Really? Charlotte's been haranguing me to get copies made every chance she gets. She claimed you wanted them. It's been tough because the station's kept me so busy, but I did print them out. She snatched them up before we started the séance. I thought she'd given them to you."

"I'm gonna throw up!" Charlotte bellowed. She opened the window and stuck her head out.

"No you're not," Francine said. "We all know you're faking it. Now be quiet so I can hear about this."

Joy pulled a couple of 4x6 photos out of her purse. "Charlotte took the two best ones, but here are a few others. I saw them when I put the cell phone away, which is what made me think to say something." She passed them directly to Francine. "Those are sexy, Francine, and I don't say that just because Jonathan is a fine-looking specimen, even at seventy. Or because I feel I coaxed the best facial expressions from you."

Francine held the four photos side by side. The first three showed her and Jonathan in various stages of disrobing in the carriage, all while passionately kissing. The desperation in their eyes, which could be interpreted as anxiousness to get to making love, was palpable. It almost made her laugh, since the desperation had been all about getting the photo shoot over. But the fourth photo was the one that made her uncomfortable. It had been taken through the window of the carriage. Jonathan was laid back on the seat bare-chested with Francine lying on him, her blouse unbuttoned provocatively low. Though it was unclear just how much of their lower bodies might be unclothed, their hips were snug together. Francine's face was the focal point of the picture, and her expression was a vacant one, like she was sliding into ecstasy and could think of nothing else.

Her face flushed. "This one can't get out in public."

"It's too bad I'm driving," Jonathan said, "because I need to see these. They sound hot."

"Mary Ruth thinks this one should be December's photo," Joy said, leaning up and stabbing at finger at a picture, "because in her opinion if it doesn't define 'sexy,' she doesn't know what does. Period costumes, an unusual setting, a lot implied without revealing too much skin. I agree. Wow. I'm almost sorry the only other people who see it will be those few we give a calendar to."

"That's the reason I was pushing to get it," Charlotte said, too quickly in Francine's opinion. "I needed to get this to my friend who's putting the calendar together. We reserved October and December for Francine's photos. Now the calendar can be finished and printed."

"To what end?" Francine asked.

"So we'll all have copies to give our significant others for Christmas. Plus, I can check this off my Sixty List."

Francine did not buy this. "It's only mid-October. How long would it realistically take to get a few copies printed?"

"She's very busy and needs time to make it look right before printing."

Joy nudged Charlotte from behind. "That doesn't change the fact it's only mid-October."

"Just what are you accusing me of? Because let's remember that we are in strange circumstances right now, what with two cases of arson under investigation and William's death. Plus we have Mary Ruth's challenges trying to manage a food booth at the Covered Bridge Festival when she can't stop selling out of food. We have too much going on. What any of us is experiencing here is hardly normal behavior. Who is to say how any of us should respond under such circumstances?"

Francine caught Joy's eyes in the rearview mirror and they exchanged glances. Finally Francine said, "We're not accusing you of anything. And you have a point. But the calendar has nothing to do with any of those things."

"Of course it does. It's the starting point. If we hadn't been at the Roseville Bridge that first morning, we wouldn't be wrestling with any of this but Mary Ruth's food booth, and it may not have reached the popularity it has without the additional television exposure."

It all made no sense to Francine. She promised herself she would keep one eye on Charlotte to make sure she did nothing with the calendar.

But once they pulled in the driveway back at the mansion in Rockville, that promise became complicated. Sitting in the driveway was the Buick she and Charlotte had searched for twice. The one belonging to William and his wife, Dolly.

TWENTY

ALICE MANEUVERED FRANCINE'S CAR around the Buick and parked in the garage in the back. Jonathan followed in the truck but didn't park in the garage since there wasn't enough room. When they got out, Dolly was walking toward them, her pumps clicking on the concrete. She was dressed in a charcoal gray suit with pencil skirt, the type one might wear to a funeral. She carried a handkerchief and seemed distressed.

Francine and Jonathan hurried to meet her. "Dolly, I'm so sorry," Francine said. "I'd hug you but I'm a soggy mess from falling in the creek at Bridgeton." For that, Francine was actually grateful. She shook hands with Dolly. Jonathan followed her lead and did likewise. "Are you doing all right?" Francine asked. "Let's go inside."

Dolly allowed herself to be whisked into the house and settled in the kitchen. Francine introduced everyone, and they expressed their condolences. Charlotte offered Dolly tea while suggesting Francine change her clothes before she caught her death of a cold. Francine went upstairs to do that, taking Charlotte's jacket with her. The other women excused themselves to hang up their jackets as well.

Francine changed into comfortable jeans and a non-ugly sweatshirt, grateful to be dry again. She hid the photos she'd obtained from Joy to prevent Charlotte from finding an immediate use for them, even though she knew it would easy for additional copies to be printed. Then she hurried back down to the kitchen.

Charlotte was questioning Dolly over tea while Jonathan sat quietly. The others took orders from Mary Ruth getting food ready for tomorrow. Two of the apple-cinnamon scones Alice had made the previous day were in front of Charlotte and Dolly, which surprised Francine since she thought they had all been sold earlier in the day. But the appearance of Charlotte's large purse lying open made her think Charlotte had obtained them one way or another before they had reached the public.

At least she's sharing.

Francine sat next to Dolly and across from Charlotte. She noticed the teacup was empty. "Can I get you any more tea?"

"No, thank you. Your friend Charlotte has already offered."

"Dolly was telling me that William's funeral will be here in Rockville on Wednesday," Charlotte said.

Dolly filled her in on the details. It would be at Brooks & Nay Funeral Home. The visitation would be on Tuesday in the early afternoon.

"I'll be there," Francine said immediately. "Is there anything you need in the way of help? Anything I can do?"

"Not that I can think of. My sister is here now, and she's been a big help to me. I don't know what I'd do without her."

"Yes, your sister. Did she help you find William's car? Charlotte and I went looking for it but weren't able to find it, were we, Charlotte?"

Charlotte shook her head in exaggerated fashion. "No, not at all. Now that I think of it, Francine, we still have William's key. Let me go get that for you." Charlotte wielded her cane energetically and hightailed out of the room.

Francine had no idea what Charlotte might be up to, but she felt the need to keep a conversation going with Dolly while Charlotte went to get the key. "It feels right that William's funeral should be here in Rockville."

"William never strayed far from his roots in Parke County," Dolly said, giving a rueful smile. "I used to joke that his blood was locally made maple syrup."

Francine smiled at her remark. "You could never take Parke County out of William. He always called it home."

"And I wouldn't take him away from it now. One of the reasons I managed the nursing homes in Terre Haute and Clinton while he took care of the ones here was because of his affection for the area. He knew everyone."

Francine tried to think kindly of her cousin, especially considering he had just passed away. But all she could think to say was, "And I'm sure everyone knew *him*," knowing that it was true because William was so awkward socially. Once people met him, they knew him and tried to avoid him. She moved on to a new topic. "I understand he was a historian?"

"He thought of himself as one. Used to scour the antique markets around here looking for old items—correspondences, diaries, anything from the past. He was always poking around in the archives at the Rockville library. Do you know the old family cemetery?"

The mention of it brought back sad memories to Francine. She remembered her grandmother being buried there. She was pretty sure she could find her way there. Her mother had taken her there a few times to visit the graves. But her own mom and dad were buried in Evansville. "I think so. It's out by the old family farm, isn't it?"

"Your side of the family, yes. William had it registered in his name and was taking care of it. We'll have the graveside ceremony there. It was where he wanted to be buried."

There was a silence that grew awkward the longer it lasted. Dolly took a bite of the untouched scone in front of her. "This is delicious," she said. "I heard that Mary Ruth's Fabulous Sweet Shoppe has been a big hit."

Mary Ruth, who'd been working in the kitchen, came over. "Thank you. I'm glad you like it. My partner Alice made those. She's really catching on."

"I don't know what could be keeping Charlotte," Jonathan said. "Let me go check on her."

Thanks, thought Francine.

Mary Ruth and Dolly made small talk for a couple of minutes. Francine found herself drumming her fingers on the table. She had been thinking about the cemetery when she remembered Zed's surprise assertion that William had been poisoned. At the next opportunity, she asked about it. "Do you know what caused William to pass away like that? When we'd last talked, you'd indicated he was doing well."

Charlotte burst into the room. "Here's the . . ." She noticed Dolly's downcast expression. "Sorry." She laid the key to William's car next to Dolly's hand.

Francine patted the seat where Charlotte had been sitting originally and Charlotte took the hint. "I had just asked Dolly if she knew what caused William's condition to decline so rapidly."

"I don't have any idea. I think the coroner might do an autopsy. I'd just as soon his body be cremated and buried, but I guess rules have to be followed. To have to wait for an autopsy when he was in the hospital and in a coma just seems senseless. I mean, given his age and his condition, it was clearly something related to his going into the coma that killed him."

"Clearly," Charlotte said. "Which implicates Zedediah Matthew."

Dolly looked up. "Yes, it does. Especially given that it was Zededi-ah's shots that caused his fall into the creek and began all this trouble."

"We don't know that, do we?" Francine asked. "The sheriff hasn't established whose rifle those expensed cases came out of. Not that I recall."

"Do we know that?" Charlotte asked. "Has the sheriff established whose rifle those expensed cases came out of?"

Dolly became indignant. "Whose else would they be?"

"That's the thing," Charlotte said, giving Dolly a studious glare. "There were likely two shooters at Roseville Bridge. One who might have been Zed chasing William out of his property. But there was also someone upstream shooting at the bridge. They almost hit us. We were in the bridge."

Dolly sat up in alarm. She seemed surprised by this information, but Francine couldn't place in what way. "This is the first I've heard of it," Dolly said. "Why would there be a second rifleman? And why would he be shooting at you?"

Francine noticed that Dolly said *rifleman*. No one had said the second shooter used a rifle. But then, it might have been a logical assumption.

Charlotte continued trying to read Dolly's eyes. "We don't know the answer, but all of the events seem too coincidental to not be re-lated. This unidentified shooter might have something to do with the arson at the Roseville Bridge or at Zed's house. Or William's death. How do you think they might be related?"

Dolly averted her eyes angrily. "I have no idea how, other than Zed is probably guilty of all three. Why are you asking me?"

"Charlotte is an amateur sleuth," Francine said. "She sees connections everything. She didn't mean anything by asking you. I'm sure."

"I think your view would be helpful," Charlotte said. "You yourself admitted the events could be related. One must have caused the others. Set them off like a chain reaction. The first was William's accident. I presume it's the starting point, at least until we discover some event that occurred ahead of it. What we need to figure out is the motive that ties the three together. Like revenge."

"Are you saying I had something to do with the others?" Dolly flipped back a lock of hair in a manner befitting an actress. It reminded Francine that Dolly was ten years younger than William. Honestly, she looked twenty years younger. Some people just had that gift, and others desired it.

"I'm not accusing you of anything, only using revenge as an example," Charlotte said. She put on her innocent face, which annoyed Francine.

"You still don't have any idea what William was doing on Zed's property that morning?" Francine asked. "Or why he would be carrying a vial of some liquid?" She wanted to mention the mason jar she and Charlotte had found in the trunk of William's car, but that would give away the fact they'd searched it.

Dolly glanced toward the ceiling as if pondering the question. After a few seconds, she leveled her gaze at Francine. "I've thought and thought about it since you brought it up the first time, but I don't have a rational explanation."

"I'd settle for an irrational one at this point," Charlotte said.

Dolly stood up. "Thank you for the tea and scones but I need to be on my way."

Francine rose as well. "Thanks for dropping by to let me know about the funeral. I appreciate that you drove all the way from Montezuma to tell me. You have my cell phone number, don't you?"

"I do. You gave it to me at the hospital along with your address here in Rockville. I needed to come this way anyway to see about a funeral tomorrow. Something had happened at our memory care unit here in Rockville. William had been seeing to it, but now it's fallen to me. It gave me a reason to stop by instead of call."

"You don't have someone who can handle the nursing homes while you're going through this difficult time?" Charlotte asked the question in a sympathetic way, but there was also a touch of disbelief in it. Francine hoped that Dolly didn't pick up or react to it.

"It was out of the ordinary," Dolly said defensively. "One of our longtime residents. William and I were close to her. Only one family member ever came to visit her, and the manager couldn't get hold of him. Sadly, we have to contend with this sort of thing all too often."

"Was that the woman you were telling me about at the hospital?" Francine asked. "The one who told stories like *Little House on the Prairie*?"

"Yes, it was. Room seventeen. She'd been on a downward trajectory for some time now and had difficulty eating and drinking. Sad. Now I really must be going."

Francine had a flashback to the slip of paper she'd found in William's car with the number seventeen on it. She had a feeling it wasn't a coincidence. The three of them walked to the front door. "I'll be there early on Tuesday for William's visitation. I'd be happy to help you and your sister with anything you need. A tragedy like this makes us appreciate friends and family, doesn't it?"

Dolly said, "You don't know how much," but Francine didn't think it sounded sincere.

Dolly hustled down the driveway toward her car.

Charlotte stood at the window in the front room, watching her.

"What was that all about?" Francine demanded.

"All of what?"

"All of that questioning about the nursing home and William's death and everything being related."

Charlotte moved away from the window. "Don't you think it's odd that Dolly is busy with someone else's death while she has William's to cope with? She doesn't seem particularly moved by any of your efforts to help. And you know better than I how Alzheimer's patients can die a slow death. I see it as so similar to William's comatose state. I wonder if the two deaths are connected."

"You are such a suspicious person."

"Because I see so many possibilities here? A shooting, a death, two cases of arson, now another death. And who is the person still standing? Dolly."

"You forget Zed. If he didn't have so much faith in me, I'd say he's a better suspect."

Charlotte gave her a devious smile. "And also the one more obvious. In mystery stories, it is rarely the most obvious suspect."

"But this is real life."

"You know what we could use right now? William's tablet. The one he was writing his history on. Because it might shed some light on what it was he found so fascinating about Zed's property."

It dawned on Francine why it had taken so long for Charlotte to bring back William's key. "You snatched it out of William's car, didn't you?"

"I did, and handed it to Jonathan for safekeeping so I could get back in here as soon as I could."

"Let's go find him."

TWENTY-ONE

THEY FOUND JONATHAN, BUT he was in the kitchen, having been recruited by Mary Ruth to help with food prep for tomorrow. The pink apron looked out of place over his black shirt, but no worse than Toby, who had his over an ugly camouflage sweater with fall decals he must have picked up at Bridgeton. The men looked out of place next to the four baker-helper women from the Festival Committee.

Alice worked on creating scones for the next day, which were cranberry-orange. Joy wasn't around but Francine presumed she was doing something for Channel Six. The whole place smelled of cookies and scones baking.

Talk of murder and computers snatched illegally from cars to see what they might reveal took a back seat to Mary Ruth's need to get food prepared for tomorrow's rush.

Francine slipped on the pink apron Mary Ruth handed her. "That's fine. We're glad to help."

There was a knock on the kitchen door that opened to the outside, and Marcy walked in without waiting for someone to let her in.

Mary Ruth acted like she expected Marcy to be there. "I switched out the flavors of cookies and scones like you suggested. Some of them, anyway."

Marcy slipped off her jacket. "Exactly," she said. "Ramp up the anticipation by swapping out a few items every day. Not the corn fritter donuts, which are becoming quite the attraction, or the cinnamon rolls, but the easier things."

Charlotte narrowed her eyes as Marcy donned a pink apron. "I'm confused. Whose publicist are you now? Ours? Joy's? Merlina's?"

"I'm Mary Ruth's publicist officially now, so you don't have to pay me anymore, Charlotte."

Charlotte's eyes went wide as she put a finger to her lips, hoping Marcy would stop talking.

Francine knew instantly what was going on, like a bubble of understanding had suddenly risen up in her. It made her smile. "Item fifteen: Be more generous and philanthropic," she said.

Charlotte cleared her throat loudly. Marcy realized what had just happened. She tried to cover. "I'm also handling Joy's bookings and Merlina's bookings," she announced, "but Merlina's are mostly local and easier to accommodate. Mary Ruth's are national!"

The news took Francine by surprise. "National?"

Marcy clapped her hands. "I'm pleased to announce that Food Network is back and interested in Mary Ruth Burrows! As it happens, a camera crew for Robert Irvine's new show will be making a detour stop through Rockville for a look at Mary Ruth's Fabulous Sweet Shoppe."

"Ooohhh!" Charlotte said. "Isn't Robert Irvine the one with really big biceps?"

"And the very cool British accent," Alice added.

Francine went to the refrigerator and extracted four sticks of butter according to the peanut butter cookie recipe. "But I thought he was the guy who's always trying to fix what's wrong with things, like restaurants and recipes and stuff. What's this new show about?"

Marcy waved her hand in a dismissive way. "I'm not sure, but I think it's about how to sell more product."

"That's the only thing Food Network seems to be focused on," Alice said. "Selling more of *their* product. That and creating competition shows. What ever happened to cooking and baking?"

"That's on the Cooking Channel," Mary Ruth observed. "It's not as popular. The economy's recovering, and people are cooking less and eating out more. Food Network is all about celebrating chefs."

"Or being a celebrity chef." Francine threw the butter into a stand mixer.

"Precisely what we're aiming for with Mary Ruth," said Marcy. "We want Robert to see the lines of people, taste the baked goods, and have him give an excellent report."

The group was ordered back to task by Mary Ruth. Within minutes the kitchen was humming with activity.

They worked until suppertime. No one felt like making dinner, so Jonathan ordered Mexican from a restaurant on the square in Rockville. It was within walking distance. Francine volunteered to go with him to get it. She knew it was far enough away that Charlotte wouldn't volunteer to go with them. Besides, Charlotte was dying to get her hands on William's laptop. Francine, on the other hand, had the second diary tucked away in her purse and hoped they would have to wait for the food and she could skim the entries while she waited.

Francine and Jonathan walked at a good clip toward the square in Rockville.

"Tell me," Francine began, "did you know Charlotte had taken William's tablet out of the back of the car when she gave it to you?"

"She came in from the outside, so I'd wondered where she'd gotten it. I had no idea it was William's."

"She's probably scouring the tablet right now looking for clues."

"Not unless she finds someone who knows William's password. It was password protected. Charlotte tried to get me to turn it on, but I couldn't get past the first screen."

"Toby might be able to do it. He's done it for her before."

As they walked along, Francine couldn't help but marvel at the large historic homes in the area and how many appeared to still be homes. In the greater Indianapolis area, such homes were largely turned into businesses because the upkeep was so great. Langley Funeral Home on the other side of the street seemed to be the exception.

She gave it more than a passing glance and saw William's car parked in the lot. There weren't many other cars. Langley wasn't the name of the funeral home Dolly had given Francine for William's arrangements. *Must be that nursing home resident she mentioned.*

El Monterey Delgado was doing a brisk business, mostly from Hispanic-looking faces, so Francine hoped it would be authentic food. She could detect cumin and adobo in the air, and the aroma of tortilla chips being fried was strong. Jonathan checked on their order and found it would be a few minutes. The place was mostly take out; there were a few tables, but there was no waitstaff that she could see. The tables were already occupied. They found a spot on an empty bench inside the restaurant that seemed to be specifically for waiting. She opened her purse and took out the diary.

The first entry in this diary was much later than the other diary, October of 1944. Francine did some calculation and determined her grandmother, Ellie, would have been thirty-nine years old at the time. Francine's own mother was twenty, and expecting. Francine would be born in April of 1945.

She tried to speed-read, knowing that it wouldn't take long for the order to be ready, but the handwriting didn't lend itself to that. She found herself absorbed in the context of the entry.

I do not think it is inappropriate for my mother to consider marrying a man who is not a doctor. She is, after all, a widow, and has been for five years. She loved my father in her own way, and she has remained faithful to his memory, at least in public. Having proven she can live on her own, must she, forever? She has had suitors of my father's station, but none of them have interested her. I would defend her ability to fall in love with a simple tradesman like a gardener, let alone someone who has an international following like Doc Wheat. It does not matter that he has no degree; he has proven that he can produce marvelous remedies. Some people say he's a huckster, but Mother does not believe that, nor do I.

Francine stopped. Her great-grandmother married Doc Wheat? Surely she would have known that. Wouldn't her mother have told her that? Or her grandmother?

She began to skim the entries looking for key words like *marry* or *Doc Wheat*. Two entries later, she found a reference.

Mother and I cannot believe the stir that has been created by her relationship with Doc Wheat. One would think she has chosen to marry someone whose brain is not right in his head. Even my husband believes it is not for Mother's well-being. "Doc Wheat is a fortune hunter," he has opined. "He is only after the money she has inherited from her father and from her husband." I grant that this is a substantial sum, but Doc Wheat is himself successful. Years before he took up with Mother, back when Father was still alive, he had purchased additional land adjacent to his farm and paid for it in cash. At least that was the talk. A brook runs through it, and also a good deal of forest land. I have toured it with Mother. There are places where it is hilly, and it has a lovely meadow where the brook emerges from the ground. Doc Wheat has a garden there where he grows his medicinal herbs.

And then there is the matter of love. It would not appear to me that he is after her money. I have known of their secret relationship for the past three years. They took great pains to hide it then. You, my diary friend, know that I have written of how I have witnessed their love many times. I accompanied them on summer picnics when my husband had business out of town. Doc would hitch up his horse and carriage and we would take paths deep into his property to where the sycamores and the maples provided shade from the noonday sun in a perfect grassy spot. I watched him spread out the blanket for us, and he and I would sit in anticipation as Mother retrieved the food she had prepared. She made simple meals but beautiful ones. Then they would hold hands as we sat and talked and ate. The passion they had for each other, the way he would caress her hands, the way Mother's breath shortened at times when she would get back in the carriage and he was close behind her, helping her, their bodies briefly in contact. It was as if they were my age instead of theirs. Would that my husband made me feel this way!

"Jonathan!" a heavily accented voice called. Francine jerked her head up from the page and saw a Hispanic man put two large paper bags with handles on the counter. She found herself momentarily confused, jerked out of an idyllic scene to return to the sights and smells of El Monterey Delgado.

Jonathan, fortunately, was more together. He leaped up from the bench and went to the counter.

The diary had a fabric placeholder in it. Francine marked the spot she was at and carefully returned the diary to her purse. She met Jonathan at the counter. She checked over the order to make sure it was correct. When they left the restaurant, she noticed it had only been ten minutes.

"Did you learn anything?" Jonathan asked.

"They were certainly in love, at least in my grandmother's eyes."

"Who is they?"

"My great-grandmother and Doc Wheat."

"Did we know they were in love?"

"No. This is the first I've heard of it."

They took the same path back to the mansion. It took them past Langley Funeral Home once more, but Dolly's car was not there. A few cars remained in the lot, and Francine wondered about the older resident for whom Dolly and William had such affection that they were willing to arrange for a funeral. Would she recognize the name if she saw it?

"Would you mind taking dinner back to the group without me?" she asked. "I want to check out the visitation at the funeral home. William's car was there on our way to the restaurant, and now it's gone. I'm curious what Dolly was doing in there. It's not where William's body is going to be."

Jonathan made disapproving noises. "I could come with you."

"And then everyone's order would get cold. I'll be along in a few minutes. Really."

"You spend too much time around Charlotte. Her penchant for being a snoop is rubbing off on you." But Jonathan let her go and headed toward the mansion toting both bags of meals as she'd asked.

Believing the cars in the lot meant the doors would be open, Francine walked up the concrete sidewalk. She tentatively tried the door handle, not wanting to make much noise, but the door swung open easily. A small directional sign with removable letters stood in front of her. BELINDA MILES FLOWERS, it read, with an arrow pointing to the left. She noted that the calling was from four to five o'clock tomorrow afternoon. Francine was struck by the Miles name, which was her own maiden name. She tried to think of any relatives named Belinda, but none came to mind. It was a common enough name, especially in the area. She couldn't help but take a peek into the room, just to find out if there were any clues as to who Belinda might be. She wasn't at all certain it would be the woman Dolly had spoken about, but the fact that Dolly had been there ten minutes earlier and that there were no other funerals listed fueled her desire to investigate.

Ahead of her were double doors that led into a smallish viewing room. The doors opened into the back of the room. As she approached it, she saw chairs set up, ready for visitors to sit while they shared their grief over the death of Ms. Flowers. Francine could hear someone grieving, and she hesitated before sticking her head in. She didn't want to disturb whoever was in the room. But she was certain the person would be facing away from her, focused on the front of the room, and she still wanted to know if it might be an acquaintance or relative of hers from long ago.

She peered into the room. Zedediah Matthew sat in a plush turquoise funeral chair in the front row, his head in his hands, weeping.

TWENTY-TWO

FRANCINE DIDN'T QUITE KNOW how to handle the situation. What was Zed doing there? Who was Belinda Flowers that Zed would be weeping over her death? Was she even sure that Belinda Flowers was the woman Dolly had mentioned?

Francine ducked her head back in to the hallway. Her heart was beating rapidly. She wasn't sure she wanted Zed to know she was there. Moving slowly so her jacket wouldn't rustle against her clothes, she slipped away from the room and back to the entryway to look at the signage. Belinda Flowers was the only name listed as having a funeral tomorrow, exactly as she'd thought. She'd seen Dolly here earlier. So Belinda was the woman from the memory unit, right? And Zed was in there weeping. So Zed must have a connection to her.

It *was* Zed, right? She'd only seen him from behind. Now that he was clean-shaven with a neatened hair style and blended into society better, her first impression that it was him might be wrong. She snuck back up on the room and peeked inside again.

The room was empty.

Francine could feel the goosebumps begin to form on her arms. This would be the time in the movies when the heroine would turn around and find the person she was trying to spy on, spying on her. She turned around, fully expecting to see Zed. Her mind was wrestling with what she would say to him.

But he wasn't there.

She peeked one last time to be sure. But the room was empty. He was gone. Had he known someone had been spying on him and exited from the front?

She didn't question whether or not her eyes had played tricks on her. She strode back to the front door, pretending that her being in a funeral home with no scheduled showing was perfectly natural. She prepared herself to nod at anyone as though it were an expected encounter. But no one saw her.

She hurried back to the mansion, breathing easier once she was inside.

Or would have, if Charlotte hadn't been at the mansion's front door to accost her.

"It's about time you got back," Charlotte said. "You know I can't eat spicy food too late in the evening or I'll have acid reflux that feels like the inside of a two-liter soda pop bottle when someone drops Mentos down it."

"You could have started without me."

"We did. We're snacking on chips and salsa. But we're holding up on the main meals. Mary Ruth has them in the warming oven. Jonathan said you'd be along in a minute. Where were you?"

"He didn't say?"

"Nope."

Francine didn't feel like being challenged by Charlotte just then. She took her jacket off and laid it aside on one of the chairs. "We can talk about it over dinner."

She marched into the kitchen and Charlotte followed. She spotted Jonathan in the dining room setting the table for dinner. *Probably trying to get away from Charlotte.* Toby was also in the dining room. He had moved a television in from the media room and was hooking it up.

Francine sidled up to Mary Ruth. "Are we set for tomorrow?"

"Amazingly enough, yes. Even with most of you spending part of the afternoon in Bridgeton, we'll be done after the last of these cookies come out of the oven. The rest of the food is either in the freezer or the refrigerator." She spread her arms to indicate four sheet trays of cookies that were ready to be placed in the two wall ovens. "For now, let's eat."

Francine helped her pull the Mexican food out of the warming oven. She, Mary Ruth, Joy, Alice, Charlotte, and Marcy joined the men in the dining room.

Toby turned on the television. "Good thing they have cable here. Otherwise we wouldn't be able to get the Indianapolis stations."

Joy had a chair closest to the television. She nibbled on a taco and stared at the screen. "I know you're not thrilled that I had to interview you, Francine, but I think it came out all right."

"I guess we'll see," she said.

Charlotte carried in the chips and salsa, which she was still snacking on. Toby sat next to her and began to wolf them down. Mary Ruth finally glared at him. "Eat the bean and rice burritos," she said. "They haven't been fried."

"But I'm starved," he protested. "And anyway, I promise, I'll eat those too."

"You know what I mean."

Joy's reporting from the Covered Bridge Festival came later in the news program since there really weren't any new developments on the fire that consumed the Roseville Bridge. It was mainly about the minor fire at Bridgeton, which was believed to have been started by Zedediah Matthew, who was escaping from police wanting to question him in connection with the death of William Falkes. Joy reported that the fire had been quickly contained, but the crowd had stampeded. The report ended with Francine's emergence from Big Raccoon Creek after escaping the crowd's rush toward the bridge. Joy's interview with Francine consisted of questions about the scariness of being caught in a mob scene, but the anchors ended the segment by reminding viewers that Francine was one of the Skinny-Dipping Grandmas, and they dredged up a photo of Francine in the wet sundress from the summer fiasco.

"I'll never live that down," Francine said, her head in her hands.

"You don't want to live that down," Marcy said. "You want to embrace it."

Francine ignored Marcy.

"Eat some more of your fajitas," Charlotte suggested. "Fajitas make everything better."

"I can't eat another bite. And I thought *chocolate* made everything better."

"It does as well." Mary Ruth rose. "And I created a smaller version of the peanut butter chocolate chip trio cookies for us to have for dessert."

They had no sooner finished when the doorbell rang. "I'll get it," Joy said. She almost leapt from the table to go answer it. She disappeared out of the dining room.

"The amount of energy she exudes drives me nuts," Charlotte muttered.

Jonathan began to gather up the empty Styrofoam containers.

Alice helped him. "We all know she's the Energizer Bunny of the group. But I think she might be expecting someone."

"Ahhh!" they exclaimed all at once.

Jonathan took into the kitchen the containers he and Alice had collected.

Joy returned with a dejected look on her face. "It's for you, Francine. A courier of some sort."

Francine wrinkled her nose. "A courier? Do they even have those in Rockville?"

Charlotte got up from the table in a much slower manner than Joy. "It's probably not his regular job. I'll come with you."

Francine couldn't think of a reason to stop her, so she let her come along.

A short man in a brown suit stood inside the front door. Francine figured Joy must have invited him in. He looked to be in his twenties. He held a manila envelope in his hand.

He looked from Francine to Charlotte inquisitively. Francine didn't let him remain confused for long. "I'm Francine McNamara."

"Could I see some kind of identification, please?"

Now Francine was confused. She frowned down at him. She could see the top of his head. "I could go get my purse, young man, but is it really that important? Don't I just have to sign something? What is this about?"

"I'm with Frost & Associates Law Firm. I have a notice here to deliver to Francine McNamara."

Charlotte answered him. "She's Francine. You can be sure of that. She's one of the Skinny-Dipping Grandmas. Don't you recognize her?"

The young man blushed. "Well, I do. Sort of. But you'll need to show me some ID anyway. It's required. I mean, if you want the document."

"Why wouldn't I want it?"

He seemed completely flustered now. "I didn't mean to say it like that. There's nothing wrong. It's just that you're invited to the firm tomorrow."

Francine crossed her arms over her chest. "Why would I be invited to a law firm tomorrow?"

"For the reading of a will."

"Whose will?"

He opened his mouth and then shut it.

"You might as well spill it," Charlotte said.

"Please. I need some kind of ID. So I can say in all honesty that I saw it."

Francine exhaled noisily. "All right." She turned and went upstairs and returned with her purse. She pawed through it.

"What's going on?" Jonathan asked, joining Francine and Charlotte in the living room.

Charlotte was visibly excited and answered before Francine could. "It's a summons."

Francine removed her driver's license and thrust it at the young man. He recorded the license number on a form he had and handed it back to her. "Thank you," he said. He made a little bow, handed her the manila envelope, and left.

"I kept an eye on him while you were gone," Charlotte said, "so he couldn't pull any funny business."

"I don't think funny business is what he had on his mind." Francine took a seat on a leather couch by the door, sinking into the cushions. "I think he was just an intern."

Charlotte settled into the spot next to her. Jonathan crossed his arms over his chest and stood in front of them. "So, what is it?"

"I'm getting there." She examined the envelope. It had her name on it, and then "c/o" the address of the mansion. "I wonder how they knew where I was staying."

"Will you just open it?" Charlotte said.

Francine did. She pulled out a notification and read it. "It says it's for the last will and testament of Zedediah Matthew." She folded the paper and laid it on her lap. "But that can't be right, because I just saw him."

"You mean at Bridgeton?"

Francine looked at Jonathan, not sure if she should reveal to Charlotte where she'd just been. But then, Jonathan didn't know either. She hadn't had a moment alone to tell him. He shrugged.

"No," she answered. "I mean not less than a half hour ago. On my way back from the Mexican restaurant, I stopped at Langley Funeral Home because I thought I had seen Dolly's car in the parking lot on my way there and I wondered what she was doing there."

"But instead you found Zedediah?"

"In a manner of speaking. There was only one visitation on the schedule for tomorrow, and I went to that room because I was curious about the woman it was for. I wondered if it was the older woman Dolly had mentioned, the one she and William had been close to. I heard someone weeping, and it was Zed."

"*Weeping* is a strong word. Did you talk to him?"

"No, I was so surprised that I backed out of the room to check the name of the woman a second time. When I went back less than a minute later, he was gone."

"You're sure it was him?" Jonathan asked.

"Pretty sure. Although he's cleaned up now, not so much the mountain man since he's trying to get away from the law."

Francine told them the name of the woman whose funeral would be tomorrow had her maiden name, Miles.

"We have to assume whoever arranged the service—maybe Dolly—wanted to emphasize her maiden name," Charlotte said with her usual authority.

"Maybe. But that still doesn't answer the question of who she is."

Charlotte waggled her eyebrows. "Because, Watson, that has been left to us to figure out."

Alice entered the room. "You three have been gone a long time. Who was that at the door?"

"Francine has been summoned to a law firm tomorrow morning to hear the last will and testament of Zedediah Matthew," Charlotte blurted out.

Alice looked confused. "But you and I just saw him today. Jonathan did too."

Francine nodded. "But he told me it's his plan to disappear."

Charlotte tried to get off the couch and found herself too deep in the soft cushion to gain traction, especially with her short legs. She held out a hand to Jonathan. "Help me out of this couch, please. I have work to do."

Mary Ruth and Joy came in behind Alice. "Did I hear Charlotte say she has work to do?" Mary Ruth said, taking off her pink apron. "Now's a fine time for her to decide that, when we've already cleaned the kitchen for the evening."

Jonathan held Charlotte steady so she could pull herself forward and get her feet on the floor. She leaned forward and came to a standing position. She steadied herself with her cane, which was parked nearby. "The work we have to do is planning for tomorrow.

Somehow, even though we'll be staffing Mary Ruth's dessert booth, supporting Joy's reporting duties, and getting ready for the Food Network to stop by, we've got to figure out how to free Francine up to make the reading of the will, get time for a subgroup to visit the funeral home to see who this mysterious woman is that Dolly and William cared about, and anything else we can figure out needs to be done."

"A visit to the retirement community might be a good idea," Jonathan suggested. "Before you jump to too many conclusions, you should make sure the woman who died in the memory care unit is, in fact, Belinda Flowers."

Charlotte weighed that in her mind. "Good point. Although I'm pretty sure we're right on that point."

Mary Ruth scratched her head. "Back up a minute. What will? What funeral home?"

A lot of catching up was necessary, which under Charlotte's direction involved being back in the kitchen, having coffee and eating more cookies. At the end of Francine and Charlotte's summary, Mary Ruth was the one who had the ideas.

"Marcy's gone for the day, but she'll be back here early tomorrow morning. She had to make a bunch of calls to the local press to alert them to the Food Network being here tomorrow around noon. If I can redirect her energy in the morning, she can help Alice, Toby, and me finish off the prep work and get the booth up and running. That will free up you and Charlotte to do your sleuthing. Joy will be off reporting. Jonathan, I assume you'll be around tomorrow too?"

"I'm here for the duration of the Covered Bridge Festival. At this point, I'm afraid to leave. I don't know what trouble you'll get yourselves into."

"No offense to Toby," Charlotte said, "but I'm glad to have another man here. Jonathan's been around the block a few more times. Plus, he has a permit to carry."

"Speaking of which," Jonathan said, "where is Toby?"

Charlotte snapped her fingers. "I forgot. He's down in the basement examining William's tablet. It was password protected. He couldn't crack the code earlier so he sent a message to one of his hacker friends looking for help. Maybe they've figured it out by now."

She started to head for the back staircase, the one that led downstairs. "Francine, please come help me with the stairs."

"Maybe Alice can help you. There are a couple of things Jonathan and I need to discuss."

Alice took the hint. "I'll be happy to help."

Charlotte was clearly highly suspicious, but she had no alternative with Alice firmly moving her toward the stairs. Francine was thankful that as friends, their group knew exactly what kind of help to provide each other, at the exact times they needed it.

Because she had an idea she wanted to check out with Jonathan. It was kind of leap of faith, but there was something she wanted him to check out the next day. She'd go with him, too, if she could get away, but it might involve a search that would take time.

TWENTY-THREE

When Francine joined Charlotte in the basement, Toby had both his laptop and William's tablet open. He was wearing a headset, the microphone in front of his lips. Francine could hear what he was saying, but it made no sense to her. They might as well have been speaking a foreign language.

"He's communicating with his friend," Charlotte whispered. "The one who's the expert hacker."

Toby looked from one screen to the other. "I'll try it one more time with the Frankenstein variation on the sequence," he said. He typed something into William's tablet. The screen lit up. Francine could see icons on it. "Got it!" Toby announced. "Thanks for your help, Ace."

Toby signed off and spun around in the chair so that he faced the two women. He had a wide smile on his face. "What do you want the new password to be?"

"I don't want there to be a new password," Francine said. "I want it to be the old password. This needs to get back into William's car.

At least, eventually. If it has a different password, she won't be able to get in."

"Francine, think," Charlotte said. "If Dolly has already noticed that it's gone, then she'll know something's up when she finds it again. If she hasn't, then it likely means she didn't know it was in there, and she won't ever notice that it's gone. It doesn't make any difference. It's our tablet now."

Francine couldn't help but feel how similar this was to the way Charlotte had obtained Friederich Guttmann's iPod, and how it held the smoking gun that eventually flushed out his killer. She hoped this didn't turn out like that. The tablet was here, and they should probably read the book William was writing, if they could find it. But she didn't have to make the decision Charlotte wanted her to make about not returning it, not if the password didn't change. "It stays the same, at least for now."

"I'll write it down for you," Toby said. "It's kind of interesting." He picked up a pen and scrap piece of paper and jotted down *itstheWATER*. He handed it to Francine. "The password is case sensitive."

Francine stared at it. "Curious password."

"Given that the symbol for water was carved in the message under the bridge, yes," Charlotte said.

"But we don't know what the significance is, do we?"

Charlotte shrugged.

"Can you find out if William was writing a book on the history of Parke County?" Francine asked Toby. "We were told he spent hours and hours at the library researching it."

"I'll need some kind of keyword to search the database."

"Try *water* and see what comes up."

Toby found the manuscript pretty easily. *Water* was a common word in it. He also found several emails. Unfortunately, William used a different password for his email program so they couldn't get into it.

"I could try to break that code, too, but I'd need the tablet for a while," Toby said.

Before Charlotte could say anything, Francine said, "No. Bad enough we're reading his book. We're not going to do the email thing."

Toby showed them how to get into the manuscript. "Anything else I can do for you?"

"Actually, yes," Charlotte said. "There's something that's been bothering me, and I think you might be able to help."

"What now?" Francine asked.

"I thought about this when Joy pulled out those photos earlier today of you and Jonathan. Zed *had* to know it was the start date of the Covered Bridge Festival. With all the problems with the law he's had when he's tried to run people off his property, would he have fired on us when we were on public property? He couldn't be sure we were a part of whatever William was doing there."

"But I thought that you thought he had something to protect."

"I did," said Charlotte. "That's where we were wrong. I don't think Zed would fire on us unless he was certain we were a danger to him. And anyone who was with him would do the same. Therefore, the second person, the one who fired on us, was not with Zed."

"You say that as though you have a suspect in mind."

"I don't, but I have a motive in mind. The person who fired on us was there to rendezvous with William. William and whoever his friend was had expected that if Zed had found him on the property, there would be consequences. So the friend was there to provide cover fire, if necessary, so William could escape."

"And why did the friend fire on us?"

"Also cover. What if William was *supposed* to descend into the creek? Only he'd gotten injured, but the friend didn't know that because he couldn't see it. All he could see was that someone else was there, someone possibly with Zed, and William needed additional cover to get back to the rendezvous spot."

"I think you're overthinking this, but even if you aren't, what's the point?" Francine asked.

"What's bothering me is why we never had someone blow up the photos to see if we could see the shooter. Those photos were taken with a camera with a lot of pixels. Toby here could probably blow those up and find out who the shooter is. Where are the photos Joy took of you and Jonathan? They faced the direction the shots were coming in from."

"That would have been at quite a distance, Charlotte. I don't know if it could be magnified enough and still have the definition to see who it is."

Toby's head stopped bobbing between the two women. "There's only one way to find out. Get me the photos and let's scan them in."

———

Francine clenched and unclenched her fists as she watched Toby methodically search the background of the photograph of her and Jonathan in a compromising position. Part of her hoped he wouldn't find anything. She couldn't imagine how bad it would be if these photos got out into the public realm, which she knew would happen if he spotted anything unusual and they had to turn them over to the police. On the other hand, she could use a break in trying to solve the mystery of who shot at William.

Toby went to the limit of the photograph's resolution. It allowed them to clearly view much of the brush along the creek, but not to the point of distortion. He used his finger on the touchscreen to drag different segments of the photograph into view. Every time a new segment showed up, they all studied it.

Toby abruptly stopped. "There. Right there. Someone's in the brush." He pointed to the spot.

"How in the world did you spot that?" Charlotte asked.

"He has young eyes." Francine brought her face close to the computer screen, tilting her head up trying to put the face in the sweet spot of her glasses. Once she did, she was fairly certain who it was. The thought made her straighten up. "Can you blow this up any more?"

"If I do, it will only distort the image. You won't see it any more clearly."

Francine felt Charlotte poking her. "Out with it. I can tell by your reaction you know who that is."

"It's Dolly. William's wife."

"Yes!" Charlotte crowed. "My hypothesis fits. She was there to cover him, and we were the wild card. They were going to meet at the Roseville Bridge, but we showed up. She couldn't explain what she was doing there, so she hid. And then William is discovered and is chased out of the cornfield. She's horrified, but she can't do anything about it without giving away the fact that she's there."

"Because if she does," Francine continued, "that raises the issue of what they were trying to do."

Charlotte, whose voice had gotten loud with excitement, now dropped a notch. "Which is what? Retrieve a diary? Steal a vial full of water? It sounds weak."

Francine scratched her head. "It does. Zed so much as told me the diary belonged to William. And it's difficult to believe they would put so much into water samples."

For a moment, both of them were silent. Then Charlotte pointed back at the screen. "We don't know that it was, in fact, the water. What we do know is that William was there, and now we know Dolly was there."

Toby played with the keyboard. "I've cropped that part of the photograph and saved it as a separate file. I want to go back and look at the video Joy took after the shooting began. I want to see if she has anything else pointing in that direction."

"To see if Dolly is still there?" Charlotte asked.

"Yes," Toby said. "And to see if she's carrying a rifle."

A half hour later, after fast-forwarding through the video and a cursory examination of the photographs, Toby came to a disappointing conclusion. "The part of the creek Dolly was in was too far out. It never came into Joy's video. She focused on William's fall and Jonathan's rescue, and that was all down by the creek."

"I'm not giving up on this line," Charlotte said. "We could still establish something from the ballistics. Francine, what do you know about Dolly? Does she have a rifle? Could she tag a squirrel from a hundred yards or is she lucky to hit the side of a barn from fifty feet?"

Considering that Charlotte had a rifle and was a scarily bad shot, Francine thought it wasn't right for her to demean someone else. "I don't know if Dolly has a rifle or whether she's a good shot. But while I hate to stereotype anyone, Dolly is from Kentucky and the Appalachian area. If I had to guess, I'd guess that she grew up shooting."

Charlotte put a finger in the air. "I knew it! Now we just have to get Roy motivated to investigate her. The police have the bullets that were used to shoot up the bridge. Proving they came from Dolly's rifle—"

"If she even has a rifle," Francine cautioned.

"—will be a snap. They do it all the time on *CSI*."

"There's such a thing as self-incrimination, Charlotte. Dolly will be wary, and the crime here is William's death. If, as you hypothesize, Dolly was protecting him, that doesn't make her guilty of the crime."

Charlotte checked her watch. "I wonder if Joy could get Roy back here so we could show him what Toby uncovered. Once he sees that Dolly was there, I bet he'll want to question her as much as he wants to question Zed."

Francine thought about that. Just how important was this anyway? William running out of the cornfield with a vial of clear liquid and her grandmother's diary still only boiled down to trespassing. The clear liquid was a more vexing problem, but not necessarily indicative of a crime. Or was Zed hiding something? Was he the source of some kind of terrible pollution that William and Dolly were collecting proof of? Unfortunately the vial was now in the hands of the police. There had been a mason jar of something they'd pulled out of William's car, possibly the same thing, but they couldn't be sure since she'd insisted on putting it back. The *itstheWATER* password made her think twice, but in the end, the only thing she could rationalize was trying to get the water analyzed.

"I don't think we have enough to call Detective Stockton tonight. Let's try him in the morning when he's on duty."

Charlotte was clearly disappointed, but then she brightened. "You're right. We *should* wait until morning. In fact, we should wait until after your appointment with the lawyer. We might have more information then, and more information is always good."

Toby held out William's tablet. "What do you want to do with this?"

Charlotte made a grab for it. "I'll take it," she said.

Francine was one step ahead and snatched it away just before Charlotte's hand got there. "I know it was through your efforts we've obtained this, but as William's cousin I claim dibs on it." Charlotte started to turn red, so Francine said, "Why don't you read over my grandmother's diary? I read it last night, but I was very tired. Maybe I missed something in it."

That seemed to pacify her. "Is it hot?"

"Lurid," Francine answered, "at least for that time period."

"All right," Charlotte said, and she grabbed the photos of Francine and Jonathan off Toby's Apple computer. "But I get to keep the photos too. Consider it blackmail material."

TWENTY-FOUR

FRANCINE HAD ANTICIPATED GOING straight from the law firm to the food booth, so she felt a little underdressed in a pink Mary Ruth's Catering t-shirt and jeans when she arrived at the address on the notice. Frost & Associates sounded like a long-established law firm, and it looked like it from the outside. The office was part of group of suites that had been carved out of an old bank building located across the street from the courthouse. Francine opened the glass-paneled door—frosted, she noted wryly—and found herself in a wood-paneled office that radiated decorum and old money. But the smell was of Febreze. With no one in the office at that moment, she peered around the receptionist's desk and saw an electric scent outlet plugged in behind the desk.

The desk sat between two office doors. Both of them had shiny nameplates on them. One of them said DENISE FROST. The other one was a man's name. She thought he must be the associate who brought her the summons last night.

The door to the one labeled DENISE FROST opened, and Merlina walked out. She was not wearing an old Hungarian dress but a black skirt and white blouse. She wore a tailored turquoise blazer over it, and her hair was pulled back behind her head.

"Hello, Francine."

"You're Denise Frost?"

"No, my real name is Marla Frost, and I'm Denise's paralegal. Also her daughter. Mother felt that I should have a day job. Aunt Marcy is a bit more accepting."

"You're a paranormal paralegal?"

"If you only knew how many times I've heard that joke."

"Sorry."

"But as a paralegal, I've been working with Mr. Matthew on this. Since I've been doing all the work, Mother thought it best that I be the one to meet with you. Besides, she had to be in court today."

"So that's how you knew Zed."

"It is. But I couldn't say. Client confidentiality and all that."

Francine felt her mouth opening and closing like a rusty gate as she tried to process all this.

"You must have a million questions," Merlina told her. "Please have a seat. Tea? Coffee?"

"Tea would be nice."

"I'll get it. It's part of my job, anyway."

Just a few minutes later they were seated on opposite sides of a round hickory table in a corner of Denise's office.

"I don't understand why Zedediah Matthew would leave me anything," Francine began. "And I'm not sure that he's dead. I could have sworn I spotted him yesterday at a funeral home. Do you have any insight on that?"

"Sorry, I don't."

Francine wondered if Merlina had insight on anything, which made her think of a question she'd been wanting to ask. She almost felt awkward asking it because she wasn't sure she would believe an answer even if it were a logical one. "Who did you channel at the séance?"

Merlina thought for a moment. "It was a woman. I think. I'm not always sure. Unless the spirits reveal things to me, all I know is what they say."

"Doesn't Zed have other heirs? Where are they?" Francine gestured toward two empty chairs at the table as if they should be occupied.

"There are no other heirs. Mr. Matthew was married once, but they had no children. He was very sad about that."

"Where is his wife?"

Merlina paused as if she were trying to figure out how to word her answer. "Something terrible happened to his wife, and he never remarried."

"I'm so sorry to hear that. What happened to her? And in what way am I related to him?"

"I was under the impression that he had given you some documents that explained that."

Francine was even more confused. "All he gave me was a diary my grandmother had written about her mother marrying the man who became Doc Wheat."

"I see." Merlina smiled at her. It made Francine think that despite protestations to the contrary, Merlina knew more about her past than she did. Merlina steepled her fingers. "From what I know of Mr. Matthew, I'm sure you have to read between the lines to figure out what that means. Aren't you curious about what he left you in the will?"

"Of course I am."

Merlina went to a locked cabinet in the opposite corner of the room, unlocked it, and removed an old wooden box. She returned with it, opened it, and presented Francine with two documents. One of them was a detailed will. The second was an irrevocable living trust. The will looked to be older, so Francine considered the trust first. She flipped to the last page. It had been signed two days before. "Perhaps..."

"Basically, he has left you everything that is not money. Mainly that's his property, which is fairly substantial. He owned three hundred acres of land in Parke County, including some forty acres that he maintained as pristine as it was when he purchased it. That's according to him."

"Who did he purchase it from? And what did he do with the money? Did that go to another heir?"

Merlina shook her head. "I told you, there are no other heirs. He donated it to charity. A hospice care organization, if you must know."

That would have been Francine's next question, if Merlina hadn't answered it. "Let me back up a step. How do we know that Zedediah Matthew is dead?"

"We don't. But it's not a problem for you legally. May I?" She indicated the papers Francine was holding. Francine dutifully passed them back to her.

Merlina flipped to the next to last page. "This is an irrevocable living trust. He transferred all the property into it. As of yesterday, that trust became yours. Even if you or anyone else cannot prove that he is dead, you own that property."

"But what if he wants it back?"

She shrugged. "It's yours. He can't get it back. You'll find the will has the same goals in mind. You are heir to the ranch. Have you had a chance to look at the property?"

Francine was overwhelmed by the sheer number of questions in her head. Why hadn't she asked Jonathan to come here, instead of sending him on a mission? A mission that now she'd have to attend to anyway, as soon as she got out of the office. "No. The only time I was there you were with us. We saw the house and the greenhouse. I know the house burned down. I trust the greenhouse is still standing."

"I'm pretty confident it still is."

Merlina said it in the stage voice she'd used at the séance. Francine wondered how much of that was playing a part and how much of it was some kind of supernatural knowledge she didn't understand. Then she remembered the will had been signed the same day the arsonist struck. "Who was the beneficiary before me?"

"A woman named Belinda Miles Flowers."

Francine would have to process that. Had Belinda died before the irrevocable trust become effective, or after?

"I was told to tell you to make sure you see the lovely rolling hills in the preserved section. It's beautiful there." Merlina handed over the box that had contained the will and the trust.

Francine took it from her. The box was about the size of two shoeboxes set side by side. When she opened it, it smelled of cedar and reminded her of her grandmother's hope chest. It looked old enough to have been constructed at the same time.

But what got her attention was that there was another box inside it. She lifted it out and set it on the table. Carved into it was the heart icon she'd seen on the beam of the Roseville Bridge and on the cover of the two diaries. It had a tiny lock on it. The lock was strikingly similar to the unlatched lock that was on the two diaries, neither of which had required a key. But when she tried to open the lock on this box, it wouldn't budge. "What's this?" she asked.

"I don't know what's in it. It's been in my possession now since I first met Mr. Matthew. He referred to it as the key to his ranch. He said that what was inside would make sense only to the person who could open it. That's all I know about that, really. I assume that you have the key?"

Francine tilted the box right and left, examined the bottom, and then ran her hand over the lock. She remembered the phrase carved into the bridge under the heart: *You are to mine.* It made no more sense now than it did then. But she believed if she could figure out one, she would be able to solve the other. "I don't have the key, and I don't know where to find it."

"Pity." Merlina stood up. "I'm afraid that's all I know. I need to leave for another appointment. I'm trying to get them all out of the way this morning because Aunt Marcy has me booked for another gig this afternoon, much to Mother's chagrin." She smiled, and for a moment she looked more like the Merlina Francine knew, despite the professional dress. "It looks to me like you could break the box open, but if I understand correctly, until you find the key, it may not be worth it. Both boxes and everything in them are yours to take. If you have more questions for me after you've had a chance to think this all through, please let me know. I don't know that I'll have answers, but you may find some help in just asking them."

Francine found it an odd phrase—*you may find some help in just asking them*—but she understood what Merlina meant by it. That was her experience often with Charlotte. Just putting voice to a question often helped shed light on the answer.

She put the second box and the documents back in the first box and carried it out.

TWENTY-FIVE

FRANCINE LEFT FROST & Associates with almost as many questions as she'd had going in, but she knew what her next move was. She needed to get hold of Jonathan and tell him of her change in plans. She called him on the cell phone. "Did you check out Warm Memories?" she asked.

"I did, and you were right about someone stopping by to see Belinda before she died."

"I was pretty sure. Where are you?"

"I'm headed for Zedediah Matthew's place, as you requested. I'll be there in about ten minutes."

"Good. Change in plans. Now I'm going to meet you there. We can search it together."

"What about Mary Ruth's Fabulous Sweet Shoppe?"

"I'll stop by and clear it with them, but I think they'll want me to go. I just inherited Zed's ranch."

"You *what*?"

"I'm as mystified by it as you. Wait for me by the driveway. I'm on my way."

Francine had no problem convincing Mary Ruth that she needed to go to Zed's ranch instead of staying to help, which surprised her. The line was longer than the previous day, and Mary Ruth seemed as frazzled as ever when she told Francine she was pretty sure they'd be out of food. Again. Plus, Marcy had learned that not only would Food Network be there, it was possible Robert Irvine might also. They just had no idea when it would happen. Marcy bustled about, tweeting photos of the crowd and assuring Mary Ruth that as long as she held back some corn fritter donuts to fry for Robert, they were fine.

The rumor that Robert Irvine might appear worked in her favor in dealing with Charlotte. Charlotte was beside herself with excitement, and she was only mildly interested in where Francine was going. Francine simply assured Charlotte she'd tell her everything when she got back, and that seemed to placate her. But Francine hadn't defined *everything* in her own mind yet.

Jonathan was leaning against his truck when she pulled up in the driveway at Zedediah Matthew's property. He walked up as she put the car in park. When she got out, he pulled her close into a hug.

"Are you okay?"

"I'm very, very puzzled. But I'm fine. We just need to do some exploration."

They walked warily up the driveway. Both of them felt spooked a bit. As they approached the turn before it cut toward the house, Francine saw that the arch that identified the property as Matthew's ranch had burned. The sign lay a few feet off the gravel driveway. She went over to it.

Something was different about the sign. She had interpreted the sign to have said MATTHEW 1844 RANCH, but now that she could see it up close, she could see the lettering had been doctored. It was intended to be MATTHEW 13:44 RANCH. She fingered the lettering that was burned into the wooden sign. "Look at this, Jonathan."

"What is Matthew 13:44?" he asked.

"I don't know offhand, but if Zed's sometimes on/sometimes off cell phone booster is working, I could look it up with my Bible app." She was getting a signal, so she looked it up quickly. "It's the parable of the man who found a great treasure buried in a field, and went off and sold all he had to obtain it."

"That jibes with the idea that Doc Wheat buried his fortune here."

"But Zed kept using the word *treasure*, not *fortune*. And the carving we found on the bridge that had the same graphic as the diaries had, 'you are to mine' written under it. Now that I think about it, one doesn't *mine* fortune, but one could *mine* a treasure. Sort of. I'm sure it all means something, I'm just not sure what."

They left the sign and walked to where the burnt out bones of the house lay in a heap on the ground, yellow crime scene tape squaring off and preserving what remained. Francine was more interested in seeing the greenhouse, which hadn't been touched by the fire. She dragged Jonathan back there. While he perused the plants, she went to the back hoping the off-road vehicle she'd seen was still there. It was, in the back corner with a tarp thrown over it. She uncovered it. Fortunately, the key was in it. She satisfied herself that the key was too big to fit in the tiny box's lock, and anyway, what kind of sense would it have made if it had? She hailed Jonathan over. "Do you know how to ride one of these things?"

He threw one leg over the seat. "Hop on and let's find out. Where do you want to go?"

She climbed on behind him. "Merlina mentioned the rolling hills like it was a clue of some kind. And last night when I read the history of Parke County William was writing, it made reference to a location on this land in the hills."

"Do you know where they are?"

"From William's description, I would guess that since the woods are in front of us, and I know where the cornfields are, the hills are between them. Can you get through the woods?"

"Only if there's a trail of some kind."

"Let's find out."

Jonathan drove out of the back of the greenhouse and skirted the edge of the woods until he found a narrow path that looked passable. Once they got a little farther into the woods, the path broadened and became more hard-packed. He took them through the woods at a higher speed until, some fifteen minutes later, they burst out of the trees and into a meadow. Beyond it was the beginning of another forest, but unlike the flat terrain they just left, this forest rose on a gentle incline.

"Would you call that a gently rolling hill?" she asked him.

"It could be."

Jonathan sped across the meadow, slowing as they went into the new forest. This time the path was not hidden. He followed it until it pulled up on the top of one of the ridges. Below them was a canyon, not deep, but lush with growth. At the rounded end, in a grotto, a small geyser started up and sprayed water widely into the air. It covered the immediate area, sprinkling drops over all the plants, but not a lot on any of them. A copper basin sat next to the geyser collecting whatever water came its way. There was a long pause of several minutes before the mini geyser went off again. Then it went dormant.

The sun shone through a clearing above them into the canyon. Francine examined the trees surrounding the clearing. They were either barren of leaves or in varying stages of color. The green growth below stood in direct contrast. "How do we get down there?" she asked, getting off the ATV. She had no idea what to make of the contrast.

Jonathan followed her off the vehicle. Together they paced the ridge. "I feel like there must be an easy way down," he said, taking her by the hand. "Look on that side." He pointed to his left into the canyon. "Doesn't that look like a path?"

Francine knew what he meant. The other side of the canyon dropped away quickly, but this side, after an initial drop, smoothed out and seemed to wind gently down to the grotto. She traced what she could make of the trail toward the top. It seemed to lead to a space not far from them, a space marked by a stand of five trees. They stood like sentries blocking the way, like they'd been planted there some time ago. In contrast to the deciduous trees of the forest, these were spruces, evergreens.

Jonathan was a few steps ahead. He pushed through the branches, his arms flailing in an attempt to deflect the limbs from snapping back toward him. He disappeared from view.

Before Francine had a chance to worry he'd fallen, she heard him. "There's a rope and chain ladder on the backside," he called. He reappeared on her side of the trees and held back branches for her. "It's only five steps down the ladder. Not easy, I think, especially the last step, but it's doable."

Francine wasn't thrilled when she saw the makeshift ladder. It was not stable. Thick black chains anchored into side of the canyon served as steps. The rope could be grasped as a handrail. She would have to back down the ladder, trusting that her feet would make the next step without being able to see it. The last step, as Jonathan said, was a steep one. "I'll let you go first," she said.

Jonathan didn't hesitate. He grabbed onto the rope handrail with both hands and lowered himself step by step to the bottom. "Just go slow," he reassured her. "I'll help you on the last step, but your legs are long. You'll be fine."

She didn't breathe until she was on solid ground, but as Jonathan predicted, she was able to step off. "I don't know how I'll get back up, but now that we're here, let's search the grounds."

Once they reached the bottom of the canyon, she could see that the copper basin drained into a funnel. Under the funnel she expected to find a mason jar, one exactly like she'd seen in Zed's greenhouse and in the trunk of William's car. But there was nothing there.

"It's the water," she said.

"Yes, but what *about* the water?" Jonathan asked.

The little geyser went off. Francine stuck her hand in the spray. "It's warm, almost to the point of being hot."

Jonathan did the same thing. "I didn't think there were any mineral springs in this area. I associate that with southern Indiana, like down around French Lick."

"Not so," she replied. "Montezuma had hot springs. A sanitarium and hotel was built on one until the place burned down in the 1930s. And we had Cartersburg in Hendricks County too. Didn't you have that in your Leadership Hendricks County class? I know I did."

"You're right. I remember it now." He looked at the green growth that had grown up around the stream. "But I didn't know about Montezuma."

The geyser had stopped, but then it started up again. Francine knelt so she could get closer to the funnel that came out of the copper bowl. She cupped her hand and waited until she had gathered enough in her palm to have a sample. She brought her hand to her nose and sniffed. Then she used her tongue to taste the few remaining drops.

"Francine, don't! You don't know what could be in that water."

She had already assessed the risk and had decided to test it anyway. Her eyes closed, she ran her tongue around in her mouth. At first she felt the warmth of the water, and then the taste she expected was there. "This has that exact same metallic taste that was in the tea and date-nut bread Zed served me."

"I still don't think you should taste any more of it until we can have it analyzed."

Francine stood up and wiped her hand on her jeans. "I agree. Too bad we didn't bring a container."

They were silent for a few moments. Francine studied the beauty of the impossibly green valley. "What do you think it means?" she asked Jonathan.

He shook his head. "I don't know. Let's follow the reach of the spray and see how far it goes."

The answer was only a short distance. Within a few hundred feet they could no longer feel the geyser when it went off. The plants were brown and dried up. Even a stream that came out of the ground and trickled to the right into a wooded area didn't revive the lush growth. Here, autumn returned. Leaves that had fallen from neighboring trees drifted in the water as it meandered out of the canyon toward an unknown destination. Francine thought it likely to be Big Raccoon Creek.

Francine had only worn a lightweight jacket, and without the sun, she felt chilled. "Let's go back."

They returned to the grotto. Francine studied the plants. "These are the same varieties that Zed has in the greenhouse. I'd bet money on it. I remember that some were familiar, but there were a few I didn't recognize. Zed told me they were native species."

"Do you think it's the heat of the water that keeps them alive?"

Francine briefly wondered about everyone's obsession with the water itself, but then dismissed it. "Possibly. Or maybe it's the unique position here." She pointed to the sun directly in front of them. "They have unblocked southern exposure. Unless the wind is directly out of the south, they're protected from the weather by the narrowness of the canyon."

"Surely they die at some point during the year. It gets too cold in Indiana, and snow's going to be whipped in here and blanket the canyon no matter how protected it is."

Francine couldn't argue with Jonathan's logic. "I guess that's why Zed has the greenhouse." She began to trek back toward the all-terrain vehicle. "I'd like to come back here and get a sample of the water. Maybe not today, but soon. I want to know what's in it, and why Zed served us tea that I'm certain was made from this."

When they got to the top, Jonathan went ahead of her and helped her up past the pine trees. He drove slower on the way back. Francine was grateful, although she was certain her hair must still be a mess from the quick drive there.

They parked the vehicle in the greenhouse, put the tarp over it, and arranged everything so it looked like it had when they arrived.

"There," Jonathan said. "When the owner comes back, they won't know we were here. Oh, wait. You are the owner."

She put her arm around him and pulled him close. "*We* are the owners. Don't think you're going to get out of this one. What's mine is yours. For whatever reason, this property is now ours."

Francine felt a buzz in her pocket and discovered she'd missed a phone call while they were gone. The grotto must have been out of range of the wandering signal. It was from Mary Ruth. Francine returned the call.

"We're out of food, and Robert Irvine had a flight delay, so he if comes in, it won't be until four o'clock. Alice and I are heading back to the house to make some more scones, cookies, and of course, the corn fritter donut dough to have ready, just in case. Joy and Toby are off recording B-roll. Can you come back and keep Charlotte busy?"

"I thought she was being helpful."

"Only so long as the promise that Robert Irvine would arrive held out. Now that there's no guarantee he'll be here, she's less interested. In fact"—Mary Ruth's voice dropped to a whisper—"she's being a pain."

"We're just wrapping up here." Francine checked the time. She and Jonathan would make it back in time for her to try to solve yet another of the mysteries she'd encountered. "Tell Charlotte I'm taking her to a funeral."

"Is it someone we know?"

"No. But tell her it's the woman I thought I saw Zed crying for, and who might have been poisoned. Tell her it's a mystery yet to be solved."

"I'm sure she'll love it."

TWENTY-SIX

Francine had not thought to bring clothes suitable for a funeral visitation, mostly because a funeral had been the last thing on her mind when she'd packed for the Covered Bridge Festival. She had several bright pink Mary Ruth's Catering t-shirts that would not do, along with turn-of-the-century clothes she'd rented for the photo shoot. Ugly fall-themed sweaters weren't going to cover it, either.

With that, she had set aside nearly everything in her suitcase. The only things left were black jeans that looked kind of dressy and a white long-sleeve shirt that buttoned up the front. She thrown them in on a whim, thinking that if Mary Ruth had needed her for something a little more formal than the food booth, she'd at least look the part. They, and the scuffed black flats she wore often to keep from looking so tall, would have to do. As she checked herself in the mirror before leaving the room, she noticed scarves on a shelf that the owner of the house had left behind. Several of them had subdued colors that would help dress up her outfit. She selected one and tied it around her neck as was fashionable nowadays. *I'll put it back when I'm done and no one will be the wiser*, she thought.

She was grateful William's funeral had been scheduled for the day after the Covered Bridge Festival was over. Either she'd have time to run back to Brownsburg and prepare for it, or she would have Jonathan bring the clothes the next time he came back. For this visitation, he would be able to get by much better than her, since he had his business casual clothes.

Francine knocked on the bathroom door. "Charlotte, how are you coming in there?"

"Fine." The answer was brusque.

Francine glanced at her watch. "Please be ready in five minutes. The visitation is only an hour, and I don't want us to be there long enough to have to stay for the actual funeral."

Charlotte opened the bathroom door. She was dressed in an electric-blue sweatshirt with a photo of the Bridgeton Bridge on it, and words that screamed *I Shopped Bridgeton! Parke County Covered Bridge Festival.*

"Looks like someone went shopping yesterday in Bridgeton," Francine remarked.

"Don't stare, Francine. It's the best I've got."

"I wasn't staring."

"You're also a bad liar. Is Jonathan ready? Let's get this over with."

Charlotte grabbed her cane and they proceeded down the stairs. "I hope there aren't too many people there."

Francine reached the bottom of the staircase well before Charlotte, who took the stairs one step at a time, and turned to make sure her friend didn't fall. "I imagine there will be a few nurses from the memory care unit, and then Dolly. We need to keep our eyes peeled in case we spot Zed lurking around, but if Merlina is right, he's gone."

"Merlina had to have had some long conversations with Zed if she prepared that irrevocable trust," Charlotte said. "We should ask her more questions."

"You're right, but she seemed short on time yesterday. The whole thing came as such a shock that I didn't have time to even formulate questions."

"That's why you should have brought me along. I'm quick on my feet." Charlotte finally reached the bottom of the stairs and realized what she'd said. "To use a cliché," she added.

Francine knew Charlotte could move decently without the cane. She'd seen her do it many times before. But for whatever reason, Charlotte liked to appear more handicapped than she was. "Maybe we'll go see Merlina tomorrow. If she's doing her day job and not holding séances."

Jonathan was waiting for them in the front room, seated on one of the leather couches. He stood when they entered. He was wearing tan chinos and a black sweater. "Ready?" he asked.

"Is there never a time when you don't look good, Jonathan?" Charlotte asked.

He laughed. "You can be so sweet sometimes."

"Sometimes," Francine echoed.

Charlotte looked up at her. "I only let my friends see me at my worst. So you know this is hardly my worst. I may look like I'm more ready to roast wieners at a bonfire, but at least I'm clean and have makeup on."

The women flanked Jonathan, each taking one arm, as they made their way down the sidewalk to the Langley Funeral Home. As expected, there was not a crowd.

Francine's phone rang before they went in. Francine looked at the phone number. "Caller ID says it's Roy Stockton."

"Let me answer it," Jonathan said. "I'll tell him you're not here once you're inside. Then I won't be lying."

The two women went in.

Dolly stood at the front of the room, talking with a young woman Francine guessed to be a nurse from the ward. Dolly wore a long-sleeved black dress and her makeup and nails looked perfect as always. Francine wondered if it didn't say something about the relationship with William that Dolly didn't even have bags under her eyes from being awake all night or mascara running down her cheeks from crying.

The casket, to her surprise, was open. There were a few pictures of the woman who had died, all of them fairly recent. They were in small black frames. A couple of stands of flowers were there. Francine checked the names on them as she and Charlotte waited for Dolly and the nurse to finish up. One was from Dolly, another from the nursing home. A third, which was larger than the other two modest displays, was filled with white roses intertwined with fall flowers. Francine read the inscription.

She pulled Charlotte over. "This card says it's from Doc Wheat."

"Doc Wheat, really? You'd think he'd be pretty old by now."

"Stop it! You know he's dead."

"It's a bad practical joke."

The two stared at the flowers. "Pretty elaborate display for a practical joke," Francine said.

Dolly and the nurse finished talking. The nurse left. Dolly turned and saw them. At first Francine thought the look she gave them was one of dismay, but then she wasn't sure. It might have been one of puzzlement.

"Charlotte and I wanted to stop by and express our condolences," she said, nearing the casket. "I know you said you and William were close to her. It's difficult to lose a good friend, especially at a time like this."

"She was a sweet lady," Dolly said. The words sounded hollow to Francine.

"Had she been sick long?" Charlotte asked. "Or did she go suddenly?"

The question made Dolly visibly uncomfortable. "She had Alzheimer's for years, but when her time came, she went quickly. Which in many ways is a blessing."

"So did you know her before she had Alzheimer's?"

Francine worried that Charlotte was being too direct in questioning Dolly. She wanted Charlotte's help in solving this mystery, but not to the point that she alienated Dolly. She glanced in the casket at the dead woman.

"We knew her when the Alzheimer's had finished settling in. That was when her husband brought her to the memory unit of our nursing home. I think it's been about ten years."

"So she had lost her short-term memory by then? Did she still remember things from way back, or had she lost that too?"

Without looking up from the casket, Francine gripped Charlotte's arm.

Charlotte pried her arm loose and didn't skip a beat. "I was only wondering because I had a friend who was like that. No short-term memory but thought I was her mother and used to tell all kinds of stories. Only some of which I thought were true."

But Francine had not gripped Charlotte's arm to stop her. She'd been surprised. The woman in the casket was wearing a necklace with a charm. The charm was a duplicate of the heart-and-arrow graphic she'd seen on the diaries. In fact, it was really an echo of the one on the bridge, because it had the further inscription below it, *You are the key to my heart*. And then there was another charm, a bit larger than the heart-and-arrow. It was a key. Small enough to fit the lock of the diaries. Sturdy enough to fit the lock on the box she had inherited from Zed.

Francine pulled Charlotte close.

"Ouch, you're hurting me," Charlotte whispered. "I thought you wanted to me to help question her."

"Never mind that," Francine hissed. "Look at the necklace."

Charlotte's eyes lit up. "It's the same thing we saw on the bridge."

"Yes, and I need that key." Francine glanced back to see what Dolly was doing. Dolly had edged away from Charlotte and was looking at the flowers that were supposedly from Doc Wheat. *Thank goodness for Charlotte's questioning, however direct it might have been.* "My guess is, it unlocks the box Zed left for me."

"What box? You didn't tell me about a box. You only told me you inherited the land."

"I was *going* to tell you, but I didn't exactly have much to say about it until I could open it, and there was no key. But if that is 'the key to my heart,' then it should open the box."

"But who is Belinda? How did she get it?"

"I don't know. But right now that's not as important as how we're going to get it."

"Oh, boy, that's going to be a tough one. You can't just reach in and get it."

A group of elderly people shuffled in, accompanied by a middle-aged woman with a strict face. "Please sit here," she said, a little louder than custom would have dictated. She directed them into the front row. She and Dolly huddled in the back of the room.

"I need you to create a distraction," Francine said.

"I'll give it a try." Charlotte sat in the chair next to the last of the seven people to have been brought in. She looked to be in her late eighties, a good fifteen years or more older than the Summer Ridge Bridge Club group. "Do you watch Food Network?" Charlotte asked. "Have you heard of Mary Ruth's Catering? I have one of her famous corn fritter donuts." She opened her cavernous bag and pulled out a donut wrapped in a bakery sheet. "It's yours if you want it."

The woman had a blank look on her face, but she tentatively took the donut from Charlotte. She sniffed it suspiciously. Then she bit into it, taking a big mouthful. She began to chew.

The amount of donut didn't fit well in her mouth. Crumbs began to fall from her mouth onto her lap.

"Here's a napkin," Charlotte offered, pulling one from the bag.

"What's that you've got there, Biddy?" asked the woman next to her.

"It's a donut," Biddy said. Her mouth was so full the words were almost unintelligible. A large piece tried to escape from her mouth, but she used a finger to shove it back in. "Cake of some kind."

"Is it good?"

"Better than good, Cassie. They never let us have donuts any more. Do you remember donuts?"

"I loved donuts."

"It's so good. Did you bring your teeth?"

"Sure did." Cassie had a small purse sitting on her lap. She pulled out a case that presumably had her dentures in it. She rustled around and came up with a tube of Fixodent. "But I need to find a bathroom so I can put them in first."

Charlotte dug into her purse and pulled out another donut. She waggled it back and forth. "It's yours when you get back."

Cassie got up and darted for the exit.

"Where's she hustlin' off to, waving that tube of denture cream?" the man next to Cassie asked.

"Going to put her teeth in," Biddy said. "Though this cake donut is soft enough she probably don't need it."

"Can I have one?"

"You'll have to ask this nice young lady here, Eddie." Biddy indicated Charlotte.

"I'm not Eddie," he said. He turned to the woman to his left, who was wearing a heavy blue sweater button up to her neck. "At least, I don't think I'm Eddie. Am I Eddie?"

Francine hoped this would all play out quickly, though she couldn't remember the last time any of them had been called "young lady."

Charlotte made eye contact with Francine. It was a look of alarm. "This is my last donut," she mouthed.

"Find something else," Francine mouthed back.

Charlotte dug through her purse.

The blue sweater lady stood up. "I want a donut too." She bypassed the man who may or may not be Eddie and stood in front of Charlotte.

"I called dibs on it," he said.

Biddy stood up and elbowed Blue Sweater out of the way. "Actually, it's Cassie's. You'll have to call dibs on the next one she pulls out."

Charlotte dug faster.

"I'll just take that half donut you're waving around," Eddie told Biddy.

Biddy swallowed whatever was left in her mouth and shoved the rest of it in. She held up her hands triumphantly.

All six of the remaining seniors were now out of their seats clustered around Charlotte trying to shove each other out of the way, like little kids. Dolly and the strict nurse rushed to separate them. They were a handful, though.

Francine knew she'd have no better time. She reached into the casket and pulled on the necklace, looking for the clasp. She brushed against Belinda's skin. It felt tight and cold. As a nurse, Francine had been around dead people before, especially right after they died. But this was different. This person had been dead for days and went through the embalming process. It made Francine not want to touch her.

"I've got something you'll like better," she heard Charlotte say. "You like hot women?"

Francine fumbled around the dead woman's neck, trying not to touch her again but still get the necklace undone so she could grab the key. She leaned closer in.

"Hot dog! I love hot women!" Eddie said. "Harry, look at this."

Francine heard pages rustling in the background but she tried to focus on the necklace. Her bifocals were in the wrong spot so she was squinting at the same time she was feeling around the chain. She found the clasp.

"I'm not Harry," said a second male voice said. "But I know who that is. That's her!"

Francine had a bad feeling about this, but there was no letting go now. She almost had the clasp undone.

"Her? The one bending over the casket like she's ... well, I used to know what that was called. Ever done it in a casket?"

"Ever done what in a casket?"

"You know."

"Give me that calendar," Dolly said.

"No," said Harry.

Francine felt a hand on her rear end. "Hi, Tootsie."

Francine turned her head briefly. It was Eddie. Or whoever. "Get your hand off me. *Now!*" she ordered.

She turned back to the dead woman's necklace.

"Heh, heh. I bet you like to play games."

The clasp came undone. Francine tightened her fist around the necklace and the key. She pulled herself to her full height and towered over Eddie. "I don't play games, and I know self-defense."

Eddie backed up into Harry, who was holding a full-sized wall calendar opened to December. Harry showed it to Eddie. "You're right. She *is* the one."

Francine looked on in horror. The photo was the one of her bending over Jonathan in the carriage, the one where her breasts could be partially seen. "Give me that," she said, lurching for it.

Harry danced away. "Pretty hot mama."

He bounced off Dolly, who was standing behind him. She grabbed the calendar. "What's this?" she asked.

Cassie entered the room smiling, her dentures evident. She marched up to Charlotte, who was wrestling with Blue Sweater, trying to get into her purse. "Where's my donut?" Cassie demanded.

The lone remaining corn fritter donut bounced like a hot potato between Biddy and two other women from the nursing home. Cassie spotted it and pounced on Biddy, who at that moment happened to catch the donut.

Charlotte whacked Blue Sweater with her purse and leaped at Dolly. She caught her by surprised and wrested control of the calendar momentarily.

A melee broke out.

But it ended just as swiftly as Jonathan entered the visitation room accompanied by Detective Stockton and two deputies. The deputies and the nurse from the care home restored order while Stockton addressed Dolly.

"Dolly Falkes, I am placing you under arrest for the murder of your husband, William." He recited her rights.

It was then Francine noticed that the whole episode was also on tape. Joy stood in a corner recording it all.

TWENTY-SEVEN

"WE'RE GRATEFUL THAT YOU tipped us off to the poisoning," Roy Stockton told Francine, Charlotte, and Jonathan later. They sat in the detective's office in the Parke County Sheriff's building. There were certificates of accomplishments on the wall behind him and on an adjacent wall were photos of him with various Indiana dignitaries. In all the them he wore his signature Stetson. "The coroner rushed the results of his blood analysis. William died of poisoning from the toxin tremetol. We were able to find a tiny vial laced with it in the wastebasket in his room. It had Dolly's fingerprints on it. We obtained a search warrant and found a container of it in her house. We believe she may also have used it to kill the woman whose funeral she arranged for, Belinda Flowers."

"What's the motive, though?" Charlotte asked. "Why kill her husband?"

"She has clammed up on the advice of her lawyer, which is to be expected. The prevailing theory is the sizable life insurance policy. She'd gain control of the company in the case of William's death, of course, but it looks like she pretty much controlled it anyway from the interviews we've conducted. In comparison to the equity they had in their company, the insurance policy wasn't that much, so it's tentative. Still, people have been known to kill for less."

Francine could tell Charlotte was less than satisfied by the way she jabbed her pen in her notebook, scribbling sentences in it as the detective discussed the case.

Charlotte paused, holding her pen to her lips as though she had a sudden thought. "What about an affair? Could she have tossed William over for another man?"

"Do you have a person in mind?" Stockton asked. "The only person we can determine she had some kind of strong relationship with is Zedediah Matthew, and from all appearances it was acrimonious."

Francine loved that Roy used words like *acrimonious*, though she might have used something stronger. "I thought she might have been behind the arson at Zed's house," she said. "Zed told me at one point he said he would get revenge on the person who torched his house."

"Which brings up the arson point," Charlotte said. "Do you know who did that? Was that Dolly too?"

"We have circumstantial evidence, like the containers placed at the food booth, that might indicate she was behind it. But it could be planted evidence as well. It could be someone was trying to frame her, or frame you, Francine. We understand you have inherited Zed's property. But you have an iron-clad alibi."

Francine was offended by the suggestion. "Why would I burn down the very house I stood to inherit?"

"The property is worth much more than the house. You might have done it to kill Zed so you could inherit the three hundred acres right away."

Jonathan put his arm around her. She reached up and felt the warmth of the hand on her shoulder. "I still haven't figured out why he left it to me."

"You might never."

Francine patted his hand and sat up. "I would think Dolly would have an iron-clad alibi. She was at the hospital with William when the two fires were set."

"She left for a period of time during the afternoon, supposed to go meet her sister at her house. But it turns out she wasn't with her sister. So Dolly was gone long enough to set the two fires or rig them up to go off later."

"All for Doc Wheat's treasure," Francine said. "Whatever treasure that was."

"When did Zed buy the property from Doc Wheat?" Charlotte asked. "I couldn't find any record of the sale when I searched the county databases. Somehow it became listed as Zed's property in the late 1960s, but Doc Wheat had disappeared before that."

"Doc Wheat vanished from the county in 1969, long after his business as an herbal healer had closed. As far as we know, there is no record."

Francine was as disturbed by Charlotte as the lack of answers. "Who was Belinda Flowers to Dolly? Why would she have poisoned her like she poisoned William?"

Stockton shrugged. "Again, we don't have an answer to that. We know that Dolly and William were particularly attached to her. Perhaps it was an angel of mercy act. The woman had been in a vegetative state for over a year."

The "angel of mercy" comment struck Francine. *Zed knew Belinda Flowers too*, she thought. *She wore a necklace with the same graphic that was found on the bridge and on my grandmother's diaries.*

What if Zed were the angel of mercy? But that wouldn't explain William's death.

She wondered if opening the box Zed left her would shed any light on the subject. She hadn't had a chance to try the key on it yet. Charlotte was anxious to see it opened as well. They needed to get some time alone to do that. She'd told Jonathan about the box, but he didn't know yet she had a key that might work. He'd assured her, though he hadn't seen the box, that it likely could be pried open. She thought he was right, but she only wanted to use that as a last resort. Merlina's words about needing the key to understand the contents of the box, at least according to what Zed had told her, haunted Francine.

You are to mine. Those were the words they'd uncovered on the Roseville Bridge. But Zed spoke of a treasure. Was Belinda Flowers the key to Zed's heart or his treasure, or both? And what was the treasure? Love? The grotto? The water?

She could hardly wait to finish up here to unlock the box.

———

"I don't like Dolly as the person who torched Zed's house, burned down the Roseville Bridge, and killed two people, one of which was her husband," Charlotte said. "She doesn't seem, I don't know, *nasty* enough."

Charlotte said this from the back of Jonathan's truck. They were driving back to the house in Rockville. Francine sat in the front seat with Jonathan. Her thoughts were scattered, but they were running along the same lines as Charlotte's.

"That's your intuition again," Jonathan said. "The facts seem to say otherwise."

Francine defended Charlotte. "The facts don't seem conclusive to me, either, Jonathan. Not until there's motive to back them up."

"Then how did Dolly's fingerprints end up on the bottle of whatever poison was used?"

Francine threw up her hands. "Who knows? But it doesn't make sense as we see it now."

"Tremetol," Charlotte said, consulting her notes. "That's the poison Dolly used."

Francine pulled out her phone. She did a Google search. "Tremetol is derived from the white snakeroot plant." There was a photo on the website that had come up, and she clicked on it. When she saw the plant, she did a double take. "Look at this," she said, thrusting the phone in front of Jonathan.

He glanced at it, but then went back to driving. "I can't get a good look," he said. "Tell me what you think it is."

"It was the white blooming bush we saw at the grotto."

"You're certain?"

"As certain as I can be without having it in front of me to compare."

Charlotte unbuckled her seat belt and perched on the edge of the seat behind Francine. "What bush? What grotto?"

The seat belt light on the dashboard showed an unbuckled passenger and a dinging noise began to sound in the car. "Charlotte, please put your seat belt back on," Jonathan said.

"Here." Francine handed Charlotte her cell phone.

She slid back into place and dutifully buckled in. The noise stopped. Charlotte studied the image. "You saw this where?"

"In Zed's greenhouse," Francine corrected.

Charlotte gave Francine a suspicious scowl. The affected look, which wrinkled Charlotte's already wrinkled face, scrunching up her nose and pushing out her upper lip, almost made Francine laugh. "You said something about a grotto."

"No, Francine's right," Jonathan said. "It was in the greenhouse."

"Why do I think you two are hiding something from me?"

Francine tried to divert Charlotte's focus. She turned back to Jonathan. "But if Zed was in possession of the plant used to make tremetol, that would imply that he was the one to poison William and Belinda Flowers. First of all, how would he do that without being seen, and what would be his motive? And how did Dolly's fingerprints end up on the bottle? And I can't see Zed setting fire to his house and to the Roseville Bridge."

Charlotte handed the phone back to Francine. "Excuse the pun, but could Zed have planted the evidence?"

Francine performed some mental gymnastics in her head. Four crimes, two suspects. Who did what to whom? Or were there other possibilities? Were there other persons involved who could have aided or abetted the criminal or criminals? It required too much concentration, like a sudoku puzzle at the highest difficulty rating. She didn't have the energy for it right then. "It all boils down to motive, and until we understand that, I don't think we'll have the answer."

The car settled into silence as they motored to the Rockville mansion.

In the kitchen, Mary Ruth, Alice, and Toby were mixing, baking, and otherwise preparing for tomorrow's Covered Bridge Festival. In all the excitement over Dolly's arrest, Francine had nearly forgotten why they were in Rockville in the first place and that Mary Ruth had to have things ready for another day of selling her goods.

Charlotte opened the oven door and looked in, steaming up her white framed glasses. Mary Ruth shut the oven door and nudged Charlotte out of the way. "The scones need the heat, not you."

"I couldn't see them anyway. Smells like oranges in here."

Alice put down a microplane. "It's because I'm zesting oranges for the scones. They're cranberry orange."

Charlotte's mouth turned down. "I missed Robert Irvine, didn't I?"

Mary Ruth pulled a tray of cookies out of the second oven and used a spatula to shuttle them off onto a cooling rack. "Yes, but he's coming over here this evening to get some background footage of us prepping for tomorrow. He's also going to ask a few more questions."

Francine saw the clock on the oven. "It's almost six o'clock. How much later is he going to be?"

"They didn't say. As I understand it, the organizers took Robert over to Bridgeton and Mansfield to get B-roll of him walking around and sampling some of the other food offerings."

The corners of Charlotte's mouth turned up as she smiled. "I'd like to see that. Can you imagine him checking out the beef jerky and the lemon shake-ups? I'll bet he'd have a lot to say about that."

Francine and the others had a laugh at the thought of Robert Irvine sampling some of the less sophisticated offerings. "I suggested they take him to the mill at Bridgeton," said Mary Ruth. "That would give viewers a more favorable impression since they grind their own flours that are available for sale."

Charlotte perused the few items that were finished. "Do you need our help?"

Mary Ruth let out a sigh. "Yes, I could use it. We've been short-handed with you and Francine being gone and Joy out filing stories for the station. She stopped by briefly and told us the killer had been arrested. We're sorry to hear it was your cousin's wife Dolly, Francine."

Francine tried to be honest. "In some ways, it doesn't quite make sense still. I think we'll all feel better when we know what the motive is."

Before Mary Ruth could get them started helping her, the doorbell rang. Charlotte used her cane as a third leg and beat Mary Ruth to the front door. "It's Robert Irvine!" Francine heard her say.

Jonathan tugged at Francine's hand and indicated they go upstairs. He leaned toward her ear and whispered, "While everyone's distracted, this would be a good time to open the box."

Francine wanted to meet Robert Irvine, but she'd been on television enough for one day. She and Jonathan scuttled up the back staircase.

TWENTY-EIGHT

FRANCINE PULLED OUT THE box Merlina had given her at the law office. She inserted the small key she'd taken off Belinda Flowers's body and smuggled out of the funeral home in all the confusion. The key fit perfectly in the lock. She turned it and the box opened.

It, too, smelled of cedar and was smooth on the inside. Several items were stacked in the box. Francine lifted a leather bound notebook, slightly larger than traditional paperback size, from the top of the stack. She flipped through it. It was not a diary in a traditional sense, although it did have dated entries that went back to the late 1930s. The handwriting was clearly different than her grandmother's.

She skimmed the first few entries, adjusting her bifocals as she read.

Jonathan stood behind her as she turned the pages. "I wish I'd brought my reading glasses."

"I wish you had too. It's hard for me to fathom this, but this appears to be Doc Wheat's journal on his natural remedies. What he tried, what worked, and what didn't."

"His formulas?"

"Yes. The key seems to be that they were made from the water at that spring."

"Then he believed the water had some kind of special properties?"

Francine continued to skim. "Right from the start. He presumed that from the growth around the grotto that stayed green so long."

"Apparently others bought into that. He had a worldwide audience for a while. Does it say why he stopped selling his remedies?"

"I'm sure it's in here somewhere." She turned to the end of the notebook, hoping the answer might be there. But what she saw made her heart falter. "Jonathan, the last entries are dated two weeks ago. The formula he was experimenting with calls for white snakeroot."

Jonathan didn't say anything for a moment. "Is the handwriting the same?"

Francine almost said yes, because it looked nearly identical, but the implication was difficult for her to get her mind around. If the handwriting was by the same person, then Doc Wheat would be … Zed? It would account for the reason there was no record of the land being sold to Zed.

She flipped back and forth between entries at the beginning and at the end. "I'm no handwriting expert, but it seems to me they are very similar."

Francine went back to the small cedar box and sorted through the remaining contents. The next item was yet another diary from her grandmother. This time Francine went immediately to the end to check the dates of the last entries. "This diary goes up to the last week of her life, right before the automobile accident. Look! She mentions me."

"How old were you?"

She stopped reading for a moment and put the book in her lap, her thumb marking the page she was on. "I was seven. I'll never forget it. It was my first encounter with the death of someone I loved very much."

Jonathan rubbed her shoulder. Francine went back to the diary. "*I took care of Francine today while Jane did chores,*" she read. "*Being a grandmother is one of the best experiences there could be. Tempting as it is to keep her at this age, I understand why the treasure mustn't be shared until adulthood. Even Jane needs a few more years before she learns the truth. My father has undergone three transformations already, the last one being the most difficult to manage. He says with the advancements in record-keeping, it will only get more challenging to hide the treasure, but to let the secret out would only invite disaster.*"

"The 'treasure' again. My grandmother died shortly after this. But did my mother ever know about the treasure? Who was her grandfather? What does she mean by transformations? She couldn't mean Doc Wheat, or Zed, if that's what she's talking about. That would put him well over a hundred years old, and he appears to be younger than us."

"I'm starting to get a picture I'm finding hard to believe," Jonathan said. "Your grandmother died in an automobile accident. You never knew your grandfather. Your mother died of cancer at an early age. Your father disappeared sometime after your mother died. None of those were from old age."

"Are you saying what I think you're saying?"

"What happened to your great-grandmother? Where is she buried?"

"Her gravestone is next to Grandma and Grandpa's in a private cemetery on the land we used to own here in this county."

"I think it might be a good idea to go see that grave."

"When?"

"As soon as we can shake Charlotte, Robert Irvine, and whoever else is downstairs."

They heard cane taps on the hallway outside the room. There was a knock on the door. Francine rushed to put everything back in the box and whisked it under the bed. She kissed Jonathan hard on the lips just as the door flung open and Charlotte bustled in.

"You have to come downstairs and meet Robert Irvine!" Charlotte said. Francine unlocked her lips with Jonathan's and gave Charlotte a stare. "Am I interrupting something?"

"Not anymore," Jonathan grumbled.

"I would have thought you'd snuck away to try to open the box, now that you have the key."

"Turned out to be more complicated than I thought," Francine said. She stood and straightened her clothes. Jonathan did likewise. He cleared his throat like it was thick from desire.

Charlotte looked from Jonathan to Francine. "I'll just be waiting in the hall." She backed out of the room and closed the door behind her.

Francine put a finger to her lips to indicate Jonathan shouldn't say anything. She tiptoed toward him, but the floor creaked anyway. The two of them choked back a laugh.

"We got away with it for now," Francine whispered, "but we'd better not push it. Let's go downstairs and see what's happened."

Charlotte, true to her word, leaned against the wall outside the room, waiting. "You need to know, he's seen the calendar. In fact, just about everyone's seen the calendar. Joy caught a good part of what happened at the funeral room and filed a report that's already aired."

Jonathan crossed his arms. "I don't detect any remorse in your voice about that. I thought this was just something that would stay inside the group."

"And how does this play into Robert Irvine's visit?" Francine asked.

Charlotte was already working on the stairs, one step at a time. "Come down and find out."

———

Robert was gracious but didn't stay long after they came downstairs into the kitchen. Mary Ruth had several bowls out, and it looked like she'd been demonstrating the prep work for corn fritter donuts while he had interviewed her. He shook Jonathan and Francine's hands and told them he enjoyed their photos in the calendar and hoped he was in as good as shape as they were when he was in his seventies. Francine felt it was a sincere comment, even though Robert Irvine was built like a Mack truck. She imagined him as a Jack LaLanne who would be forever in shape, pulling train cars into his eighties. When the Food Network camera crew finished packing up, they left.

The Bridge Club was all atwitter with what had transpired while Francine and Jonathan had been upstairs. "Between the footage he got at the booth today and this last bit here, he's going to do a very positive segment on my food booth at the Covered Bridge Festival," Mary Ruth said.

The women crowded around Francine and Jonathan in their excitement. "And using our status as the Skinny-Dipping Grandmas and Joy's position as a reporter for *Good Morning America*, he's going to help us promote the calendar to raise funds to rebuild the Roseville Bridge," said Alice.

Francine was stunned. "But I thought we were all in agreement that this was to be very private."

"Not after Joy's next segment on *GMA*," Charlotte said. "You heard Robert. The two of you look good. You'll probably come out of this with another appearance on Dr. Oz."

"I don't want another appearance on Dr. Oz."

"Too late," said Marcy, coming out of the dining room into the kitchen. She pressed a button on her phone like she had just hung up after a conversation. "I've got a press conference lined up for tomorrow at what remains of the Roseville Bridge where you'll announce the calendar will be for sale by the end of the month to raise funds. After that and Joy's segment on *GMA*, I have you all booked on several local morning shows in Indianapolis, Terre Haute, and Fort Wayne. I also have a call into *Ellen*, *Wendy Williams*, and *The Tonight Show*. It's only a matter of time before the Dr. Oz people are calling me."

"*The Tonight Show*!" Charlotte exclaimed. "I *love* Jimmy Fallon!"

All except Joy looked at her like they didn't know who she was talking about. "He's no Johnny Carson or David Letterman, of course," she said.

"Don't tell him that," Marcy said. "And I think this calendar is the kind of thing that might go viral too."

"When did you become our publicist again?" Francine asked.

"I re-hired her," Mary Ruth said. "To help me, not the Bridge Club, but I feel like my business is inextricably linked with the group."

"Don't think of this as promoting yourself," Marcy said. "You're saving the Roseville Bridge."

As much as Francine didn't want to admit it, the Roseville Bridge was an important piece of history to her, even more so now that she was coming around to learning the truth.

———

Francine and Jonathan made their excuses as to why they couldn't stick around for dinner. The group was ordering out again, this time Chinese. Francine knew Charlotte suspected they were up to something because both she and Jonathan loved Chinese food. But with the mystery already solved as to who had been behind the deaths of William and Belinda as well as the two fires, Francine aimed to keep Charlotte's curiosity contained. "We just need to have dinner on our own," she insisted. "And Mary Ruth, we'll be back in time to help finish up prep work for the food at tomorrow's booth. I know the visit from Robert Irvine put you behind."

"Even if all you have left to do is dishes," Jonathan offered.

Mary Ruth looked up from the batter she was preparing for a batch of corn fritter donuts. "You're on. Dishes would be much appreciated. Charlotte, don't try to stop them. We have a deal."

Apparently even Charlotte couldn't argue with someone else doing the dishes.

Francine drove since she knew exactly where the cemetery was. The property was out past the burnt-out remains of the Roseville Bridge, so Francine slowed when they went by it. She shook her head. "Such a sad thing. I still have a hard time believing Dolly was behind it all."

Jonathan wasn't looking in the direction of the bridge; he was looking in the opposite direction toward the Rock Run Café. "I know exactly where we should eat for dinner."

Francine turned west onto a county road and they drove for a while through a wooded section. When they reached the intersection with a southbound county road, she took it and slowed to a crawl. "It's near here."

They turned onto a dirt road that led deeper into the woods. Within a quarter mile they came across a small cemetery with an iron fence completely surrounding it. The gate to the cemetery was open.

Jonathan and Francine got out of the car and stood at the gate. The cemetery was not a large one. Francine went ahead of Jonathan walking toward the east side.

He followed, audibly reading the gravestones that were still legible. Several of the earliest ones were tablets that had weathered to almost nothing. "I thought you said this was private, not primitive."

"It's both." She stopped. "Here's what I was looking for."

The gravestone she'd stopped in front of was a more modern one—large, solid, and upright with the decorative engravings still intact. Francine's great-grandfather's name was there, but she knew now that he had not been a biological ancestor. Her great-grandmother's name was next to it.

And the ground where her great-grandmother was supposed to be buried was freshly dug out.

TWENTY-NINE

"So has she been dug up or never buried?" Jonathan asked Francine.

A male voice said, "You know the answer to that."

They both turned. Zed stood there with a shovel.

The sight of the him clad in well-worn jeans and a heavy flannel shirt grasping a spade in one hand made Francine think of an unpredictable horror movie villain, even though he was now neatly groomed. She was glad Jonathan was with her. "Where were you hiding?"

"In the trees. Your car is quiet when it's running on battery power, but the road is bumpy enough I heard the chassis bouncing as you came in."

Francine felt Jonathan shift his stance to one of preparedness in case they were attacked. She had no idea if he was carrying his gun, but she assumed so.

Zed did not make any threatening moves. In fact, he acted jovial. "Well, congratulations, Francine! You figured it out. You found the key, you know the secret. You are our worthy successor."

"I'm not sure I understand it all, but let me try. You are my great-grandfather, the carriage driver who inspired such passion in my great-grandmother that you had a tryst with her."

"*Tryst.* An old-fashioned word. But then, we are old-fashioned people. Please continue."

"The woman who died, Belinda Flowers, was my great-grandmother. Somehow, you discovered this land and the geyser on it. The water has … restorative powers. You used them to develop remedies and re-created yourself as Doc Wheat."

"And your great-grandmother?"

Francine had read enough of her grandmother's diary to know the answer. "She never stopped loving you."

Zed approached the gravesite. He seemed anxious to finish shoveling the remaining dirt on the grave. "Again, you are correct. Our love affair continued during the arranged marriage."

"More than that. When he died, she came to live with you. And my grandmother knew the truth."

"She was one of us. We started her on the waters too young, though. We were still in the experimental phase then. We didn't know how it would affect aging. She seemed eternally young."

"Her death was a blow to my great-grandmother."

"The water can restore, but it can't prevent death. Accidents, fires, diseases that act too quickly—they all proved to be too much."

"Is that why you gave up your Doc Wheat identity?"

He shook his head. "That came long before her death. Authorities were starting to look too closely. To protect the secret, we re-invented ourselves again."

"As Zedediah Matthew."

He didn't say anything.

"Did my mother know?"

"We had planned to tell her when she got older. We had decided amongst ourselves that she would need to reach a certain age before we introduced the water, so she wouldn't look so young, like your grandmother had. Sadly, she never reach the age at which we could tell her. So your grandmother had died, and then your mother, and Belinda became depressed. And then I discovered one other disease that we couldn't fix. Alzheimer's."

"That's how William and Dolly found out who Belinda was, didn't they? When she came to live in the nursing home, she told stories that made her of an age that seemed impossible, but because of the family connection, they guessed."

Zed simply looked at her. She didn't think he would confirm or deny anything else, but she pursued the line of questioning.

"Who killed William?"

"I'm surprised you have to ask that question. The police have established who did it."

"But Dolly had no reason to inject poison into his saline solution, not really. Not unless ... she thought it would cure him." She knew she was only guessing, that there was no way to prove the conclusions she was reaching. "You set her up."

His stance became rigid and tense.

"She and William were getting too close, weren't they? In fact, they had already discovered the water, the source of your remedies."

"It started off innocent enough. William was wrapped up in the whole Doc Wheat legend for his historical project. I allowed him to learn a little too much. Then he found where I hid my collection of water from the geyser."

"He stole a jar of it, didn't he? A jar you let him steal. It had the poison in it. Charlotte and I found it in the trunk of the Lucerne."

Zed threw a shovelful of dirt on the grave, looking like he didn't want to answer Francine. She waited him out.

"I had been watching for him since I first discovered the missing jar," Zed explained. "I wanted to catch him in the act. I'd moved the jars into the greenhouse and locked the greenhouse and the cabinet. But he'd done something I hadn't anticipated. He discovered the source of the water, and he'd gone straight to it."

"That explains why he only had a vial of it."

"It takes a long time to collect a pint."

"If you weren't expecting him, how did you know he was there?"

"I was headed into town when I saw Dolly's car go by me. I was surprised that she would be traveling out this way and so early in the day, so I turned around and went back. I found the car easily, but after casing the greenhouse, I determined he wasn't there. I was horrified by the thought that he'd found the grotto, but he had. I took my rifle and tracked him through the cornfield headed to the Roseville Bridge."

"But that still doesn't explain how you 'know' Dolly committed both acts of arson."

Zed smoothed out the dirt on the grave. "Long memories in Parke County. Many years before she married William, Dolly was shacked up with someone infamous. The man arrested for burning down the Jeffries Ford Bridge. And he always claimed he was innocent."

Francine blinked. So Dolly really was an arsonist, and she'd done it again to get revenge on Zed. Revenge for tricking her into poisoning her husband. "I'm still sorry for what happened to William. Aren't you?"

He shrugged. "Not my descendant. Although he was seeking to prove he was a relation with his version of our family history. If he'd been successful, he would have inherited this place, and not you."

So heartless. "But he's still my cousin!"

"But not a worthy successor. I never believed he could be trusted to make the right decisions once he knew the truth."

Francine had a sudden flash of insight. "Dolly didn't kill Belinda. You did."

Zed choked back a cry. "Belinda had fallen into a vegetative state. She wasn't there anymore. If the waters hadn't extended her life, she would have died by then. I decided I loved her too much to let her live like that."

"You're going to let Dolly take the fall for those murders? She never meant to kill anyone!"

"Dolly burned me out of my house and took down the monument to the love Belinda … Victoria … and I shared for nine decades. The arson will be much harder to prove. So let her be put away for something. You are my heir."

Francine looked at Zed's face and saw only grief there now. "What about you?"

"I'm going away, far from this place. I'm leaving the water behind and I'll age again. When I die, I die. I suspect it won't be long."

"What if Dolly talks about it?"

He smiled sadly. "She would have to admit to her wrongdoing in order to make the case. And then, who would believe her about the water?"

"What am I supposed to do with it? If this is all true, it's like winning the lottery. It is both a blessing and a curse."

"Yes," he said, nodding. "But it's yours now. You will have to decide which you want it to be."

The wind picked up. Leaves that had fallen to the forest floor stirred up around them. "Let's go," Jonathan said. "He should be allowed some last moments here alone."

"You're a good man, Jonathan," Zed said. "I trust you to support Francine, whatever she decides."

Jonathan gave no reply. When they turned to walk back to the car, Francine whispered, "You're not calling the sheriff's department, are you?"

"By the time they got here, he would be gone. I don't like that Dolly will be convicted of something she was duped into doing, but let's wait and see how the trial plays out. I think, in the end, it will be easier to allow the greater sense of justice play out."

"Meaning let God take care of it?"

"Yes."

They got in the car.

"I don't know what I'm going to tell Charlotte about this," Francine said several minutes later.

"A lie," Jonathan said, and then laughed. "Or tell her a truth that makes sense to tell her. She's a pretty good detective. It will take something good to keep her off the case."

————

Francine and Jonathan stopped at the Rock Run Café for dinner. There was a crowd, but the owner recognized them and set up a table in one of the back rooms for them. "We don't usually use this room," he said, "but I can tell the last thing you want is attention. I'll serve you myself back here."

He set candles on the table and lit them. The soft glow of the candlelight seemed magical, like the only thing that existed was what they could see by its light, and that was a very small world. Light jazz played in the background. The owner brought table settings, two menus, and a bottle of brand-name sparkling water. He presented it to them as though it were a fine wine. "We don't serve alcohol so this is the best we can do. But it's on the house."

He poured them each a glass and left, promising to come back in a while and take their orders.

Jonathan held up his glass of fizzy water. "Here's to your good fortune."

"Our good fortune," she replied, clinking his glass with hers, "if it's to be believed."

"It's an amazing story."

Francine swallowed a sip of the water and felt the bubbles tickle the back of her throat. In spite of her tiredness, the surreal story she was contemplating as truth, and the knowledge that she and the Summer Ridge Bridge Club would be back in the spotlight tomorrow at the press conference, she smiled. "A bit ironic, isn't it? To be sitting here in the restaurant where we started down the path to answer the riddle of what happened to William, to have the journey turn out to be nothing like what we'd imagined, and now to be sipping a glorified version of spring water, which, let's be real, is the answer to the riddle."

He tipped his glass toward her, nodded, and took his own swallow of the water. "You're not only a good detective, you also have a bit of the muse in you." He gave her a crooked smile.

She eyed him curiously. "You say that like you have thought of a solution."

"Not me. You have." He picked up the bottle of water, turned it around so the label faced her, and handed it to her.

"It says Pellegrino."

"Yes, but it's much more than that. Read the label."

"It's bottled at a source in Italy."

"What if it were bottled right here in Parke County? What if William's history of the county were modified to make that suggestion?"

Francine thought a moment. "Jonathan, you're a genius. The geyser is the source of the water Doc Wheat used in his remedies. William and Dolly wanted to bottle the water for their own purposes. A craft water with 'restorative' powers, at least that's the ages-old myth. Zed wouldn't permit it. No more, no less. It sounds like a snake oil proposition, doesn't it? Best of all, no one will believe there's any truth in it."

"Not even Charlotte," he said.

They clinked glasses again. Francine began to giggle, which made her feel silly and young and free of the worries of the world. Jonathan began to chuckle with her, and when the owner came back to take their orders, he found them dancing to a jazz version of "Love Is a Many Splendored Thing."

————

Francine, Jonathan, and the Summer Ridge Bridge Club put on their best faces for the press conference the next morning. Joy presided over the announcement of the pinup calendar and how the proceeds would go to rebuild the Roseville Bridge. Marcy prowled in the background, passing out sample copies they'd couriered the previous night from Indianapolis. In the end, the tragic story of William's death, Dolly's rampage of arson and poisoning, along with the semi-nude photos of the women baring their all, reached around the world.

Five weeks later, Francine and Charlotte sat in the kitchen at Francine's house. The Thanksgiving and Christmas holidays were Francine's favorites, and she always decorated for them. With Thanksgiving upon them, she had placed pumpkins and gourds in strategic nooks throughout the house, multicolored ears of dried corn lay on tables and hung from hooks in the kitchen, and on this particular day, the promising smell of apple pie cooling on a counter filled in the air.

"How are sales?" Francine asked. She poured Charlotte a cup of tea.

"You ask me that every week when you have me over for tea."

"I don't keep track of where we're at, but if I remember right, we're closing in the amount needed. I know you monitor it closely."

"Marcy is preparing to release the information to the press. Net proceeds from the calendar total half a million dollars, and the crowd-funding site Marcy set up has raised an astounding $2.3 million. We've passed the goal."

"So you've accomplished your Sixty List item sixty-nine, Be a Sexy Calendar Girl, and fifteen, Be More Generous and Philanthropic."

Charlotte started to say something, and then got choked up. Francine reached over and rubbed the back of her arm in reassurance. "Is everything all right?"

"It's just that we are so blessed, Francine."

"We truly are."

"I never thought that at this age I'd have so many opportunities. I remember when my husband died, I thought life might be over. I still miss him, but life goes on. Thanks to your friendship, and that of Alice, Mary Ruth, Joy, and all the people who've come into our lives, I see so many good things ahead."

"Who would have thought our Sixty Lists would have produced such a sensation?"

"It's God working in all things to bring about good. I'm sorry that the Roseville Bridge burned and that your cousin died. In some ways I almost feel responsible since we wouldn't have been there if it hadn't been for the pinup calendar on my bucket list."

"But in the end you've touched the lives of a lot of people, Charlotte. And Mary Ruth's successes at Food Network and Joy's on *Good Morning America* have inspired a lot of seniors to try new things. Alice managed to check the séance off her list, but more importantly she's realized she needs and wants Larry back in her life. It's like a miracle."

"Not like, it *is* a miracle. You didn't come out too bad, either. You inherited the ranch from Zed. I just hope you don't have the problem he had with people searching for treasure on the property."

"It was Marcy's doing, but going public with the story about William's idea for merchandising the spring has put it in the category of Pluto Water, the mineral waters they sell down in French Lick. There's only so much room for those kinds of novelties, and Jonathan and I won't participate in them. I think the matter's settled. But we are going to build a new cabin there. It'll be a nice retreat for us. For all of us."

Charlotte took a sip of tea. "What kind of tea you have made this week?"

"I'm still experimenting with some herbals I found in Zed's greenhouse. How do you like it?"

"It's nice. Has a bit of metallic taste, though."

"Is it bad?"

"No, but don't look so surprised. It's the same taste I've mentioned every week."

Francine demurred. "Let's change subjects. How's your knee doing? You seem to be walking better."

"It's the funniest thing. I don't have nearly the pain I used to. My physical therapist is excited. The new exercises he found to strengthen the muscles around the artificial knee seem to be working."

"Then let's celebrate with a piece of pie. Just a sliver. I'm sure it's cool enough to serve."

And that's just what they did.

THE END

ABOUT THE AUTHORS

Elizabeth Perona is the father/daughter writing team of Tony Perona and Liz Dombrosky. Tony is the author of the Nick Bertetto mystery series and the standalone thriller *The Final Mayan Prophecy* (with Paul Skorich) and co-editor and contributor to the anthologies *Racing Can Be Murder* and *Hoosier Hoops and Hijinks*. He is a member of Mystery Writers of America and has served the organization as a member of the Board of Directors and as Treasurer. He is also a member of Sisters in Crime.

Liz Dombrosky graduated from Ball State University in the Honors College with a degree in teaching. She is currently a stay-at-home mom. *Murder Under the Covered Bridge* is her second novel.